ALSO BY DONNA FREITAS

The Possibilities of Sainthood
This Gorgeous Game

THE SURVIVAL KIT

DONNA FREITAS

THE
SURVIVAL
KIT

FRANCES FOSTER BOOKS
Farrar Straus Giroux
New York

macteenbooks.com

Library of Congress Cataloging-in-Publication Data

Freitas, Donna.

    The Survival Kit / Donna Freitas. — 1st ed.

      p.   cm.

    Summary: After her mother dies, sixteen-year-old Rose works through her grief by finding meaning in a survival kit that her mother left behind.

    ISBN: 978-0-374-39917-7

    [1. Death—Fiction. 2. Grief—Fiction.] I. Title.

PZ7.F8844Su 2011

[Fic]—dc22

2010041294

This book is dedicated in memory of my mother,
whose real-life Survival Kits inspired this story

And to Frances Foster and Miriam Altshuler,
two women whose presence, support, and encouragement
these last years have been indispensable to my own survival

THE SURVIVAL KIT

JUNE

The Dress Made of Night

1

CAN'T GO BACK NOW

I found it on the day of my mother's funeral, tucked in a place she knew I would look. There it was, hanging with her favorite dress, the one I'd always wanted to wear.

"Someday when you are old enough," she used to say.

Is sixteen old enough?

After the last mourners left the house, Dad, my brother, Jim, and I began arguing about Mom's stuff—What were we going to do with it? Who got what? Dad wanted to get rid of everything and I wanted it kept exactly as she left it. After the yelling and the sad, alternating silences became too much, I ran off. Suddenly, I was at my mother's closet door, grabbing the cold black metal knob, turning it and walking inside, pulling it shut behind me, hearing the hard slam as I was eclipsed by darkness. I fumbled for the string to turn on the light and when my fingers closed around the knot at the bottom, I pulled. Tears sprang to my eyes with the illumination of the bulb and a wave of dizziness passed over me, too, and I collapsed onto the footstool Mom uses—no, *used*—to reach the higher shelves.

That's when I thought: this is a mistake.

Everything around me smelled of her—her perfume, her shampoo, her soap. Looking up from my crouch, knees pulled tight to my chest, I saw how her clothes were just *there*, as if she were still *here*, as if at any moment she might walk in, looking for a pair of jeans or one of her teacher smocks, splashed across the front with paint splotches. My gaze fell across skirts that would never be worn again, blouses and light cotton dresses that would likely be given away, her gardening hats in a big pile on a low shelf, everything colorful and bright, like the flowers in her garden and the wild, rainbow collages on the walls of her classroom— all except for one dress.

With my hands bracing the wall for balance, I stood up and waded through the shoes on the floor, shoving everything in my way aside, until I saw it: the dress made of night, in fabric that was the darkest of blues and dotted over with a million glittering specks of gold. My mother sometimes wore it for a walk on a summer's night or to sit in the pretty wire chairs in the middle of her rose garden, where, when I was little, she would read to me under a flowered sky.

Tied to its hanger was a baby blue ribbon, done up neatly in a bow and pulled through a small, perfect circle punched into a brown paper lunch bag. Big, sloping letters in my mother's hand marched across the front in blue marker strokes: *Rose's Survival Kit*.

My heart began to pound. Mom made Survival Kits for so many people during her lifetime—she was famous for them, but never before had she made one for *me*. I lifted the dress off the bar, the Survival Kit cradled in its midnight blue layers, and carried it out of her closet and down the hall to my room as if it were a body, gently laying it across the bed.

"Mom?" I whispered, first to the floor, then to the ceiling, then through the open window to the grass and the sky and the flowers in her gardens, as if she might be anywhere. A light summer's breeze snuck up behind me and caressed my cheek and again the word *Mom* expanded inside me, my attention drawn back to the Survival Kit that was just sitting there, waiting. The top of the bag was creased with a flap so sharp it looked as though she'd ironed it. My fingers fumbled with the fold, the crackle of the paper loud in the silence, when suddenly I stopped. My breath caught and my body shivered, and before I even glimpsed what was inside, I gathered everything into my arms, pressing it against me, and went to my closet. Gowns for homecoming and the prom vied for room among the stacks of folded jeans and sweaters and the cheerleading jacket I'd never worn. Quickly, I shut the dress away with everything else.

I closed my eyes tight. Someday I would be ready to open my Survival Kit, but not yet. It was too soon.

"Rose? Where are you?" Dad's voice rang through the now empty house, causing me to jump, startled. I'd forgotten I wasn't alone, that my father and brother—what was left of my family— were just down the hall.

"Yeah, Dad?" I called back, taking a deep breath and trying to steady myself.

"We need you in the kitchen."

"Okay! I'll be right there!" I shouted, and did my best to shove all thoughts about the Survival Kit away from my mind.

At least for now.

SEPTEMBER & OCTOBER

The Promise of Peonies

2

ABOUT A GIRL

It was the morning of September 4. Summer was over, school
had started again, and I was dreading the day. Exactly three
months had passed since my mother's death and already I'd learned
to hate this date on the calendar, the way it relentlessly cycled
around every few weeks, always looming ahead. I headed out the
door to wait for my ride and I hadn't gone two steps before I
almost tripped over a body.

Will Doniger was rigging sprinklers along the edge of the front
walk and he looked up when the toe of my boot met his back, his
eyes barely visible through his wavy hair. He didn't say a word.

"Sorry," I told him, stepping aside.

He gave me a small nod but that was it.

Will was a senior at my high school and had been working in
our yard as long as I could remember. He and I shared something important now, too: he lost his father to cancer, just like I
lost Mom. But still, we never spoke to each other, so I walked
around the rest of him and kept on going.

Before my mother died Will had only cut the grass, but afterward he became a daily fixture at our house. He ran his father's

business, Doniger Landscaping—that's what it said on the side of his truck—and we'd needed help with the gardens Mom left us. Everything would have died or become overgrown without Will's help—though I don't know that I'd have said this to him.

Before I reached the street, I glanced behind me. Will was staring off into the distance, every muscle in his body tense in the glaring sun. Words hovered on my lips, but my attention was caught by a bright red gerbera daisy that stood taller than the rest in a nearby garden. I reached out and picked it, raising it close to my nose, the long petals tickling my face. An image of my mother with a thick bunch gathered in her arms cut through my mind, and my fingers automatically released the sticky green stem as if it were covered in thorns. The flower fell to the ground, and I stared at it lying there. A car horn sounded. Chris Williams, my boyfriend of two years, pulled up in front of the house. I hurried to meet him, the sole of my boot crushing the red petals of the daisy against the brick.

"Hey, babe, you look gorgeous today," Chris yelled over the song playing on the stereo. "I like your hair down. It's about time you lost that ponytail you keep wearing."

My hand hesitated at the door handle as I tried to call up a smile. Lately I shrank from comments about my appearance, and it took some work to remember that Chris was only trying to make me feel good. "Thanks," I told him, taking a deep breath and getting inside. Before I had a chance to put on my seat belt, Chris stepped on the gas and launched into details about last night's football practice, not even noticing me turn off the music, at least not at first.

"Hey, I was listening to that," he protested after a while.

I didn't respond, just focused my attention straight ahead.

"Someday you're going to have to start listening to music again," he began, hesitating a moment. "Your mother wouldn't want you to live the rest of your life in silence."

"But it makes me so sad," I whispered. "Let's not do this today, okay? Please."

Chris sighed. "Fine," he said, and we continued on our way to school. He tapped the steering wheel lightly with his thumbs, as if a song still played and he was drumming to its beat, eventually getting back to his story. "So then I passed the ball to Jason—*forty* yards—it landed straight in his arms, and I was thinking, I just hope we can do this again at the game on Saturday. I wish you'd been there yesterday to see it." He glanced over at me. "Babe?"

I nodded, pasting another smile to my lips, and he went on talking.

Football was a big deal in Lewis, and Chris Williams was the quarterback, so he was the center of it all. He was *that* guy at our school—the star athlete, the homecoming king, the boy every girl dreamed of dating. Chris was sweet, he was beautiful, he was the life of the party, but most important he was mine. When he picked me out of everybody else to be his girlfriend my freshman year, I just smiled and said "Absolutely, positively yes." Wearing a football player's letter jacket was about the coolest thing a girl could wish for in a town like ours, and the fact that I was lucky enough to have the name Chris Williams stitched across mine made me *that* girl. I was even a cheerleader.

But that was before my mother died.

Since then I'd quit—the partying, the cheering, and much to Chris's chagrin, having sex. My body felt soft, vulnerable, like one great wound all over. Sex would be wrong, impossible even, and it had become a huge source of tension in our relationship, this wall I'd put up between my body and his. I used to like it, but now I almost couldn't bear to be touched. The only thing I'd managed to hang on to from my former life was my title as Chris Williams's girlfriend. If I wasn't careful, I'd lose that, too.

When Chris stopped at the next red light, he leaned toward me, his lips grazing my ear and traveling down my neck, and I shivered but not in a good way. I could tell he wanted me to kiss him, but I couldn't bring myself to turn my face toward his. Instead, I stared straight ahead, frozen, as if I didn't notice him there, until the signal turned green and he was forced to pay attention to the road again. The expression on his face was grim at first, and I felt awful for rejecting him, but then it softened.

"I'm sorry, Rose. I forgot it was the fourth today. How are you feeling?"

The fact that Chris remembered the anniversary hurt my heart. "I don't know," I said finally, and reached across the seat for his hand, wanting to show I was grateful. "I'm okay. I guess. Thanks for asking."

"Is it four months?"

"Three," I corrected, and he wove his fingers through mine, squeezing tight. We spent the rest of the ride in silence and soon we were turning into the school parking lot. Chris drove down the long row of cars closest to the front entrance, and sure enough, the best spot was waiting for him. The star quarterback in Lewis got certain perks, and he pulled into the space like someone accustomed to special treatment. Chris got out immediately, but I just sat there, not moving, noticing how the sun gleamed a bright streak across the metal hood of his SUV and wishing I was one of those girls who could cut school without a care.

"You coming?" Chris bellowed from outside.

"Yup," I mouthed, and turned the rearview mirror my way for a quick look. Sleep had eluded me again last night and I hoped the eyedrops erased enough of the red so that no one would comment. I pushed my arms through the sleeves of Chris's jacket, so big it swallowed my body, appreciating how it made me feel covered up and hidden away.

Chris knocked on the windshield to hurry me, his blond hair almost white in the light. As a couple we were like a photo and its negative, his features bright and colorful, skin tanned and golden, and mine a series of dark and pale hues from head to toe. When I got out of the car, Chris immediately wrapped his arm around my shoulders, shielding me from the prying eyes and sympathetic stares of others. When physical contact felt protective, I welcomed it, and only when it felt like an advance did I push it away.

We walked toward the entrance. In my peripheral vision I saw Kecia Alli, one of the cheerleaders, sitting on the trunk of her car, and immediately I felt guilty. We hadn't spoken in months—not since I'd quit.

"Hi, guys," called a melodious voice over the loud morning chatter, and for the first time today I smiled for real. Krupa Shakti fell into step with us, my best friend in the whole world.

"Hey, Krupa," Chris said, holding the door open to let us both through. "You'll be there on Saturday?" He meant his football game.

"Yes. For the first five minutes only, *as usual*," she replied.

Krupa was not a sports fan. The school paid her to sing the national anthem during football season, which she did only for the money—she was saving for Juilliard and getting out of Lewis as fast as her vocal cords could carry her. Krupa was tiny, but she had the biggest, most powerful and insanely beautiful voice I'd ever heard, as if someone had placed the singing capacity of a three-hundred-pound woman in the body of a ninety-pound girl.

"Maybe you can convince Rose to come with you this time, even if it's only a few minutes. That would be a start. Right, babe?" he said softly into my ear. "Five minutes?"

My heart sank. My moratorium on football games was the

other source of tension in my relationship with Chris lately. I had painful associations with the football stadium. The moment that split my life in two—when I found out Mom was in the hospital—I'd been at cheerleading practice.

Krupa must have read the panic in my eyes because she answered Chris before I could. "Maybe Rose will come with me another time," she said. Then to me, "See you at lunch?"

"Always," I agreed, and Krupa waved goodbye, turning left toward the locker we shared. Chris and I continued down the hall until we arrived at the door to my Spanish class. He looked down at me and smiled. Hard as I tried to pretend things were fine, every part of me felt stiff and uncomfortable and wrong, and so when he leaned down to kiss me, I wondered if my lips felt as cold and frozen to him as they did to me.

3
MY BEST FRIEND

With over three thousand students, Lewis High School was huge, and its two-story building meandered for what felt like miles. It had more wings than I'd visited and you could probably make it to senior year without seeing some people even once. Chris was typically at my side when I navigated the halls, but Tony Greco, his best friend and a linebacker on the football team, a veritable giant at well over two hundred pounds and six foot three, currently held the role of walking me to the cafeteria to meet up with Krupa for lunch. Tony would be terrifying if it weren't for his puppy-dog eyes and the fact that he was such a sweetheart.

"So, Rose," he said, his voice low and deep, as we each grabbed a blue plastic tray from the stack. "When are you going to put in a good word for me with your friend?" His body was stooped to accommodate the rails we pushed our trays along since the metal came barely above his knees.

Tony had been asking about Krupa since Chris and I first started dating. The thought of Tony and Krupa together always made me want to laugh since he was three times Krupa's size, but I refrained. "You know she doesn't date athletes," I reminded him.

"Someday she's going to change that rule," he said, the look on his face sincere.

"For your sake I hope so," I said. Before we parted ways, Tony toward the burger station and me toward the sandwiches, I tried to offer at least some small bit of hope. "I am sure if Krupa *did* date athletes, you'd top her list."

Tony placed a massive hand on my shoulder. "You're nice to me," he said, and leaned down to kiss the top of my head before loping off. People automatically cleared a path without his having to say a word.

The cafeteria was especially crowded, and half the time allotted for lunch disappeared while I waited in line to get my sandwich and Coke. With my tray balanced across one arm and trying desperately not to spill my drink, I wove in and out of the people milling about, pretending I didn't notice that most of the occupants at the cheerleaders' table were staring at me. Finally, I found Krupa, the one person in the world who made me feel safe now that Mom was gone, the friend who reminded me that there was still something of the old Rose left and that maybe she wasn't gone for good after all. The little tin cups that contained her mother's homemade Indian cooking were spread out in front of her like shiny round toys, and she speared a tiny tree of cauliflower covered in a yellow sauce, popped it in her mouth, and went for another. The delicious smell of curry hit me and I immediately regretted my boring sandwich choice. My mouth watered as I placed my lunch on the table and slid into the other chair, nostalgic for the time when my mother used to pack me yummy things to eat at school, too.

"So what's up?" I asked.

"You know," Krupa answered, waving her fork like a conductor's baton. "The usual. Classes. Quizzes. Blah, blah, blah." She pushed a cup filled with lentils toward me and I dipped my spoon into it. The taste was so transporting I wondered whether Mrs. Shakti could cook away my memory of the last few months. "Though, Ms. Halpert, the athletic director, called me in to see if I'd sing the national anthem at the hockey games this year."

I looked up in surprise. "But you hate doing the football games."

Krupa took a sip of her chocolate shake, the only thing she ever bought, and swallowed. "True. But for hockey I'd get a hundred bucks per game and that's double what I make for football."

"A hundred dollars? Wow," I responded, impressed.

"I know. Crazy, right?" Krupa's brown eyes widened, the whites bright, standing out against her skin. "And there's, like, a million games, too. Practically every Friday and Saturday night from November till March." She dipped her naan into some yogurt, and the smell of the garlic spread on the bread was so strong I could almost taste it. "That's ridiculous money for virtually no effort."

"Well, as long as you don't count the forfeit of all your weekends."

"Luckily I'll have my best friend to come with me," Krupa said with a grin, ripping the rest of her naan in two and offering me half.

"Bribes don't work, you know," I said, but took it anyway.

"But it's *hockey*. Hockey is a completely uncomplicated, lacking-in-Rose-baggage scenario, so get your sweaters and mittens ready—hey!" she protested, placing a hand over the lentils before I could scoop the last of them onto my spoon. "Eat your turkey. And speaking of Rose-baggage scenarios—"

I put my hand up to stop her. "I don't want to talk about it."

"Rose," she pressed.

"Krupa," I said in between bites of sandwich, my mouth still full.

"Stop avoiding this conversation."

"But I don't want to talk about Chris. We're fine."

"You can't keep up this perfect high school couple act forever."

I picked off the crust on one side of the bread. "It's not an act," I said, and dipped the crust into the cup filled with yogurt and long slivers of cucumber before popping it in my mouth, enjoying the cool tang of the *raita* as it slid down my throat. "Yummy."

Krupa glared as if I had sinned against her lunch.

"From now on, whenever you get annoyed about me mooching on your lunch, just think *hockey games*," I said, hoping the subject had been shifted sufficiently. "Every single Friday and Saturday during winter," I added for good measure, but to no avail.

"Rose, I know you love Chris. I know he loves you in that meathead, good-intentioned-jock way of his, and I know you've been with him practically forever—what's the tally now?"

I sighed. "Two years in October."

"—thank you. And so, for like, a year and a half of that time things were good, but something has changed. You have to admit."

"Krupa, do we really have to do this? I hate even thinking about it."

"Yes, we do. This talk is a long time coming, so why not now?" Krupa scraped her last piece of naan across the bottom of another cup, soaking up the sauce. "You'll feel better if we do."

"No, I won't. Dread is what I feel."

"But afterward, you'll feel *un-bur-dened*." Krupa pronounced each syllable slowly and carefully.

I rolled my eyes. "Fine. We can talk about it," I said, giving in when a loud electronic noise pierced the air. "The bell," I exclaimed with relief. "Got to go to lit class," I sang, and shoved the remains of my sandwich in my mouth, washing them down with soda.

"We'll continue this later," Krupa said as we got up. I bussed my tray while she packed her tins into their big mama tin. "You need a ride after school, right?"

"Yes. Chris has football."

"I'll see you in the parking lot then," she said.

As always, Chris was waiting at the cafeteria door to walk me to my next destination. The smile that was so genuine for the entirety of lunch soon faded, and I worried that Krupa had been right, that it wouldn't be long before Chris and I had to face reality.

4

HOW TO SAVE A LIFE

It took Krupa ten minutes to get her car started. Between that and the stress of whether we'd break down on the way to my house, she dropped me at home without another word about our earlier, unfinished conversation.

"See you later," she called through the open window, pulling away in a cloud of exhaust.

As I headed up the front walk an image of the red daisy from this morning popped into my head, and the memory pained me. My eyes scanned the ground for its remains but I was relieved to find no sign of it, as if it had never been there at all. A loud roar came from around the far corner of the house, and there was Will Doniger again, this time behind a lawn mower. He pushed the machine to the edge of the grass, turned, and started down another row as I waited there, watching him until he disappeared behind a long row of trees. I was about to go in the house, when I noticed that Dad's car was parked next to the Doniger Landscaping truck. I froze, closing my eyes, and it took all the willpower I had not to scream. It was way too early for my father to be home from work, which meant only one thing. My insides began to cave and I hugged my schoolbag to me, like it might stop everything from crumbling. Since the summer, my father had started drinking. It's not as though he didn't drink when Mom was alive, but lately he would go on these benders and they terrified me. Between his driving home drunk and then passing out cold, it felt as though any day now I might lose him, too.

"Breathe, Rose. Just breathe," I said out loud to no one, and put both hands on my knees to steady myself.

———————————

Taking care of everything—the house, the cooking, and the chores—was a challenge to put it mildly, and I had a new appreciation for all that my mother did now that the responsibility was on my shoulders. The only thing I didn't have to worry about was my brother, Jim, because he was away at college, though I missed him a lot, especially on the days when Dad wasn't doing well.

Lately my father was a fragile glass picture frame and I was the stand: solid, steady, ensuring that he didn't topple over and shatter. Over the last few months I'd developed a new routine for us—anything to keep him going. First thing in the morning I ground the coffee in this really loud machine that filled the house with screeching life and signaled the beginning of one more day we managed to get up for as opposed to stalling out. Eventually that beautiful coffee smell would pull Dad from his room, and if it didn't, then I pulled him myself. I lined up cereal, skim milk, and fruit on the counter so when Dad shuffled to the kitchen he could fix himself some breakfast, and while he crunched on his Special K, I'd go to his room and lay out a clean shirt, a tie, and a pair of pants for him to wear to work. Eventually I sent Dad out the door with a travel mug filled with coffee and watched as he drove up the street and out of the neighborhood, making sure he turned right toward the office and not left toward his favorite bar.

It was kind of like getting a kid off to school.

After the funeral was over and we were trying to get back to something like normal, Dad told Jim and me that he was going to work, when really, he was going to the local watering hole. Then one day around the end of June, Dad's office called to ask when he was coming back or if he was coming back at all and that's how Jim and I found out he was lying to us. We began calling around to the bars, and sure enough, Dad turned up at one of them, and not only was he drunk when we went to pick him up but he was livid that his teenage daughter and son were telling him what to do and mortified that we had found out his secret. The next day, though, he returned to the office and we went on from there.

Now Dad's work was like his day care and I was his rest-of-the-time care, until we got to those occasions when he gave in and went to a bar during lunch to let the alcohol dull every-thing. The last time my father showed any real emotion was the day of Mom's wake. Before anyone else came in to pay their re-spects, he threw his arms around her casket as if somehow he could throw his arms around Mom one last time and he wept and cried like he might never be able to stop.

It broke my heart, watching Dad hug that casket.

"Come on, Rose. You can do this," I said as I straightened up, doing my best to collect myself. Dad's car was empty so at least he wasn't passed out in the backseat. I headed through the ga-rage to the door, pausing before I opened it, nervous about what state I'd find him in. Then I barged into the house, letting the door slam against the wall with a sharp bang. My boots clomped across the floor as I thudded through the kitchen and into the living room, the noise a courtesy to give Dad a chance to pull himself together.

But then I saw him.

"Dad?" I called out.

He didn't look up.

"Daddy?" My voice rose higher. Skin tingling with fear, I rushed over to where he was slumped, his upper body curled into a ball in one of the easy chairs. He seemed so small among those big, soft cushions as I crouched down next to him, my hands gripping the armrests as I tried to steady myself. "Daddy? I love you," I whispered as if this would help, even though I knew that all the I love you's in the world didn't make any difference at all when something was really wrong. I put my hand across my father's forehead, feeling for signs of life, and tried to rouse him. "Dad? Are you asleep?"

Passed out? Dead?

"Dad!" I barked, louder, my fear escalating.

Slowly, he opened his eyes and groaned. "Rose," he said, his voice garbled and low, squinting up at me like he was having trouble focusing. "How was school?" he asked as if nothing was wrong, his words slurred.

The sour smell of liquor on his breath was strong and I jolted away. "You need to eat something," I said, my voice stiff, feeling enraged that he was still getting drunk in the middle of the day when he was supposed to be at work, and that neither Jim nor I could convince him to stop no matter how we begged, reasoned, threatened, or screamed. But I was relieved, too, because right now, this minute, Dad was alive. He was still breathing and he was just drunk, and drunk I could deal with, because by now I had plenty of experience with this sort of situation and drunk was far better than the alternative scenarios my mind was always conjuring.

Dad shifted, trying to sit up. "Isn't it early for dinner? What time is it?"

Everything about him seemed ruined, old, *fragile*, and I hated noticing this. My heart ached, and my hand reached for my chest as if I could soothe this battered part of my anatomy.

"It doesn't matter how early it is, we have to get food in you," I said furiously, and stomped my way back to the kitchen, the noise hurting his head for sure but I didn't care. "And lots of water," I yelled, grabbing a tall glass from the cabinet above the sink and filling it. When I returned to the living room, Dad was still crumpled in the chair, his elbow and hand holding up his head. He winced each time the heels of my boots hit the floor. "Drink this down right now," I ordered. "Then I'll get you another." He sighed and didn't move, his eyes barely open. I held the glass in front of his face. "Dad. I'm not leaving until it's gone." He finally took it and sipped a little bit. "All of it," I demanded.

When he began to drink in earnest I sat down on a nearby ottoman to wait, the muffled noise of the lawn mower outside providing the only sound in the house. Any evidence that Mom once livened this room with her loud voice and laughter was gone and a layer of dust covered everything. None of us wanted to touch anything, as if by wiping a cloth across the shelves and knickknacks we would erase any traces she'd left behind. Dad had removed the pictures of her, too, leaving only the dull brown cardboard backing in empty frames. Guilt stabbed me as thoughts of my Survival Kit entered my mind. Like everything in this room, I'd neglected it, and it had sat untouched in my closet since the day I found it. My eyes shifted back to my father, one hand still around the glass, the other resting on the arm of the chair, his eyes glazed and empty. Maybe whatever Mom had left inside the Survival Kit would help show me how to put our family's life back together in a way that made sense, or at least that was less painful and sad.

"Keep drinking. You're almost done. Come on," I said. "You'll feel better."

Dad put the glass to his lips again and gulped down what was left. When he was finished I stood, took it from his hand, and went to refill it, but this time I didn't wait around while he drank it down. Instead, I started dinner, taking out the eggplant, eggs, and milk from the fridge and breadcrumbs and olive oil from the cabinet. I turned on the flame underneath the big sauté pan after I poured a layer of olive oil across the bottom. Grandma Madison, Dad's crotchety mother, had taught me to cook, and Dad craved fried eggplant when he'd been drinking—something about fried food soaking up the alcohol. The rhythm of the slicing and dunking and breading and the sound of oil sizzling began to calm me, and for a few minutes I forgot about all the worries and the responsibilities and the giant mess that was Dad in the living room because cooking for me was like gardening for my mother—soothing.

My phone rang, piercing the silence, and I wiped my hands with a dish towel. My brother's face smiled up at me from the screen and I grabbed it. "Jim, this isn't a good time, can I call you back?"

"Rosey, I've been trying your cell for an hour." Jim always called me Rosey.

"Let's talk later," I said. "I'm busy with Dad."

"Busy?" He paused, taking in the meaning behind my state-ment. "Busy" was code between us for when Dad went on another bender. "Jeez. He did it again?"

"The short answer is yes."

My brother sighed into the receiver. "I thought he was get-ting better . . ."

"Well, it *has* been a while since the last time, but really, I need to get off the phone. I've got my hands full."

"But—"

"No buts. Jim, please."

"I hate that you're alone—"

"I know, I know."

"Maybe next semester I should—"

"No dropping out of college," I interrupted before he could finish. "We already decided this."

"Rosey, it wouldn't be permanent. Just for a few—"

"You know I don't mind," I broke in again. The noise from the eggplant frying became louder and I began to worry it would burn. "Really out of time, Jimmy. Don't want to ruin dinner so talk to you later, love you, bye," I said in one big rush, clicking the *off* button before he could say anything else and dashing to the stove top with a pair of tongs to turn over each of the disks so they didn't blacken. Once the eggplant was crisp, I turned off the flame, and gradually the sound of the sizzling oil quieted. The noise from the lawn mower outside was gone, too, and the house became eerily silent. While the eggplant dried on paper towels, I cleaned up, putting the pan in the dishwasher and wiping down the counters with a sponge. When I finally headed back into the living room, I managed to hold my tongue. "Eat up," I said, and handed Dad the dish piled high with his hangover food. Immediately, I stalked off to my room.

I was so tired of holding him up.

5

PRECIOUS THINGS

The shimmery fabric of my mother's dress glimmered along the edge of my closet, the shiny blue ribbon attached to the Survival Kit just visible at the top, and I stared at it for a long while, gathering my courage. I *had* to do this. Mom had wanted me to and she made this for me—*just* for me—and how could I not honor her last wish? Slowly, my fingertips brushing along the soft fabric all the way up to the straps, I lifted the hanger from the rack, careful not to let the dress touch the floor as I carried it over to my bed, the paper bag crackling from the movement. Before I could lose my nerve, I untied the ribbon and tipped the Survival Kit onto its side, the contents spilling across the comforter. Suddenly, *finally*, there it all was before me.

I surveyed the items Mom had placed inside:

A photograph of peonies
A shiny silver construction-paper star
A light blue iPod
A tiny crystal heart on a chain
A box of Crayola crayons

And the one thing I knew would be there without having to look:

A bright green diamond-shaped kite.

"Rose, will you do the kites again?" Mom asked me two Augusts ago now, as if this was even a real question; as if I wasn't already looking forward to our family's annual Survival Kit–making event and as if putting together the kites wasn't my job every year.

"Mom," I said, giving her a look.

"Well, I don't know. Maybe you're getting too old for this. Or maybe you have plans with Chris." She let his name hang in the air. She couldn't believe I was only going to be a sophomore and already I had a serious boyfriend. She worried that I'd tie myself to one person for the entirety of high school.

"Of course I'm making them," I told her.

"Oh, good. I just wanted to be sure," she said, and smiled. "So will Chris be joining us, too?"

"Mom," I protested.

"Okay, sorry, sorry," she said, and continued to unpack the supplies she'd brought home from the craft store and the drugstore and wherever else she'd shopped so we could begin.

Dad's job was to count the contents of each lunch bag—the crayons, the pencils, the construction-paper stars, among other things. Jim organized the assembly line, and I helped Mom make all the labor-intensive items. Since she was the head nursery school teacher at Lewis Elementary, most people from my school had either had Mom as their teacher or knew someone who did, and just about every parent in Lewis had some connection to her because of their children. Because of this, everyone knew about her Survival Kits, too—she was famous for them. Mom came up with the idea when she noticed that parents had a tougher time handling their children's first day of nursery school than the kids did, and every September she would be left with a bunch of inconsolable mothers and fathers. The Survival Kits were meant to help them cope, and Mom filled them with objects that were symbolic of the various things parents needed to think about or do to make it through this transition year. The most important item of all, and certainly my favorite, was a tiny, diamond-shaped piece of construction paper, a white line of string attached to one corner with little ribbon bows tied along its length at the bottom.

A kite.

It symbolized the obvious: being able to let your children go, while at the same time hanging on to them, being there as they discovered their way in the world but being willing to let out more and more line when necessary, too.

I loved making those kites.

———————

I tipped the paper bag upside down and shook it to make sure it was empty, and one last item fell out onto the bed. It was a note folded neatly into fours with scalloped edges. Nervous to read her last words to me, I opened it, my breath coming in uneven gasps.

> *My beautiful Rose,*
>
> *I remember when my own mother died how it seemed the whole world went dark. Everyone is different, of course, but I hope I can offer you some wisdom as you get used to life after I'm gone.*

The word *gone* went straight to that raw part of me that I didn't think would ever heal. Through blurry eyes I forced myself to continue.

> *There is no order to this. Just a collection of things I want you to consider, to think about, that I never want you to lose, my daughter, my Rose. Do your best to humor your mother one last time. My one and only piece of advice: use your imagination! Always. It's such a gift. I love you heart and soul.*
>
> *MOM*

That was it. No *goodbye* or *always* or *yours*.

Just *MOM* in swirling capital letters.

Right then my cell vibrated on the bedside table, startling me, and I wiped my eyes with my sleeve before leaning over to see who it was. Chris's face had popped up on the screen but I didn't pick up. Instead, I lay there, stretched across my bed with my mother's dress pulled close against me, my mind going over each item in my Survival Kit again and again, wondering which one I should deal with first. The directive to use my imagination was daunting, and I wished Mom had left me a clue or just told me where to start. These questions about what and how and why went around and around in my mind until the sky grew dark, and eventually I fell asleep.

That night I dreamed of peonies.

When I woke the next morning, I had my answer.

I was ready to begin.

6

ALL AT SEA

"'Peonies can be floriferous,'" I read out loud from a thick book that lay open across my arms. The sun was out, bright above, and I was standing barefoot in the front yard. "Floriferous? Is that even a real word?" I murmured. "'A single stem often produces multiple buds, the top one blooming first, the second highest next, and so on.'" A few steps to my left a spot where a line of shade darkened the grass caught my eye, but I shook my head. "Not enough light."

September was flying by and more and more I was spending time with my head buried in one of the gardening manuals I'd checked out from the library—beginner's guides, general guides, guides specifically on how to care for seasonal flowers. A pile of large, heavy hardcover books rose up on the desk in my room, and every afternoon after school I studied tips for planting peonies as if they would be on a test the next morning. Then I would wander about outside testing various locations in the yard for a new peony bed, squinting toward the sun, at the grass, then back at the sun again, hoping for some insight. Sometimes Will

Doniger was working nearby in one of the gardens, and I wondered if he overheard my muttering or was curious about what in the world I was doing. But mostly I didn't worry about anything other than the job my mother had left me, and in truth, the more I learned the more daunting this task became. Any number of things could go wrong. Research was one thing, but actually getting started was another, and I hadn't inherited my mother's green thumb.

I was scared I would fail.

One Saturday late in September I woke to bright sunshine and jumped out of bed, trading my pajamas for a pair of ratty old jean shorts and a tank top. However much I demurred, the promise of peonies in the spring was drawing me out of the house regularly for the first time in months. In the bathroom I leaned closer to the mirror, applying lip gloss, wondering if this had been my mother's plan all along when she assembled my Survival Kit; that she knew I'd wallow indoors forever if she wasn't there to remind me how a day of sunshine could transform moodiness to hope like magic, so she'd left me a reason to bask under blue skies when she wasn't there to do it herself. I tiptoed into the kitchen, careful not to make a sound—on weekends Dad slept late. We had yet to talk about his last drinking binge, and if I had to bet, we would probably never discuss it.

After making myself some coffee, I took the mug in one hand, grabbed a pair of flip-flops with the other, and padded through the front door to sit on the porch. Ages had passed since I'd lounged out here. The gray slate of the stone floor was cool against my bare feet and the pale blue cushions of a patio chair beckoned so I sank into them, putting my feet up and admiring the way my red toenails caught the sun's glare. Steam from my coffee rose in pale white wisps, made visible against all the colors of the yard. Planters were scattered everywhere, big ones filled with geraniums and smaller ones brimming with purple violets. Fuchsia and tiny white petunias dripped down from their hanging pots. The gardens throughout the front yard flowed like streams, forming vivid ponds across the lawn, and individual blades of grass shone silver in the sun. The ancient beech trees yawned across the sky, the weeping beech with its glossy, thick leaves that cascaded in jagged lines all the way to the ground like a green waterfall. Everything seemed alive, as if Mom were still here taking care of it all.

Was she really and truly gone forever? The sound of rushing water filled the air and reminded me who was actually doing all the work and Will Doniger appeared, dragging a garden hose across the grass. He glanced my way and nodded hello.

I nodded back.

I used to think Will must be a snob, the way he never said anything, not even hello, though we went to school together at Lewis—he was a year ahead of me, and a senior like Chris—but lately I wondered if Will was just sad a lot of the time. His father had died of cancer, too, a couple of years ago, and I'd never said a word to him about it. Suddenly, this lack of acknowledgment on my part seemed horrible, and I was tempted to stand up right then, walk over to Will, and say how sorry I was about his dad even though I knew from experience that those words were poor condolences. But then, he hadn't said anything to me about Mom either, so I stayed put and drank more coffee instead.

A black SUV turned down the street and parked along the edge of the yard. Chris got out, Tony with him. They waved and I waved back as I got up from my chair and slipped my feet into my flip-flops, which made a satisfying thwacking noise as I headed toward them to say hello.

"Hey, babe," Chris said when I got close. He smiled.

"Hey, yourself," I said, and smiled back, realizing that for once I was in a good mood. "Hey, Tony," I said.

"Nice to see you, Rose. As always."

"So, can I have a hug or what?" I asked Chris, looking him in the eyes—something I didn't do much anymore—and feeling unexpectedly shy.

His face lit up and before I could say another word his arms wrapped around me so tight he lifted me off the ground, and one by one, my flip-flops fell from my feet. He held me against him like he would never let me go. "I've missed you," he whispered in my ear, and I leaned into his chest, listening to his heart pound. "It's so nice to see that smile of yours again," he added, and suddenly I felt the distance between us disappear.

Maybe Chris and I were headed back to that place where we'd been happy for so long, that time in our relationship when my pulse raced every moment I was near him. Despite all of the walls I'd put up, Chris had stayed with me, and this meant a lot. Maybe out of the blue everything could become, I don't know, *fixed*.

"Um, hello . . . third wheel present," Tony said after a while, chuckling.

"Sorry, man," Chris said, and put me down, the grass tickling my feet. I recovered my flip-flops and went to stand next to Tony.

"You're not a third wheel," I said, nudging him. "Shouldn't you guys be at practice right now?"

"Coach canceled today," Chris explained, eyeing me. "If you came to our games, you'd know that we won big last night so we earned a Saturday off."

I blushed. I was such a terrible girlfriend. "That's great," I said, and tried to look away, but my eyes met Tony's instead.

He crossed his arms. "Your boy threw three touchdown passes and rushed the goal line for another. You should've been there."

I stared hard at the ground. A ladybug crawled up an individual blade of grass and I was tempted to pick it up. "Maybe next time," I said, but knew this was probably a lie because if I had my choice I wasn't stepping inside the football stadium again. Ever.

"So what's the plan today?" Chris asked, changing the subject, and my heart swelled with gratitude. "We're heading to the diner for burgers. Why don't you come?"

"That's a nice offer, but I've got work to do around here today," I said, gesturing toward the yard. I hadn't told Chris about my Survival Kit, or anyone else for that matter. Not even Krupa. "You know, stuff in the gardens."

Chris laughed like I was joking. "Since when do you garden?"

"I don't know. Since today?"

Tony brightened. "Listen, the yard will be here when you get back. And we could swing by and pick up your friend."

I gave him a look. "Krupa's a vegetarian."

"They have pasta on the menu," Tony said. "Come on. Take a break. Hang out with us. It'll be just like old times."

Old times. Two little words and the weight of the world came rushing down on me again. No matter how I tried or pretended, things would never go back to the way they used to be. "I wish," I whispered.

Tony screwed up his face when he realized what I must be thinking. "Rose, I'm sorry. I didn't mean—"

"Tony, it's okay. Really," I said. "It's fine. Maybe I'll go with you guys another time."

Chris reached out, pulling me close again, his hand grasping my waist, his fingers finding the bare skin between my tank top and shorts, and my whole body stiffened—I couldn't help it—and he felt it. I felt like a bottle of soda that had been shaken and gone suddenly, completely flat. Chris sighed but he didn't let go, and I stood there, rooted to the spot, determined to make things right again, to feel like it was normal to have my boyfriend touching me whenever he wanted to, because it *was* normal, when all the while my heart was sinking. If I kept this up—inexplicably warm one moment, cold the next—Chris was going to break up with me. Why is it that when we lose something big, we begin to lose everything else along with it?

"Babe, I guess we're going to take off. Gotta eat something soon," Chris said, kissing me on the cheek and walking away without another glance.

Tony shrugged apologetically. "See you later, Rose."

"Bye," I said, raising my hand to wave, the grass and sky and street becoming one big blur as tears filled my eyes. I waited as they got in the car and sped off, all the promise of the day disappearing with them, like a fog burned away in the sun's heat, leaving everything bare again.

Later on I was in the kitchen fixing a sandwich when I heard Dad's car pull up. He'd left the house around three and stayed out a long time so I braced myself, listening for signs that he had been drinking. The car door slammed and I heard the heavy but sure sound of his shoes coming through the garage. This told me he was sober and I wondered whether he was becoming stable again.

"Rose, I'm home," he said when he came through the door and into the kitchen.

"Hey, Dad. Want a sandwich?"

"That would be great," he said, and turned on the old radio in the kitchen to a baseball game. The Red Sox were playing. He sat down and went through the mail as the announcer shouted the play-by-play of what was happening on the field.

I walked over and kissed him on the cheek, which made him look up at me and smile. My father hadn't worn a happy expression in a long time and seeing it made me realize how much I missed the Dad he used to be, the Dad who would take care of me and not the other way around.

"What was that for?" he asked.

"I don't know," I said. "I just love you."

"I love you, too, sweetheart." He lowered the radio. "So how are things with you and Chris?" he asked. "I haven't seen him in a while. Though he's on the front page of the sports section every week."

"Everything's fine. He's having a good season. You know, the same, I guess."

"You guess?"

Talking about boyfriends was Mom territory, and I wasn't

about to tell my father about the rocky state of my relationship with Chris. "So, Dad," I said, changing the topic and opening the packages of turkey and cheddar to make his sandwich. "Remember when you took Mom to pick out flowers at one of the farms?" His eyes shifted away from me to the letter in front of him and he didn't say anything. While I waited for his response, I piled the meat and cheese onto one slice of bread and spread mustard evenly across the other, doing my best to be patient.

Back when I was in eighth grade, when Mom was first diagnosed with cancer and was sick from chemo, Dad, who hadn't gardened a day in his life, offered to plant anything and everything Mom wanted that spring. They came home one Saturday with a car full of flowers and seedlings. Dad set Mom up outside in a chair and got down on his hands and knees and, armed with her gloves and tools, weeded and planted all weekend according to Mom's directions. It was the sweetest thing I'd ever seen him do.

My father picked up another piece of mail and slid the letter opener across the top of an envelope with a long, loud rip. "Of course I remember. Why do you ask?"

After placing the sandwich in front of him, I sat down to finish mine. "I was thinking of putting in some new flowers. Peonies, actually. Mom never . . . I mean, I just thought—" I stopped, backtracking. "I was wondering if you remembered any good pointers."

"I wish I did, sweetheart. But I'm afraid I didn't absorb her talent that one weekend." My father stood up and stared out the sliding glass door into the backyard. There was still enough light to see the outline of Mom's rosebushes.

"It's okay," I said. "Don't worry about it." I finished my sandwich and took my empty plate over to the sink to rinse it.

"I'm sorry, Rose. I wish I could be more help." His voice was sad.

"It's all right, Dad. Thanks anyway." I opened the dishwasher, and as I unloaded glasses into the cabinets I tried to manage my disappointment that Dad didn't have the magic answer, or at least a better memory of that time.

"I do know someone else who can help, though," Dad said suddenly. "Why don't you ask the Doniger boy? He's probably the only person other than your mother who knows those gardens. He's done a wonderful job."

I almost laughed at this suggestion. How had I not thought of Will myself? All this time, every single day, I saw him, I walked right by him, I watched him take care of Mom's gardens. The answer to my problem had been standing in front of my face—it was obvious now that Dad suggested it.

"Of course," I said finally. "I'll do that, Dad. I'll ask Will for help. It's a good idea."

"He has a green thumb, that kid, just like your mom," he said. I was about to go to my room when Dad called after me, "I'm glad, Rose."

I stopped and turned, curious what he meant. "Glad about what?"

"That you're going to plant some flowers. It would make Mom happy. It makes me happy, I can say that much," he said, and disappeared again behind a letter.

7

NICE GUY

The moment the bell rang to end school the following Thursday, I was on my way to the parking lot. Dad's suggestion that I ask Will for help had been rattling around in my mind since the weekend. Originally I had planned to do it on Monday, and then on Tuesday, and then on Wednesday, too, but I soon found out that approaching quiet, shy, stoic, and maybe a little intimidating Will wasn't an easy prospect. He never showed any emotion or betrayed what he was thinking, and for some reason I couldn't bear the thought of his eyes on me, like he might immediately know my secrets without having to ask. Each time I geared up to approach him, rehearsing my opening words in my head, the moment I saw him I did a one-eighty and hurried in the other direction, and I'm pretty sure he noticed me do this at least once. But then I reminded myself: Will was just the landscaping guy, someone I saw every day at my house, not a clairvoyant or a magician, and I truly doubted he would be mean to me.

"Where are you rushing off to?" Krupa asked as I flew by our locker.

If I stopped to talk to her I would lose my courage so I kept on going. "Tell you later," I yelled over my shoulder. I went over the plan in my head: Will would be paid extra for helping me, the money tacked on to what he made each week, since I didn't want Will to feel like I was asking for favors. When I reached the end of the hall I shifted my body into the metal bar across the exit door and soon I was outside in the sun. People rushed by on their way home or hung out in groups, loitering on the lawn, enjoying the nice day. A few gave me a small wave but no one stopped to talk. I cupped a hand over my eyes, searching the grounds, but still no Will.

Maybe I would find him at his truck.

I took the shortcut to the parking lot and skidded my way down a steep grassy bank and onto the pavement, sliding sideways between cars so close together they almost touched. People were sitting on their bumpers in groups, talking and laughing. Kecia Alli was putting a bag into her trunk, already dressed for cheerleading practice—and I made a quick left at an SUV and headed down another row. The noise of football practice reached out to me and I thought of Chris. Would he care that I was going to ask another guy for help instead of him?

Right when I was about to give up, I saw the Doniger Landscaping truck, gray and battered and towering over the little four-doors parked nearby, and I made my way there. I leaned against the driver's side door to wait, the metal burning hot through my T-shirt. Occasionally I glanced around to see if Will was anywhere in the vicinity, and eventually he was. Through the windows I watched him say goodbye to a few other guys, and when he came around the front of the cab he halted, surprised to see me I think.

"Hi, Will," I said.

"Hey. What can I do for you?" he asked, straight to the point, as if he already assumed my reason for being there could only be business-related.

The lack of small talk threw me off but I could be all business, too. "Um. Well. I guess I sort of have to figure out how to plant something in our yard that's supposed to grow in the spring. Peonies. Apparently they are kind of tricky and I don't really know what I'm doing and it's important—"

"Are you asking for my help?" he interrupted.

I swallowed, unnerved by those eyes of his. "As a matter of fact, yes. I am. I'd like your help."

"Sure." He looked at his watch and a sliver of white flashed along its side where his skin hadn't tanned. "How about Saturday? Around one or so?"

"This Saturday?"

Will nodded, his expression blank. He hooked a thumb into his jeans pocket, waiting there, looking awkward.

"Okay, that would be great," I agreed, and then remembered my speech, quickly launching into it. "So about getting paid—"

He shook his head and waved me off. "Don't worry about

it. I'll pick you up at your house," he said, reaching toward me, and his fingertips grazed my arm.

My heart responded by pounding hard.

"Do you mind?" he asked, gesturing at his truck.

I was blocking the door. "Oh. Sorry," I said, embarrassed, and stepped aside. The door opened and shut with a loud groan as he got in. "See you Saturday then," I added, though I don't know that he heard me. Will didn't look back. Not once.

I watched as he drove away.

8

HOW IT ENDS

The next morning I raced past Will like yesterday's conversation had never happened. He was walking across the lawn, far enough away that I felt my ignoring him wouldn't be overly conspicuous. I didn't know if we were supposed to act differently now that we had plans for Saturday, or just the same as always, barely acknowledging each other's existence. Luckily I didn't have long to debate this because Chris's SUV was already idling in the street, waiting to take me to school.

"Hey, babe, how are you?" he asked as I climbed inside.

I responded with an all too enthusiastic "I'm great!" because I was feeling uneasy about my Will-and-Rose field trip. I knew I should tell Chris that I would be missing his football game *again*, and that, by the way, it was because I was going somewhere with Will Doniger, but as we raced toward the end of the street, these things went around in my mind and stayed there.

"You're in a good mood again," Chris observed. "It's nice."

I tried to force myself to tell him, but all I managed was "Sure. I guess I am." We came to a stop sign and Chris pulled me toward him, laughing softly in my ear. He placed a hand on my cheek and turned my face toward his, leaning in for a kiss, and for the first time in months I made myself kiss him back like I always used to.

"Maybe we should take advantage of your good mood tonight," he said, a thread of hope running through his voice. When he settled back into his seat and stepped on the gas, the anticipation on his face was reflected in the window.

I wanted to make him happy, and I wanted to make me happy, too. Maybe if I just dived back in, things would return to the way they used to be between Chris and me, so out of my mouth came the only word Chris wanted to hear and that I was capable of getting out at the time. "Okay," I agreed, and shut my eyes tight.

———————

Chris and I were standing by my locker when Krupa appeared. My back was against the metal and Chris's hands were pressed against it on either side of my head. "So I'm done at practice around seven," he said, and smiled at me.

I knew that look. "See you then," I said.

"Absolutely." He gave me one last kiss and sauntered away, giving Krupa a nod.

"Now *that* is something I haven't seen in a long time," Krupa said, spinning the combination into the lock and opening the door.

"I know. But I think things are starting to go back to the way they used to be," I said. "He's coming over tonight."

Krupa raised her eyebrows. *"Really."* She grabbed her chemistry textbook and slammed the locker shut.

"Really," I said, even though unease settled over me like a dark cloud.

"I hope you know what you're doing, Rose," Krupa murmured, and took off to class.

———————

By eight o'clock Chris and I were in the basement watching a movie on the old, scratchy orange couch that had a spring poking up just under the fabric, the only light in the room coming from the television. We lay there, talking occasionally, or getting up to grab more soda from the fridge upstairs, and everything was fine. At first. But when the credits began to roll across the screen, I waited for the inevitable, becoming numb, like someone had shot Novocain through my limbs and little by little they were losing feeling. By the time Chris leaned over to kiss me it felt as though a stone statue had replaced the living girl, or that I'd suddenly left my body and become a ghost, hovering above.

Chris's lips met my mouth, but my mouth didn't respond, and when he pushed me back onto the couch, the metal spring stabbed right into the most vulnerable spot of my back, where my lungs ached for breath. Chris fumbled with the button on my jeans and I gasped, but not in a good way, and his hand froze. He moved off of me and I slipped from the couch onto the floor, curling up tight on the rug by the coffee table and watching as Chris sat there, raking his fingers through his blond hair.

"I'm sorry," I said.

"Don't you like me anymore?" Chris asked, his voice vulnerable, showing me a side that he kept hidden from everyone else. "You used to be so into things."

"I know," I said, and hung my head. Kissing, sex, and everything in between used to be so easy with us. Whenever we ran out of things to say it always filled in whatever was missing, smoothed over our disagreements when we fought. But now, when we needed it to help us leap over a difficult place, we ended up staring out over this wide gap with no way to cross. I didn't know how to be in my body anymore—not after seeing my mother's wither and die and take her life with it. Those final images of her taught me that bodies were places for hurt and pain, not pleasure. "I'm sorry. I really, truly am," I told him.

Chris stood up, his body outlined by the light of the television flickering behind him. "Is there a time frame you can give me or something? How long do you need, Rose?"

I stared at him, thinking about how my entire world was broken in pieces and I didn't know how to put them back together again. "I don't know, I really don't. I wish I did. I wish I could fix this. I wish I could fix everything."

"Is there something *I* did?" Chris asked. "What is making you like this?"

"My mother died," I whispered, and each time I uttered this it felt impossible.

Chris's hands, both of them, went up to his head and ran down his face. "I know. But that was like, five months ago."

"Almost four," I corrected him. "And it still feels like yesterday."

"What can I do to help? What do you need from me, Rose? Do you want space? Do you want to break up and you're just too afraid to tell me? Is that it?"

My head jerked up and my eyes fixed on his. Inside, part of me screamed *no*, but another part wanted this drama over, for the raw feelings that kept tearing at the seam of a deep, far from healed wound to stop, and to be left alone once and for all. "Do *you*?"

Chris stood there, not moving, not answering—not at first. I could feel his eyes on me while mine shifted away, studying the individual tufts of the rug, like short blades of grass. Then I heard him say, "I don't know anymore. Maybe we should end this before it gets any worse because it doesn't seem to be getting any better."

"Okay," I said.

"Okay," he repeated. "Really? That's all you have to say? You're fine with breaking up?"

I shrugged—I didn't know what else to do. "But you said—"

"I didn't think you would agree," he yelled.

I shrank away. "I'm sorry, I—"

"I thought you'd tell me, *No, Chris, I love you, Chris, we can work things out, Chris, I'm so grateful you're here for me, Chris, and soon I'll feel better and things will go back to normal!*" His tone was mocking and his breath came in angry heaves.

"But I don't know if they ever will," I said in a small voice.

There was a long pause. "Fine. I guess that's it." Chris's voice was even again, a mixture of hurt and fury. "We're done. Good-bye."

His footsteps were heavy on the wooden stairs that led up to the kitchen from the basement, and when he slammed the front door, the force of it reverberated through the house. I crawled back onto the couch and stared at the television for what seemed like hours, too in shock to fall asleep. Eventually I dragged myself to a standing position and headed to my room. Once I was in bed, tucked under my comforter and sheets, the words "Chris and I broke up" tumbled through me, sickening my stomach. It wasn't real. I couldn't believe it. Wouldn't. We'd get back together again because that was what we always did. When I finally drifted off to sleep I tossed and turned and woke again, staring into the darkness, feeling lonelier than ever.

———————

At one p.m. sharp the next day the bell rang and then it rang again. I dragged myself from bed, rubbing my eyes as I headed to the front door to see who was there. For a minute I thought it might be Chris, come to say that last night was a mistake, that he didn't want to be broken up, but then I remembered he had a football game so it couldn't be him.

Which made me remember who it actually was.

I looked through the window and saw Will Doniger standing on the porch, waiting for me. Oh my god. I couldn't believe I forgot and even worse, I couldn't do this. Not now. Not after Chris. I didn't want to go anywhere or do anything this weekend other than stay in bed and mope and talk to Krupa about what happened. I felt horrible for a million reasons at once, but I took a deep breath and opened the door anyway. "Hi," I said.

Will looked at me. I was dressed only in a tank top and shorts, barefoot, and though I hadn't looked in the mirror I was sure my hair was a knotted mess. "Did you forget—"

"No," I interrupted. "Well, yes. Sort of. It's complicated. I'm sorry. I had a bad—" I stopped. I didn't need to tell Will why, I only needed to apologize and hope he was forgiving enough to come back another day. "Listen, I know you are busy, *really* busy," I began, searching for the right words, "and I hate to ask this, I'm really sorry to, but is there any way we could do this next Saturday instead? Something important came up and today

I just can't." Will's eyes were on the ground so I couldn't tell what he was thinking. "Please?"

After a long silence, he said, "Sure. Next Saturday then. Same time."

"Wow, thank you so much—" I started to gush.

"Feel better," he said, and turned and left.

He walked all the way to his truck before I shut the door.

9

OVER YOU

The smell of coffee was strong through the house. Monday morning arrived and with it a feeling of deep dread. Chris and me in a fight was one thing—people at school were accustomed to our spats, and all couples fought, especially when they'd gone out for so long like Chris and I. Our stalemates had always ended with us making up and usually making out in the hallway by Chris's locker. These public kissing sessions were like an official school bulletin that Rose Madison and Chris Williams were back together again. But this time was different. We hadn't spoken since Friday, and today would mark the first occasion I'd walk through the Lewis High School hallways as just Rose and not Chris Williams's girlfriend. Who I was without him, I didn't really know and I didn't feel ready to find out either.

As if this were a day like any other, I got Dad's travel mug ready and made sure he ate his breakfast before sending him off to work. But afterward, as I stood under the scalding water of the shower, I wished that I could erase Friday night and replace it with a different outcome or that I'd just imagined my breakup with Chris and today everything would go back to normal. As I was getting dressed, my phone vibrated and Chris's face filled the screen. I stared until it stilled. Was it good or bad that he was calling me? It vibrated again and I closed my eyes, thinking I should pick up, that maybe if I did, we *would* make up and everything would be okay again, and finally on the fifth ring, I reached for it. "Hey," I said as if nothing was wrong.

"Rose," Chris said, his tone quiet and even.

Nerves rattled my stomach. "I'm glad you called. I thought about calling all weekend because I'm worried that maybe we were too hasty, breaking up like that on Friday." I was rambling but I didn't care. "I don't know what happened the other night, I just—"

"I've done some thinking, too," he interrupted. "I've been patient and I've tiptoed around your needs and stuck by you through all your craziness—no music because it makes you sad, no sex or even kissing for god's sake because you don't want to be touched, no football games because you don't want to go back to the stadium, no talking to the cheerleaders because you quit and feel awkward, no drinking because of your dad's drinking. No this, no that."

My body grew cold as I listened to Chris's list of my hang-ups and the various other things I'd been avoiding since spring. "You're right. It isn't fair."

"No, actually, Rose, I get it, to a point. Your mother dying is a huge deal and who am I to understand what you're going through and how you need to get through it? What I *was* right about, though, was telling you that we needed space, because obviously we do. *Obviously* that's what you've wanted all along or you would have disagreed when I first brought it up."

"But I was confused and I was having a hard night," I said, my hand balling up into a fist.

"When *aren't* you lately?"

Like a fish searching for air, I opened my mouth then shut it again and there was a long silence.

Then Chris said, "The reason why I called is because I want my jacket back."

I felt slapped. "What?"

"Don't make this more difficult than it already is," he said.

"But—" I started, but didn't know how to finish.

Chris's football jacket was so symbolic of our relationship and of who I was that returning it felt almost impossible. I'll never forget the first time I wore it. We were on our second date, at the diner where all the football players went after their games.

"Turn around," Chris said to me, holding his jacket in front of him by the bright-blue-and-white-striped collar.

"Really?" I asked, excited by the gesture. My face flushed from happiness and I tilted my head a little to watch as Chris slipped one bulky sleeve up my arm to my shoulder and then the other so I could shrug myself into the rest. My fingertips were just barely visible at the ends. It felt like Christmas, putting on that jacket, and wearing it said to everyone that I, Rose Madison, was Chris Williams's girlfriend.

"Keep it," Chris told me. "I like it better on you." He smiled and I got up on my tiptoes, placed both hands against his chest, and gave him a long, slow kiss. We barely noticed the whistling and catcalls from his teammates sitting in a nearby booth.

But now this memory hurt because I knew exactly what *not* wearing it would mean to everyone at school, and this made my heart ache. Returning his jacket made our breakup more real somehow. "Chris, I—"

"Bring it," Chris said, his voice sharp. "Today."

A deep breath pushed my chest out involuntarily. "Okay," I said even as tears stung my eyes and streamed down my face. "If that's what you want."

There was another long pause and he sighed into the phone. "It is."

I heard a click and Chris's picture disappeared from the screen. The jacket I'd proudly worn for two years stared at me from the back of my desk chair, where I always put it at the end of the day, and I grabbed it. Before I left the house I took out a big canvas shopping bag from under the kitchen sink. The letters *Chris Williams* stitched into the wool caught my gaze and I gave his name one long last look and then shoved the jacket inside.

———————

Krupa was waiting by the school entrance when I arrived. "Rose, how *are* you?" she asked, her brown eyes pooled with concern.

"Really glad to see you," I said, and I held out the bag with his jacket.

She peered inside. "Wow. So this is a done deal."

"I guess. I don't know. I'm too upset to talk about it right now."

"Okay. Let's just do this. We'll make it quick and get it behind us."

I loved how Krupa said *us*, as if Chris had broken up with her, too. I glanced left, then right, feeling anxious. "Ideally without attracting too much attention," I muttered as we began to navigate the packed hallways, thick with athletes, the bag bouncing against my hip with every step. A few of the cheerleaders nodded hello but I pretended not to see them. I hoped that luck would be on my side and Chris wouldn't be at his locker—I didn't want a scene. Instead, I found Tony standing there, a giant wall blocking my way, and I almost turned around right then.

"You can do this," Krupa whispered, and gave me a little push.

At least there was no sign of Chris.

"Hiya, Rose," Tony said after flashing Krupa a big smile. "What did you do to our captain this time? He was upset all weekend. You two and your little spats." He laughed, and if I had to bet, Tony was thinking that by football practice this afternoon he'd be yanking at Chris's arm, trying his best to pull us apart so they wouldn't be late. Tony's big hazel eyes were full of teasing, but then he saw my face and his expression changed. "Are you okay?"

"I have a favor to ask," I said, and took the bag from my shoulder, offering it to him, hoping he would just take it so I could leave.

"That's Chris's jacket," Tony said. "Why would you give it to me?"

I stretched my arms out farther, my muscles growing tired from holding it up. "He asked for it back. Would you make sure he gets it? Please."

"You're broken up for real?" he asked, plainly surprised by this, and when I didn't respond he began to shake his head side to side. "Don't put me in the middle of this. Besides, you guys always fix things." Tony stepped away as if suddenly afraid to be caught near me, giving me a clear path to Chris's locker, so I pushed past him. A sudden hush fell over the other football players standing nearby, watching us, their eyes like tiny knives sliding into the soft skin of my back. Reaching into the bag, I removed the jacket, folded it neatly, and placed it on the floor in front of locker 49, the number Chris wore on his football jersey, and left it there like a tribute.

"Let's go," Krupa said, pulling me away. "Everything is going to be okay," she encouraged as we headed down the hall. "And remember, you are not alone. Don't forget. You have me."

"I know."

"And just think," she went on, steering us toward our locker, "before long, football season will end and it will be all hockey, all the time on the weekends for you and me."

"Oh goody," I said, mustering a laugh.

"Look on the bright side: we won't have to worry about running into football players at the rink, right? And I'll do my best to—" Krupa stopped suddenly, mid-sentence, switching gears. "Um, we should get to class." She yanked me in the other direction so of course I needed to see what she didn't want me to.

Chris Williams was across the hall from us, his expression unreadable. He shook his head at me, whether in anger or sadness or something else I wasn't sure.

My eyes sought the floor.

Gently, Krupa urged me to follow her. "Rose?"

I breathed deep, in, out. "Let's go or we'll be late," I said, and just like that, another day of school officially began, as if nothing had changed, nothing at all—nothing except for me—and for the rest of that week I tried to get used to it, the fact that I was no longer Chris Williams's girlfriend, but a different girl, a different Rose, and in truth, I had no idea what this meant.

10

FAN OF YOUR EYES

On Saturday afternoon I found myself alone with Will Doniger. Silence stretched between us, the only sound from the bumping of his truck as we drove along back roads, the seat bouncing our bodies with sharp jolts as the wheels hit yet another pothole. The inside of the cab was intimate, as if made for conversation. We were sitting barely a foot apart, but it may as well have been miles. Will was face front, both hands on the wheel, his eyes straight ahead, which allowed me to study him with impunity. The white T-shirt he wore made his tan from all that yard work look even deeper, his jeans were frayed in places and dirt was smudged across the knees, and there was a leather cord tied around his left wrist. His hair fell in waves to just below his ears, so it had that perpetually messy look that only a guy can carry off well. He hadn't said a word since we left the house. Maybe he was angry about my bailing on him last Saturday or maybe he was just a quiet guy. Either way, he seemed comfortable with not talking.

I sighed, long and loud, glancing over at Will to see if he

noticed or might try to strike up a conversation. He didn't, and I turned my attention to the scenery outside the passenger window.

The Touchdown Diner appeared on our right, with its familiar painted signs that advertised three pancakes for three dollars and eggs, toast, and hash browns for two. I couldn't quell the sadness that accompanied the possibility that Chris and I might never go there together again. With this thought the silence became overwhelming.

"So," I began, trying to think of what in the world we might have in common to discuss. "How long have you been doing the landscaping thing?" This was the reason our paths crossed so I figured it was a good enough place to start.

"Four years," was Will's distressingly short response.

"Four years," I repeated. "Hmm," I murmured after another long pause. This was going nowhere fast. "So . . . were you, what, twelve then? That's kind of young, isn't it?"

"I was thirteen," he replied, further proof that he was not only a man of few words but more like two or three tops.

"Thirteen is pretty early, though, right?"

"It was for my dad's business. I was already used to working for him."

I was startled by how easily he brought his father up in conversation—I certainly wasn't able to do this yet with my mother. "That would make you, what, seventeen now?"

"Yup. Seventeen."

Oh my god. You know things aren't going well when you resort to basic math as a means to further discussion. Just as I was beginning to despair, Will asked, "You?"

"Me?" I wasn't sure what he wanted to know.

"How old are you?"

"Oh. Sixteen. This past summer in July," I said, and automatically thought of how difficult my birthday was without Mom.

"How'd it go?" From Will's tone it was clear he knew what I was thinking.

"Well," I began, trying to decide how best to answer. "It was sad. Really difficult." I paused. "No, it sucked actually. It completely and totally sucked. I didn't even want anyone to notice it was my birthday."

"Sounds about right," Will said.

I glanced at Will sitting there, relaxed, his left arm stretched out over the top of the steering wheel, his right hand resting on the gearshift, barely a few inches from my knee. He put on his signal and we turned down a dirt road with a canopy of trees on either side. The leaves were already turning bright yellows and oranges and my eyes settled away from him and onto a big maple ablaze with cherry-colored foliage until it disappeared behind us. "Really?"

"The first birthday is the hardest, but it'll get easier."

I turned to him again. "I want that to be true."

"You just have to go through it. The sadness. There *is* another side." He looked at me for the very first time since I'd gotten into his truck. "I mean it," he said.

"So, are you? To the other side, I mean?" Broaching the subject of his father so directly made me nervous—I didn't want to overstep. But maybe Will was more ready to talk about this subject than I was. At least it was something he seemed willing to talk about, as opposed to our stilted conversation from before.

"I'm getting there. Doing my best." He paused. "You seem to have a lot of support. You know, like from your boyfriend."

"My boyfriend?" I said, surprised by Will's comment even as I realized that saying the word *boyfriend* made me feel a pang of regret—I'd have to practice adding the "ex" before it would come naturally.

"Yeah. Chris Williams," he said.

"Oh. How did you know?" I asked, and immediately felt stupid. Of course Will knew. Everyone at school did. He gave me a face that said something like, *Come on, I'm not blind.* "Okay, okay. That was a dumb question. People always know what Chris Williams does. Or did. God, that came out wrong. You know what I mean. Whatever."

"I see you with him," he said.

"You see me—" I started, then realized what he meant. "At my house, when you're working and Chris picks me up for school. Of course. Do you and Chris know each other well?"

He shrugged. "Not really. Only enough to say hello in passing. We're both seniors."

I nodded. It was strange to be having a conversation with Will about Chris, almost a relief to talk about him out loud as if everything was still the same.

"Last week you walked to school," Will observed.

My eyes immediately dropped from Will's face and I studied his hand on the gearshift, the way it tensed when he moved. "You noticed?"

"I did."

"Well, to be honest, actually," I stuttered, preparing myself to say out loud what came next. "Chris and I broke up," I confessed, and there it was, out in the open for the first time to someone other than Krupa. It sounded so final. Though I could tell Will was waiting for me to continue, now it was my turn to play the silent one, knowing that he would let the subject drop rather than pry.

Soon the bumping and bouncing of the truck along the road became our only background noise, the trees radiant, their colorful leaves luminous in the sunlight. It wasn't long before we turned into the dirt parking lot of the farm, pulling up alongside a long rickety wooden shed with one wall open to the cool fall air surrounded by cornfields as far as the eye could see.

"We're here," Will said, the truck shuddering and coughing before it quieted. Suddenly, he looked at me straight on, his gaze steady and holding mine. Then just as abruptly he turned away, opening the driver's side to hop out. His stare was long enough for me to notice the color of his eyes. They were dark blue, like the ocean, shimmering and deep and almost impossible to see through to the bottom.

11

CAN YOU TELL

"But these are so ugly," I said.

Will and I were standing in front of a large wooden bin that was filled with thick, gnarled roots covered in knots. The ragged cardboard sign attached to one of the planks said "Pink," the next one over said "White," and a third said "Blush."

"We're not planting actual flowers. You knew that, right?" Will watched me in between picking through the bin, choosing one root over another, using what criteria I could not imagine— they all looked the same, each equally hideous. "Did you think they would be in bloom?" he asked.

"No," I said in a huff, remembering the pictures from the gardening books of just the sort of mutant potato–looking things Will was admiring and discarding one by one and only rarely putting inside the basket I held in my arms. "I knew they would be roots. It's just that the ones you keep picking look the worst of all."

He stopped his search and cocked his head to the side. "Would you like to choose them instead?"

My eyes flickered to the ceiling. "No. I don't know how to tell the good from the bad."

"Okay then." Will continued to sort through the bin, adding roots to our pile until we had twelve, four each of the different colors.

"That's it? A dozen?" I stared at them, trying to decide whether or not these deformed objects could really turn into beautiful flowers come spring.

"I thought you wanted my help," Will said.

"I do."

"So trust me."

"But we didn't talk about numbers."

"Twelve is more than enough. These will grow big, though the first year you won't see too much. In three or four you'll have more flowers than you know what to do with."

"Four years," I cried. "I can't wait that long."

"You'll have to be patient," Will said.

"I want them to bloom in May. I kind of need them to," I added in a whisper, realizing how high the stakes felt for this one task.

"Oh, they will. You'll have plenty. But the following year you'll have even more. That's all I was trying to say."

"Really?" I asked, still wanting more reassurance.

"I promise."

"Okay." I began to breathe again, feeling mostly relieved. "What's *blush* anyway?" I asked as Will traded one root for another from the bin with that particular sign attached to it.

"A color."

"But what does it look like?"

"It's a shade of pink." Will seemed pained to admit out loud that he knew this.

I smiled a little. "What kind of pink?"

"Shades of pink are not up for discussion," he said, and I almost wanted to laugh at his sudden discomfort. He grabbed the basket from me and walked up to the register, emptying everything onto the counter.

"Hi, Will," said the girl ringing up our stuff. Between her tone and the looks she was giving him it was obvious she was flirting.

"Hey," he responded, his voice flat and devoid of any real interest, placing the last root on top of the pile. Will took off, leaving me standing there with this girl staring at me, and not in a friendly way, eventually returning with two giant bags of compost and dropping them at my feet.

"Do we really need those?"

He gave me a wry look. "Peonies love this stuff."

"But—"

"Just trust me," he said. His blue eyes widened. "Okay?"

I nodded.

To the checkout girl he said, "We're taking all of this," and drew a circle in the air with his index finger to include the bags at our feet.

She smiled sweetly. "Sure, Will," she said, before glaring at me again. While I paid, Will began shuttling our stuff out to his truck.

"Are you ready to go?" he asked once there was nothing left.

"All set," I said, and walked out. Will followed behind me, each footstep loud as his sneakers crushed through the gravel in the parking lot.

"Glad to see you wore the right clothes," he said, and I turned around. He was looking over my boots, jeans, and the long-sleeved T-shirts I'd layered on today.

"Uh, thanks, I guess." I didn't know what to make of this appraisal.

"Good for digging," he said, and I did a double take.

"You want to plant these *right now*?"

"May as well," he replied, and headed to the driver's side while I hoisted myself up into the passenger seat. He opened the door and got in. "If we wait another week," he said, reminding me of how I'd canceled last Saturday, "it might be too late. I know it seems warm out now, but frosts can happen quickly." He turned the key and started the engine. "And I'm assuming you actually want these to grow."

"Yes. I do," I said under my breath, and we drove the rest of the way to my house in silence.

Later when Will handed me a shovel from the back of his truck I looked at him, concerned. "Aren't these kind of big for gardening tools? Shouldn't we start with some trowels?" I said.

"Not if you want to plant peonies," he said, removing another shovel and walking around to where I stood in the driveway. "They need a lot of space to thrive," he added, and started across the backyard.

"Wouldn't they be nicer in the front?" I called after him.

Without turning around, he shook his head. Shovel in hand, I did my best to catch up, which wasn't easy since the blade kept scraping along the ground. Once I was by Will's side he started talking again. "I have an idea for where to put them. If you don't like it, we'll try somewhere else."

"Okay," I said reluctantly.

Will took the path that led to Mom's rose garden and stopped next to it, dropping the shovel to the grass. "This is what I was thinking," he said, going on to list his reasons. "There's plenty of room for the roots to spread out. The soil is already rich because of the roses and other flowers nearby—ideally we would have composted ourselves if there was more time but we'll have to make do. They'll get plenty of sunlight all day and peonies love bright light." Will sounded like he knew what he was talking about, but before I could say yes he told me his last reason. "And your mom and I used to talk sometimes," Will said in a quiet voice.

I looked up, startled.

He hesitated, as if instinctively he knew I needed a moment to process what he'd just told me. "Sometimes we'd sit at the table on the patio over here, or occasionally on the bench. I know it was her favorite place. And I used to see you and your mother out here together, so I thought—"

"About what?" I interrupted.

His brow furrowed with confusion.

"What did my mother talk to you about?" I asked, more specific this time.

He looked away. "My dad. When he got sick and then, you know, afterward."

"Oh. All right," I said. "Okay."

"Okay what?"

"Let's plant them here. I think it's a good idea."

Without looking at me again, he immediately began to mark out the boundaries where we would dig up the grass and soil, and we got to work. Will stuck his shovel deep into the ground and I followed, using my boot as leverage along the top edge of the metal, forcing it down into the dirt, and heaving the earth onto a growing mound. Despite the cool breeze, it wasn't long before sweat rolled down my back and he and I both were stripping off layers, making a pile of discarded clothing in the grass. It was hard work, probably the most labor I'd done in a long time, but it felt good and I began to enjoy myself. The sun gradually made its way toward the horizon and I was so caught up in the rhythm that when Will spoke again I was startled. It felt as though we could go on like this forever, digging side by side, in silence.

"Hey, hey, hey," he said, hurrying over to where I stood in

what was now a hole about a foot and a half deep. My jeans were covered in dirt from my knees to my ankles. He grabbed the shovel's handle, stopping me. "We're planting peony roots, not digging for water."

I was almost sorry to stop. "I hadn't noticed that we were done."

The scrape of the sliding glass door to the kitchen caught my attention and I saw that my father stood at the top of the back steps.

"Hey, Dad," I called out.

"You kids want some coffee?" he asked.

A hot drink after all this work was the last thing I wanted, but I appreciated that he was making an effort to do something nice.

"Hi, Mr. Madison," Will said.

My father made his way toward us. "Hi, Will. Nice to see you out here with Rose. And taking care of everything in general. It means a lot. I should say it more often." He paused, surveying the nearby gardens. "I'm sorry I don't."

"I'm happy to do it. Mrs. Madison's gardens are special."

Dad rubbed a hand across his eyes. "Yes. I know."

My father's sincerity, whenever he showed even the littlest bit of emotion, made me tear up. I blinked my eyes and turned away, straight toward the setting sun.

"So how 'bout it? Coffee?" Dad said, his voice cheering up again.

I hoped my father wouldn't notice that my eyes were wet. "Thanks for the offer. I'm thirsty, but not for something hot."

"Oh. Right," he said. "How about I put some ice in it?"

This made me laugh—he was trying really hard. "Sure, why not," I answered.

"Will?"

"I'd love some water."

"One water and one iced coffee coming up," he said.

"Two waters," I said.

"Two waters and one iced coffee," my father confirmed, and returned to the kitchen.

Meanwhile, Will disappeared around the side of the house— maybe he could tell I needed a minute alone or maybe it was just coincidence—but it wasn't long before Dad brought out a tray with three tall glasses balanced on top and placed it on the nearby table.

"Here you go," he said to me.

"Thanks, Dad. That was really nice of you."

He smiled a little and I wanted to cry all over again, reminded that occasionally my father was still capable of doing Dad-like things, like trying to take care of me, even if it was only a glass of water and some coffee. "Okay, kid. I didn't mean to interrupt. Back to work," he said, and walked away, his shoulders a little hunched, though not as much as usual, and still I felt like weeping. Before a sob could escape I saw Will headed this way again, a giant bag of compost hoisted over his shoulders, his body bent at an awkward angle. I lifted the cold glass of coffee to my lips and gulped some down, the bitter taste causing me to make a face and helping wipe away the sadness. Dad had made the coffee potent and even the ice didn't dilute its strength. Will let the bag slide to the ground next to the newly dug bed. It made a heavy thud.

"Do we really have to use this stuff?"

"If you want your flowers to grow, then yes," Will said, and drained his glass. He tore an opening in the bag and took the pair of thick work gloves hanging from the back pocket of his jeans and put them on. He began to pile compost into the shallow area, covering the bottom. It looked dark and rich and earthy next to the light brown dirt we'd piled up from digging the bed. After a while, he looked up at me. "It washes off, you know."

This comment snapped me to action. I didn't want him to think I was afraid to get my hands dirty so I walked straight up to the bag and stuck my arms elbow deep in the stuff, not even bothering with gloves, and brought up a giant handful. I dumped it in the bed, trying to mimic the way Will was shaping the piles of compost so each would cradle one root.

He stared at me.

"What?" I demanded. "Am I doing something wrong?"

A small smile, so small it was almost imperceptible, tugged at Will's lips. "I said it washes off, not that you had to bathe in it. I have another pair of gloves you can borrow."

"Gloves are for the weak of heart," I said haughtily.

He flicked some compost at me and I yelped. Then I flicked some back, but he didn't budge. "Whatever you say, Rose."

It was the first time Will ever said my name. Before I could search his face for why, he was already busy at work again.

By the time we finished, the sun was almost set, the sky a brilliant palette of red and pink and blue. I was covered in dirt and compost and grass, certain I smelled awful. I couldn't wait to take a shower, but I also felt satisfied. If we'd done this right, there would be gorgeous flowers coming up from this ground in a few months. Best of all, I'd done something my mother wanted and I was proud of myself because today I had honored her wishes.

"Everything okay?" Will asked.

I studied the sky awhile longer before I turned to him. "Yeah. It is."

He nodded and began to pack up. When we were both laden with empty bags and tools we headed back to the driveway. "Now what?" I asked, after we returned the shovels and the wheelbarrow to the back of his truck.

"You wait till April, maybe May," he said, walking toward the driver's side.

"That's it?"

"That's it."

"Seriously."

"April is when the weather gets warm again," he explained, but that wasn't what I was asking about.

"So you're leaving, just like that," I clarified.

"Yup. See you later." Without even glancing my way, he opened the door to the cab and got inside. He started up the truck, put his arm across the passenger seat, and began to back out. Something tugged at me inside as I watched him go. Maybe it was confusion, maybe it was disappointment, but I was out of practice with my emotions so I couldn't be sure.

12
BETWEEN THE LINES

After the Saturday I spent with Will, my morning routine began to deviate. Like always, I brewed the coffee, got Dad up, and made sure he was fed and on the road to work on time, but before I left for school I went outside to check on my roots. According to the gardening books, they loved that compost Will made me buy and at least a good two inches of it should cover the bed to keep the soil rich until winter hit. Plus the bed needed watering or the roots would die. I certainly couldn't have that happen. First thing on Monday I retrieved the watering can from the back steps, filled it, and headed toward the new bed, the heavy container bumping against my legs, causing some of the water to slosh out. "Got enough of that stinky soil you like so much?" I said as I let a light rain fall across the roots. The sound of footsteps came up behind me and when I turned around Will was standing there.

He pointed at the watering can. "Don't overdo it," he advised, and reached out to palm the topsoil, picking up a handful and rolling it around in his fingers.

"I know what I'm doing," I said, embarrassed to meet him here, now, while I was talking to the dirt.

Will looked as if he wanted to laugh. "I can tell." He opened his fist, letting the soil fall through his fingers, and got up.

I glared at him. "I thought you wouldn't be back here till April."

He shrugged. "See you," he said, and walked off.

But then Will and I began to run into each other every morning. "Here to check on the roots," he announced the second time it happened.

"Me, too. They seem well," I said.

Again he left without further comment. By day four, though, we almost graduated to genuine conversation.

"You really care about these," he stated. Crisp fallen leaves rustled around us in the air, the trees almost barren from the growing cold and wind. Will's hair was getting long and it kept blowing into his eyes.

"I do," I said.

"Why?"

"Why wouldn't I?"

"Before your mother died," he began, and my eyes widened—Dad, Jim, and I almost never said those words out loud, as if by not saying them they wouldn't be true. "You didn't care for the gardens."

"I did, though." I was a bit indignant.

"That's not what I meant."

"What *did* you mean?"

"I meant, you literally never took care of them. Your mother did all the work."

"Oh. Well. That's right. But I guess that's changing."

"I guess so," he said, and that was the end of another exchange.

A full week passed and then another, and my conversations with Will piled up. I began to notice that he was expressive, that somewhere deep under the surface lived emotion—it was subtle, but definitely there. You just had to pay attention to see it.

During one of our morning talks, Will was explaining how reddish shoots and buds would push up out of the ground this spring and I started to think about how my mother used to bring her love of gardening into her teaching. I interrupted him. "My mother's kids used to love watching that happen."

Will looked at me with skepticism. "They grew peonies?"

"No, of course not," I said, and laughed because her students could barely wait for snack time each day never mind the six months of fall and winter. "It was a far more modest endeavor. Pea shoots in cups. They kept them by the window and checked on them constantly. My mother loved how excited the kids got at the first sign of green."

"Pea plants are perfect. They grow fast and they're difficult to kill."

"They'd have to be easy or you'd have traumatized children by the armful."

Will looked at me hard. "Peony plants are a lot more difficult."

"Are you preparing me for disappointment?"

"No. Just stating the truth." Then, like always, Will began his march around the house toward the front yard. But this time, he stopped.

I waited to hear what else he would say, warming my hands around my coffee mug.

"These will turn out fine," he told me. "You'll see. Come spring, they'll be beautiful."

"I hope so."

"Believe it," he said, and continued on his way.

———————

After school Krupa drove me home and during the ride I decided to show her the peony bed. It was only dirt, but it felt like an accomplishment, and after the last month, I wanted to share something that had gone right in my life. "Do you have a minute?" I asked when she turned into my neighborhood. "There's something I want you to see in the backyard."

"Of course," she said. She pulled into the driveway. The car rattled and sighed and clanked before quieting.

"Follow me."

We cut across the lawn and wound our way through the gardens until we arrived at my mother's roses, where the new flower bed pooled out next to the patio. "So this is it. It's not much, I know," I said.

Krupa stared. "What did you plant here?" she asked, her voice almost a whisper, and I wanted to hug her. When we were growing up my mother was always planting and pruning and digging, inviting us to pick bouquets when there were so many flowers she didn't know what else to do with them. Krupa knew that whatever I'd done here must be special because anything to do with the gardens at our house was about my mother.

"Peonies," I said, pointing at each individual mound of compost where Will and I had the roots. "In the spring this will be full of flowers. Hopefully," I added.

"Peonies are beautiful," Krupa said.

"They are," I said.

"It's going to be gorgeous. Your mother would have loved to see this."

My eyes started to fill. I'd managed not to cry for a long, long time, but I couldn't hold back the tears any longer. They slid down my cheeks and I wiped them away with my sleeve. "Thanks," I whispered.

Krupa reached over and took my hand. "This is good, Rose," she said. "It really is."

13

ONE OF THOSE DAYS

"Roooseyy."

"Jim, will you wait a minute? It's not like I forgot you were there." My brother was on speaker, which he hated, while I sprinkled salt and pepper across the top of a chicken. "Your face is glaring at me from the phone anyway."

The wind whistled loudly outside. Every day for the last week it rained, so my trips to the flower bed had ended. We changed the clocks and it was getting darker earlier, making the atmosphere feel gloomy, the sky already black outside the windows.

"Rooooseeeyyy!" Jim's voice bellowed again through the kitchen.

"I'm still here. I told you I'm kind of tied up."

"What picture of me is on there anyway?"

I laughed and glanced at the screen again, making sure to keep my messy hands away.

"Rose. What. Picture."

"Remember how in eighth grade—"

"Not the one with the braces—"

"—And the headgear *and* the long hair. Yup. Just before bed-time and you are wearing pajamas. I love this picture."

"Get that *off* your phone. Every time I call you whoever is around sees it."

I opened the oven door and slid the roasting pan onto the rack. "Stop being melodramatic." The timer was set for fifty minutes and I started it counting down. I washed my hands before picking up the phone, cradling it between my ear and shoulder while Jim continued to rant. "Jim," finally I cut in. "That photo cracks me up."

He sighed. "Yeah, but at my expense."

"Nobody sees your monster metal smile but me. And maybe Krupa."

Jim was silent for a moment. "What happened with you and Chris? Were you ever going to tell me?"

No one in my family knew about the breakup yet. I'd been keeping it a secret, or trying to. I didn't feel like dealing with their questions, though I should've known Jim would find out on his own since we knew a lot of the same people. "Who told you?"

"So it's true. Interesting."

"You didn't even know for sure?"

"I ran into Susan Hepler on campus and she mentioned she'd gone home for a weekend and run into Chris Williams. She no-ticed he was wearing his jacket."

God, that stupid jacket again.

"Are you going to tell me what happened or what?" Jim pressed.

"No," I said. "There's nothing to tell. We broke up, couples break up, and it's not a big deal. It just is what it is."

"Do you want me to talk to him?"

"No! Please don't. You don't need to do that."

Jim sighed into the phone. "Rosey, I'm worried. I don't like you to be alone."

"I've got Krupa."

"Krupa's not enough."

"Jim." My voice became hoarse. "It's my fault. I lost Chris because I can't handle being in a relationship. I've been so wrapped up in being sad about Mom and with Dad's dramas that I shut Chris out, along with everyone and everything else in my life. I used to have the cheerleaders and the football games and I used to go out dancing and partying and have a normal social life, but now I'm this person who is so afraid to hear music because it makes me cry that I can't even go into stores at the mall." This last bit of my rambling confession reminded me about the iPod in my Survival Kit.

The Survival Kit was another thing my family didn't know about yet. A part of me wanted to tell Jim, but what if Mom hadn't left him one? The mere thought made me feel horribly guilty.

I could hear my brother breathing on the other end of the phone. "Listen, I'm sorry, Jim. Forget everything I just said. I need to go."

"Rosey—"

"I've got to check on dinner. Make sure it doesn't burn," I lied, watching as the timer ticked down past forty minutes and counting.

"Rosey—"

"I'll change your picture, I promise. I love you. Really, I do. Bye." I ended the call and rested my phone on the counter. The house was quiet except for the muffled sound of the rain beating against the window.

I couldn't stop thinking about the iPod.

Once upon a time I *loved* music. All kinds—old, new, alternative, cheesy, danceable, moody. From the moment I hit sixth grade I began to give my life a sound track. I made a playlist for every occasion, every emotion, every kind of day, for hanging out with Krupa, for doing my homework, for hooking up with Chris, and for gorgeous summer afternoons. There was no reason too small.

But not anymore.

A few bars of anything, even dance music, and the tears started to fall. This wasn't the first time I'd cut music from my life either. In eighth grade, the year Mom was diagnosed with cancer and first went through chemo, I hated music then, too. If someone turned on a stereo or docked an iPod I'd race over and unplug it or press the *power* button to shut it down.

Without music, though, a huge piece of me felt missing.

Mom knew it, too, and that's why she added the iPod to the

Survival Kit. Maybe I was ready for my life to be one long, beautiful playlist once again.

Rushing through the house to my room, I threw open the closet and slid the bag from its ribbon. I unfolded the top, my hand fumbling inside until my fingers closed around the thin, smooth metal rectangle. Music would be task number two because I was done with silence. The bedside lamp cast a warm circle of light onto the iPod's silvery blue surface and I slid my finger gently around the click wheel. I was about to put in the earbuds when there was a knock at my door. I shoved the iPod under the covers and placed the Survival Kit on the floor on the far side of the bed. I grabbed a book off the table and opened it across my lap. "Come in," I said.

"Hi, Rose." My father opened the door and poked his head inside. "I'm home."

"I see that," I replied, and got up to give him a kiss on the cheek. There was alcohol on his breath and it was potent, but I did my best not to make a face. I guessed I was wrong and Dad wasn't doing better at all. "Dinner's in the oven. It's chicken."

"Thanks, sweetheart," he said, his voice flat and sad and slurred. "But I'm not feeling well. I'm going straight to bed."

Another dinner Dad wouldn't eat. Jim was right—I am alone. I looked hard at my father but he turned away, pulling the door shut, his footsteps shuffling slowly down the hall as the rain pounded the roof even harder. I pulled the iPod back out from under the blanket, cradling it with both hands, allowing myself the memory of Mom singing along to a song she liked. I knew she was right, that music was too important to shut out for good. I would take my time and little by little I would add it back into my life, and maybe with each song I would feel a bit more like myself again. Maybe music would give me something to feel good about again. I hoped it would, since I really needed to find that new something soon.

NOVEMBER & DECEMBER

A Sound Track for the Holiday Season

14

HOCKEY WEEK

"Ten minutes, that's all it takes. Come on." Krupa turned to me from the driver's side of her car, one hand still on the wheel. We were parked outside MacAfee Arena and the first hockey game of the school year was about to start. The rainy weather had continued throughout this week and it streamed across the windows. My fingers curled around the edge of the old cracked leather seat like she'd need to pry them away. "It will be good for you. Besides, there's absolutely no chance you'll run into Chris. Football players don't go to hockey games."

"How do you know?" I asked.

"I just do. The play-offs start tomorrow so there is no way they will be out on a Friday night. I am going to make a lot of money this weekend," she sang happily, and took a sip from her Coke Slurpee.

Maybe waiting alone in Krupa's car would be more depressing than going inside and having to see other people. "Fine," I said. "I'll go with you."

"Fantastic," Krupa said, and began to drumroll her hands

against the steering wheel. "And then we'll go have pancakes for dinner!"

"Okay," I said, and laughed. Krupa had been amazing since the breakup.

She opened the door and got ready to run inside. "Let's go," she beckoned, and I got out, putting my arms over my head to protect myself from the rain, following her through a door with big blue letters that spelled "MacAfee Arena" across the glass. Soon the noise of a cheering crowd was audible. Krupa glanced back at me, her eyebrows raised, and I shrugged. Neither one of us had been to a Lewis hockey game so we didn't know what to expect. We hurried through the ticket lobby and into the rink. The air was cold enough that I could see my breath and the arena was packed with people buzzing everywhere. We stood by the wall, taking in the sheer number of fans.

"Wow," she said.

"No kidding. Who knew hockey was this popular?"

"No wonder they're paying me a hundred bucks a game." Krupa rubbed her bare hands together to create warmth. "Where do you want to wait for me?"

I scanned the bleachers, searching for a space high enough in the stands that I could see over the boards onto the ice. I cupped my palms and blew into them, wishing I'd brought gloves. It felt like winter in here. "I don't know if I'll find a spot to sit so how about we meet by the snack bar?"

"Okay. I'd better go. I'll see you in . . ."—she glanced at the clock on the giant scoreboard overhead—"eight minutes."

"Try not to fall," I called after her. Krupa had sung the anthem a million times, but never standing on a sheet of ice. Maybe they would make her wear skates, I thought gleefully. Without turning around she waved me off just before curving around the rink and out of sight. I went in the opposite direction and climbed the metal stairs to the bleachers, the clanging of my boots against the rungs nearly drowned out by the noise. People maneuvered by as I stood at the top and sought an open seat, their Excuse me's clipped by the shouts and cheers that filled the arena.

I saw Kecia Alli sitting in the center of the stands. She waved.

I had to respond. Kecia had seen me for sure and if I didn't say hello I would officially be rude. She patted the open seat next to her and pointed to me. I didn't have another place to sit anyway so I climbed even higher toward the row where she sat with Mary McCormack and Tamika Anderson, also cheerleaders. I hadn't spoken to Kecia since my last cheer practice on the day Mom went into the hospital.

"Hey, Rose," she said with a warm smile. "Nice to see you. It's been ages."

"Hey," Mary and Tamika echoed, equally friendly. The three of them stood so I could squeeze by. I noticed Mary and Tamika wore heels, which seemed over the top for a hockey game.

"Hi, guys," I said, and took my seat, feeling rather nervous. I opened my mouth to say something else, then stopped.

The three of them wore sympathy stares. Whether the look in their eyes was about my mother or my breakup with Chris,

I wasn't sure, and I waited for one of them to mention either of these unpleasant topics, but then Kecia took the conversation in an unexpected direction. "I'm so excited that hockey season has finally started," she burst out. "I wish we cheered for them instead. It's way more exciting than football. Don't you think?"

My eyes blinked back surprise. "I've actually never been to a game. This is my first," I confessed.

"Seriously?" Tamika said, the ends of her long Lewis-blue scarf brushing the toes of her shoes as she leaned forward. "You are going to love it. Nonstop action. The refs, like, rarely blow their whistles and there's never any waiting around for those awful drags between football downs."

"And don't forget all the fights," Mary said.

Tamika rolled her eyes. "She loves it when the players get in fights."

"Really? Interesting," I said, and felt myself smile. Their enthusiasm was contagious. Even with two years on the squad I was unaware of my teammates' winter activities. Maybe this was what happened when you dated the center of the universe— you missed out on other things. "I'm not staying, though," I added.

"What do you mean? Why not? You have to," Kecia said. "Because you'll *love* it. Really."

"After Krupa does the anthem we're off to grab food and see a movie."

"If you wait one minute after they drop the puck you won't

be going anywhere. Cross my heart." Kecia made an *X* across her chest with her index finger. "Your eyes will be glued to the ice the rest of the game."

"You sound dedicated," I said.

Mary nodded. "Don't let them fool you. It's not just for love of the game, but more like love of hot guys on ice."

Kecia and Tamika laughed and eventually I joined in. I was starting to have fun.

Suddenly the crowd erupted into cheers and people stood up, screaming, clapping, stomping their feet.

"Speaking of hot guys," Kecia said, pulling me up off the bench.

The two hockey teams filed out of their boxes, the Lewis players wearing white home jerseys with blue numbers and bright blue rings around the edges and the sleeves. They lapped the rink at breakneck speed and then lined up in two rows, stopping so fast they sent shards of ice high into the air. Everyone in the stands faced the American flag that hung from the ceiling at the back end of the arena.

Krupa made her way out toward the center and everyone quieted.

I was a little disappointed she wore normal shoes.

"Wait for it," Kecia said as the crowd hushed.

At first I thought she must mean Krupa's voice, but then every player removed his helmet, revealing faces once obscured by protective masks.

"The moment we've all been waiting for," Tamika said in a dreamy voice.

That's when I saw Will Doniger. He was on the ice at the very end of Lewis's line of players.

No. Way. Will Doniger was on the hockey team? How could I not have known this?

Krupa's voice rang out but my eyes were glued to his face.

Kecia began to whisper. "The players to watch are numbers ten, twenty-two, and six. They're the best. You know, the same as in football, like with . . ." She trailed off in time to avoid saying Chris's name but at the moment I didn't care. There was a blue number six stamped on Will's jersey.

The cheers got louder as Krupa's voice rose for the final crescendo until the crowd was almost deafening. Once Krupa finished, the players took off around the rink, skating in a wide circle, banging their sticks against the ice. Kecia, Tamika, and Mary clapped and cheered and whistled.

I tapped Kecia's arm. "Am I right in thinking that number six is Will Doniger?"

"That's him. The team lost the state championship without Will these last two years. Everyone is very happy he's playing again."

"Lewis lost because he wasn't playing," I said with disbelief.

"That's what people say."

"What happened?" I asked.

"He was redshirted. You know, injured. At least technically."

"Technically?"

"Different stories were going around. Supposedly it was a back issue. Or an arm. I don't know for sure. A lot of people are here tonight just to see if he still has it in him. He was, like, rookie of the year back when we were in eighth grade and he was a freshman. Second-highest scorer in the state. Then he just kind of dropped off the face of the earth."

That explained why I never heard about Will Doniger, Lewis hockey star. He hadn't played since I began high school and when I counted back the years I realized that he must have stopped the winter his father died.

Loud techno music blared over the speakers and my body automatically tensed. The urge to make excuses and leave was powerful, and besides, Krupa was probably wondering where I was by now. I half expected my former cheerleading teammates to break into a choreographed routine like at football games, and Kecia, Tamika, and Mary *were* dancing—like everyone else their arms were above their heads and they bounced to the beat, just not in unison. Watching them made me feel wistful, especially since they looked like they were having fun. Kecia grabbed my hand and tried to raise it above my head. "Come on, dancing is an important part of the game. It helps warm you up!"

I stiffened and pulled away. "No thanks," I said, hoping she could hear me over the thumping. "I don't dance."

Kecia looked at me funny. "That's absolutely not true and you know it. You were one of the best dancers on the squad!

You love to dance. I've seen you." She waited for me to say something but I didn't. Eventually she shrugged, letting the subject drop, and turned back to Tamika and Mary.

I reached underneath the bench and felt for my bag, my fingers reaching into one of the pockets. The iPod was there, safe where I'd put it. When the music stopped, signaling the game was about to begin, each team lined up to face off on either side of the thick red line down the center of the ice. A referee stood in the middle, ready to drop the puck. I searched the jerseys for number six and there was Will, at the center of everything. Krupa must have been waiting by now, but still I hesitated. The possibility of seeing him play held me there.

"You should stay," Kecia said.

I craned my neck to see if Krupa was by the snack bar, but again my eyes were drawn back when the puck hit the ice and number six skated so fast after it he was almost a blur. "Well, maybe just for the first couple of minutes," I told Kecia. Will trapped the black disk, his stick flashing back and forth. Shouts of "Come on, Will!" rang out from the crowd. An opposing player shot in his direction, slamming him so hard against the boards they thundered.

I gulped. "Do you think he's okay?"

Kecia turned to me and laughed. "You've really never seen a game, have you?"

I shook my head, wondering if his time as a landscaper was over due to the broken bones he'd just sustained.

"Hockey is vicious," Kecia said. "They do stuff like that all the time."

"What, kill each other?"

"It's called checking," Kecia said.

"How do you know so much about hockey?"

"My older brother played. First I was forced to go to games. Then I got addicted."

On the ice number six went after the player who'd checked him less than a minute ago with such ferocity I almost covered my eyes. Again they smashed into the boards, but this time it was Will slamming someone against the glass. He was no doubt one of the team's stars, and I had to admit, I was riveted.

"Krupa's looking for you," Kecia said, pointing to the bottom of the stands.

Now I was sure I couldn't leave. Quickly, I pushed by Kecia, Tamika, and Mary, who bent to see around me so they didn't miss anything. "I'll be right back," I said, and ran down the stairs. "Krupa," I called out. She saw me and smiled, automatically moving to leave, so I caught up to her and put a hand on her shoulder. "Wait," I said, trying to catch my breath. "I want to stay."

Krupa turned and stared at me hard, curiosity in her eyes. "Really."

"Yeah. I'm kind of having fun. Sorta. I guess."

"At a *hockey* game? By yourself?"

"Well, not exactly. I ran into Kecia and a few other cheerleaders. Come sit with me."

"Um, definitely not. I have a football game tomorrow if you recall. That's two too many sporting events in one weekend for me."

"Do you care if I bag on our plans? I'm sorry, it's not that I don't want—"

"Please," she cut in. "You don't have to apologize. I can handle a night on my own."

I smiled. "Thanks for understanding."

"Kecia's nice. And you haven't spent time with the cheerleaders in ages. I think it's a good thing."

"Hanging out with them is less weird than I thought it would be."

"That's great. But I'm going to leave now," she said, bouncing up and down as she tried to warm up. "It's freezing in here."

I gave her a quick hug. "Talk to you tomorrow?"

"Of course," she said, and we parted ways.

The rest of the night, three periods of hockey players crashing, racing, and almost killing each other to get behind the puck, to take the perfect shot at the goal, fronted by a goalie so padded and monstrous he looked like something out of a horror movie, my eyes never left Will, whether he was on the players' bench for a breather or in the penalty box for doing something violently against the rules. The constant movement on the ice, how aggressive it was, took me in and kept me.

"Go to hell, ref," Tamika shouted, in the company of other, slightly more vulgar catcalls around us as the penalty clock was reset for a Lewis player. She turned to me, a smile forming on her lips. "What? Don't give me that look. I am *not* in uniform right now."

I laughed. "I wasn't giving you a look. Yell whatever you want. I'm not the cheer police."

When the final buzzer rang and the crowd let loose a frenzy of cheers on behalf of Lewis's win, I was almost disappointed—I didn't really want to leave. Amid a rising tally of penalties, Will scored twice. Watching him out there was pretty amazing and for a couple of hours I'd forgotten about everything else: my responsibilities, the sadness about my mom, my breakup with Chris. I'd needed this, though I didn't know it until tonight.

"Do you want a ride home?" Kecia asked as she gathered her stuff from under the bench and we began to file out of the stands.

"Oh. I guess I do. I hadn't really thought about how I'd get home after Krupa left. Thanks," I said, as much for the offer of a ride as for her pushing me to stay tonight. We reached the bottom of the bleachers and an interesting idea popped into my head. "Hey, do you know where the players come out after the game? Or don't they?"

I suddenly wanted the chance to congratulate Will. I wanted to tell him how much fun I'd had tonight. And I wanted him to know I'd seen his game. Though maybe I was just being crazy. "You're probably leaving right away, though, right?" I added. That this was likely made me feel relief.

"We're not going anywhere for a while. We usually hang around and talk to people so you've got plenty of time. The players come out down there." She pointed toward the far end of the rink below the stands. "If you walk in that direction you'll see signs for the locker rooms and people waiting outside. We'll be in the ticket lobby."

I hesitated. Will and I hardly knew each other, and then, he might get the wrong idea. But my curiosity about meeting Will Doniger, star hockey player, to see if he was any different from the boy I saw at the house eventually won out over my uncertainty. "Okay, thanks," I said, and headed toward the crowd of parents and girls lingering at the back of the rink. One of the mothers smiled and waved me over. She had two young girls with her and she seemed familiar but I couldn't quite place her.

"Rose," she said when I was close enough to hear. "I'm sorry. You probably don't remember me. I'm Cindy Doniger. Will's mom? This is Jennifer"—she placed her hand on the shoulder of the taller girl—"and this is Emily. His sisters." The girls were fidgeting, distracted by all the activity around them.

"Hi," I said. "Nice to meet you. Or, I guess, nice to see you again?"

"I knew your mother," she explained, and I recognized the mix of apology and sadness in her voice.

"Oh." I never knew what to say when this subject came up.

Mrs. Doniger nodded with understanding and I noticed that her eyes were the same blue as Will's. She placed a hand on top of Emily's head, patting her daughter's braids, and reached out for Jennifer, but her other daughter hovered near the vending machines. Then I heard Mrs. Doniger telling Emily, "See over there? It's your brother," she added, pointing toward the door of the locker room.

Will was wearing a school letter jacket that I'd never seen before, his dark hair still wet from the shower. The uncomfortable smile on his face grew even more so when a crowd of girls approached. He dropped his duffel bag to the ground against the cinder block wall and laid his hockey stick across it as girls corralled around him. His face was like stone as they talked at him.

I guess Will was reticent with everyone.

He nodded when parents said hello and laughed when teammates slapped him on the back, but showed almost no emotion until he made a beeline for his sister Jennifer, who was still lingering by the vending machines. He picked her up like she weighed nothing, flipping her upside down, while she squealed, "Let me go!" From the giggling it was clear she'd be equally fine if he left her hanging there. He walked over to his mother and kissed her on the cheek, still holding his sister by the feet, shrieking and laughing, banging his legs with her fists until he set her down and gave Emily some attention. Witnessing this made me wonder what it would take to get past the guard he put up.

That's when Will saw me and his eyes widened. He walked

toward me and I felt nervous again. Maybe I shouldn't be here after all.

"Hey," he said. "Who are you waiting for?"

"Well, I was at the game tonight and I thought I'd say hi."

"To . . ." He waited for a name or an explanation.

"Um, I thought I'd say hi to *you*," I said with a laugh.

"I didn't know you were a hockey fan."

"You didn't tell me you played." This came out of my mouth before I could think it through.

"Why would I tell you something like that?" His eyes searched mine, maybe for a clue as to why I'd stayed to see him afterward.

"Well, sorry. I mean, I can go, since I know there's a lot of people here to see you—"

"No," he cut in, stopping me. "I wouldn't have thought my being on the hockey team would interest you."

"It's kind of a big deal, don't you think? You and hockey?" I asked.

His expression didn't change. "It's important to me."

"And for a while there, we were talking, like, every morning."

"I know."

"You could've mentioned something. You know, for small talk's sake?"

He tugged at the bottom of his jacket, the blue of his eyes as bright as its color. "I suppose."

"Well, now I know," I said.

"I guess so."

"I met your family," I told him when I didn't know what else to say.

"I noticed."

"Your mom is nice."

"My sisters, though," he trailed off, glancing at them frantically pushing buttons on the vending machines. "They're a little out of hand."

"You seem to like them."

He nodded.

"You don't come by the house anymore," I blurted next.

"Winter's here. I have hockey practice every day."

"That makes sense," I said, looking around, feeling awkward. "Well, I guess I should go. I have to find my ride. I'm sure you've got . . ."—I paused, looking at the scene around us, a hovering crowd of parents and players, plus Will's family and a pack of girls hanging back, waiting to try to talk to him again—"things to do."

"Sure," he said, but didn't move, still looking at me in that way of his.

"Tell your mom bye," I said, and started to leave, but I'd gone only a few steps when I turned around again. "By the way, you were amazing out there," I called back to him.

"Thanks," Will said, and then he smiled.

I watched as our breath puffed wispy white clouds between us. "You almost never smile, you know."

Will's smile turned into a grin. "Neither do you, Rose," he said before turning away to greet a group of teammates who bulldozed him into the wall in what seemed like a gesture of affection—they were all laughing.

As I walked the length of the bleachers to meet up with Kecia a smile crossed my face, too. I couldn't help it. By the time I reached the lobby there was a slight bounce in my step. Almost imperceptible, but sure enough it was there.

I felt it.

15

MY BABY JUST CARES FOR ME

Sunday afternoon, Krupa and I were hanging out at my house, making a salad for lunch. She was whipping up dressing at the kitchen table and pressing me for details about the real reason I stayed to watch the game on Friday, while I sliced a tomato on the counter and did my best to avoid mentioning Will.

"What aren't you telling me?" she asked, her tone laced with curiosity and doubt about my response.

I kept my head down to hide the blush deepening across my cheeks. When I finally dared a glance at Krupa, I was startled to see the iPod cupped in her palms. She was turning it around and inspecting it from different angles.

"This isn't yours," she said.

"No, it's not," I agreed, not knowing what else to say.

Krupa hopped onto a stool on the other side of the counter and placed the iPod there. "Whose is it then?"

My lungs expanded in and out, wide and big, as I tried to calm myself and think of how best to answer. "It's . . . I mean, I found it actually . . ." I stopped. I wasn't ready to tell her about my Survival Kit. "It was my mother's," I finally said, which was close enough to the truth.

"I didn't know she even had one," Krupa said.

I stared at the cutting board, noticing the nicks and the thin lines and grooves made from years of use. Despite many attempts to put in some earbuds and listen, I hadn't yet heard a single song that was on the iPod. "Me neither. I was surprised, too."

"Have you had it since the funeral?" Her voice was gentle.

"Not exactly," I said. "Just for a couple of weeks."

"Where did you find it?"

"In her closet."

"I can't picture your mom with an iPod. I mean, she still listened to the radio, and god, I totally remember her putting records on that old turntable."

"I know." I closed my eyes at the sting of the memory. Without asking Jim and me for permission, Dad got rid of Mom's records and the player less than a week after she died. If I'd had a say I never would have given away her stuff like that.

"Rose, don't you miss listening to music?" Krupa asked.

I shrugged. "It's just . . . it's so hard. Every song makes me emotional and I am so sick of crying."

"It won't always feel that way," Krupa said.

"No?"

She shook her head.

"I wish I believed that."

Krupa held out the iPod. "So what's on it?"

"To tell you the truth, I don't know."

"Hang on a sec." Krupa disappeared into the living room and returned with the iPod dock that had been sitting on a shelf, collecting dust.

I watched, frozen, as she plugged it in and set the iPod into the cradle. "Krupa," I warned.

"Let's listen to one song," she said. "Just one. We'll do it together. It will get easier once you start. You haven't listened to anything since the funeral, have you?"

I shook my head.

Krupa placed a hand over mine. "I miss hanging out and listening to music with you, and going out dancing. We used to have so much fun. You remember, right?"

I nodded. Of course I remembered.

"Okay then. I think it's time," she said.

Every muscle in my body tensed as her fingers surfed the menu. Half of me desperately wanted her to stop and the other half wanted her to go ahead and make this task of my Survival Kit begin because I wasn't sure I could do it on my own. Maybe I couldn't do any of the tasks without help—not the peonies, not the music. My eyes became watery and I swallowed hard. I hadn't heard a single note and already there were tears. "Krupa, wait—"

"Rose." She handed me a napkin to wipe my face. "When you were in eighth grade and you imposed that ban on music when your mother was going through chemo, she literally marched you into the kitchen and told you, enough is enough, that your moratorium on music was becoming ridiculous, and she made you listen to the entire sound track of *Rocky*."

I smiled a little at the memory. "I know."

"Because she knew you loved the theme song and that hearing it would make you laugh. And she was right, too, and eventually you got over this need for constant silence."

"But eventually she got better, Krupa," I said, and my throat caught. "Now she's gone forever."

"I'm not your mom, but I love you, too, and I'm not planning on going anywhere." Then she said, "Ready? Because I've got the perfect song," but before I could answer she pressed *play*.

Nina Simone's big husky voice filled the kitchen and "My Baby Just Cares for Me" floated from the speakers. Mom loved the great women jazz crooners, and this song in particular. With my eyes closed I could almost see her standing by the sink, doing dishes, singing loud, and for an instant she was alive again, like magic. Music was so potent and powerful it could almost raise the dead. But as reality came rushing back and I remembered that Mom was gone for good, I went to shut down the power.

Krupa put out an arm to stop me. "Just wait," she said.

Nina Simone kept carrying those lyrics into the kitchen, and for the first time in ages I let myself sink into all this beautiful noise. When the song ended Krupa hit *pause* and the only sound left in the room was breathing.

"Thank you," I whispered.

Krupa removed the iPod from its dock and placed it on the kitchen table. "I have a proposal. Tomorrow you are going to bring your mom's iPod to school and we are going to commit to listening to one song every day. We can do it at lunch. Before you know it, music will be a part of your life again. Pretty painless, right?"

"Okay," I agreed. It wouldn't be painless, but I was grateful to Krupa nonetheless. She knew exactly what I needed to get through this. I wiped the back of my hand across my eyes to dry the tears. "It's a good idea. I'll have it with me at school. Promise."

"You're welcome," she said, and looked so pleased with herself that I had to make fun of her, at least a little.

"Don't get too carried away—it's not that big a favor," I said, already feeling a bit better.

She rolled her eyes at me, walked around the counter, and slid another knife from the wood block, grabbing a bright yellow tomato lined with grooves and smooth bulges around its circumference and setting it on the cutting board. "Let's eat soon," she said, slicing up one section, then another. Krupa nudged me with her elbow. "Are you going to help or what?"

"I suppose I could," I answered, smiling. Eventually I picked up my knife again to finish preparing our lunch, but not before the watery blur cleared from my vision. I didn't want to lose a finger.

16

ENERGY

At school later that week I found myself face-to-face with Chris Williams in the hallway. We stared at each other. Neither one of us knew what to say or do, and my heart began to race.

"Chris," I said, once I'd recovered enough to articulate a coherent word. My tone was formal and polite, like we'd just been introduced at a wedding. Sometimes the hurt from our breakup was still so close to the surface that it covered every inch of my skin.

"Rose," he said. The expression on his face was blank but his eyes were pained. There were no smiles exchanged between us, no pleasantries. I was about to leave when Chris spoke again. "You're listening to music," he said, gesturing at the iPod wedged into the pocket of my jeans.

As promised, every day at lunch Krupa and I listened to a new song. "I'm trying to," I told him. "It's not easy, but it's getting easier."

"You must be feeling better then," he said.

"I guess so."

"I'm glad."

"You are?"

Chris nodded, his eyes softening as he looked at me and for a second I thought maybe this was it, the moment when Chris and I somehow found our way back to each other, but then the bell rang. "I've got to get to class," he said.

"Me, too."

"Okay."

"Okay."

"See you."

I watched as he walked away, disappearing into the crowded hall, my mind full of Chris Williams and our short but significant conversation. Since the day I gave back his jacket we had managed not to talk at all.

After my next class, I saw Will by his locker loading books onto the shelves. He appeared and disappeared as people milled around between us. I leaned against the wall, trying to decide whether to say hi. This was the closest we'd been since last weekend, and for all I knew unless I walked up to him and started a conversation we might not talk again until the spring. My heart began to race.

Suddenly Krupa appeared at my side and gave me a curious look. "What's on your mind?"

Red bloomed across my cheeks. "Nothing important."

Her eyes narrowed. "Something is giving you a dreamy look."

"Nah." I pushed myself off the wall and we started down the hall. "I have to stop by our locker."

"Are you sure there's nothing you want to tell me?" she asked.

I shrugged. "Chris and I spoke today."

Krupa studied my face as we wove through the crowd. "Well, what happened?"

"We exchanged hellos. No, wait, I said Chris, then he said my name and there followed an awkward silence as if we didn't know each other at all. That part was fantastic."

"That must have been hard."

"It was. He saw the iPod and asked about it. I told him I was trying to listen to music again and he seemed genuinely happy about it. We even shared a moment."

"A moment? Please explain."

I tried to think of what it was that I felt with Chris. "You know, it's funny. For a second I thought he might bring up the possibility of getting back together, and I was so hopeful at the time. But as much as I still care about Chris, with even a little bit of distance I'm not sure it's what I want anymore."

Krupa gave me a look. "Really."

We arrived at our locker. She opened the door and retrieved her American history textbook, which landed in her bag with a loud thump.

"Really."

"You're getting over him?"

"Maybe I am."

"I knew you would."

I grabbed my book for class and slammed our locker shut. "That's enough smugness for the day."

Before Krupa could say anything else, Kecia Alli appeared. "Hey, guys," she said. "I was hoping to run into you."

"Hi, Kecia," Krupa said, slinging her bag over her shoulder, and the three of us began walking.

"What's up?" I asked her.

"Friday night is the second hockey game of the season."

"I know."

"You both should come this time," Kecia said. "I'll save seats."

"I don't know. Maybe . . ." I hesitated.

Krupa didn't. "Sounds great," she said.

I turned to her in surprise. "Really?"

"Rose and I will be there," she told Kecia.

"Perfect. See you tomorrow then," Kecia said, and headed upstairs.

We arrived at the door to our class and I laid my palm across Krupa's forehead. "Are you sure you're not sick, agreeing to go to an entire hockey game?"

People streamed around us on their way into the room. "No, *you* want to attend a hockey game, and I, your esteemed best friend, will accompany you."

"But you hate sports."

Krupa looked thoughtful. "After your enthusiastic review I thought I should give hockey a chance."

Her tone made me suspicious. "You have an ulterior motive. Spill."

"I do not," she protested.

"Right. Not buying it."

"Okay, fine. You want to know why?"

I nodded. "Please."

"Correct me if I'm wrong, but last weekend's game was the first truly social thing you've done at school since the spring."

I thought about what she'd said. "Okay. I'll give you that."

"And you used to be Miss Socialite."

"That was because I was dating Chris."

"Maybe." Krupa's eyes reached up to meet mine. "Listen, all I am trying to say is that last Friday when you came to tell me you wanted to stay for the game, I saw some sort of spark in you. One that I haven't seen in a long time."

"A spark," I repeated.

"It's a good thing," she said right as the bell rang. Before I had a chance to think too much more about her observation, class began and the teacher was passing out a quiz.

After school I was in my room studying when Jim called with news that he was none too happy about. "Guess what?" he asked, sounding annoyed.

"Are you really going to make me guess?"

"Well, no. Grandma Madison is coming for Thanksgiving."

I groaned. Grandma Madison was not known for her people skills, and the reminder that our first major holiday without Mom was around the corner didn't help my feelings either. "God, really?"

"Yeah. And get this, she's staying through Christmas."

"A whole month?"

"For my entire winter break." He made a choking sound.

"I'll be stuck with her the most anyway."

"Just stay out of the house a lot," he advised.

"I can't. Who's going to take care of Dad?"

"Grandma Madison, you idiot. I think that's the point."

"Like Dad told you that."

"No, she did."

I tapped my highlighter against the edge of the book on my desk. "She said that straight-out?"

"Well, during our conversation she implied that she was a combination of worried about and angry at Dad."

This surprised me. Grandma Madison never let on that she knew anything about Dad's up- and downhill trips, but then again, I wasn't the grandchild she called all the time—Jim was.

"She also said it was important that we fill up the house with as much life as possible during the holidays, you know, without Mom."

We were both silent a while before I moved the conversation

away from this sad place. "I don't think of Grandma Madison as someone likely to liven things up," I said.

Jim snickered. "But at least with her around you won't have to cook Thanksgiving dinner by yourself."

"True. Though she isn't very fun to cook with."

"I'll help."

"Right, Jim. Like I haven't heard that one before. The last time you tried to make something we actually had a small fire."

"That was not my fault."

"On that note, I'll be going."

Jim laughed. "You know I'm kidding. But I'll leave you alone. Love you."

"Love you, too, and I can't wait to see you."

"I know. Until Tuesday, then, Rosey girl, less than a week away."

I clicked *end*, just as a sharp sadness about Mom hit me hard and fast. I tried to focus on my schoolwork to distract myself, which didn't help much at all, but then I remembered what Krupa had said earlier today, about seeing a new spark in me, and I felt a little brighter, only a little, but it was enough to make a difference.

17

TAKE IT HOME

On Friday night MacAfee Arena was even more crowded with hockey fans than the weekend before, if that were even possible. While Krupa waited by the teams' boxes to sing the anthem, I made my way up through the stands to find Kecia and claim our seats.

"You're staying, right?" Kecia asked as I squeezed by her onto the bench.

"Yes. Both of us."

"That's great."

I set my bag down to save the spot meant for Krupa. Cheerleaders surrounded us on all sides and people smiled when they saw me and said hello, as if there hadn't been a period when I'd stopped hanging out with everyone. No one seemed to hold a grudge that I'd quit, and in fact it was the opposite. Amber Johnson, a fellow junior, even gave me a hug and said, "Stop being such a stranger. We've missed you."

"Thanks," I said. I was beginning to realize that avoiding the cheerleaders might have been a mistake, especially since they were acting like we were still friends. Maybe they were right, and we were.

Kecia reached under her seat and pulled a cup off the floor. "Hot chocolate," she explained, cradling it close to her lips so she could blow on it, while steam rose up from the little circle at the top. It smelled good and I considered asking for a sip. Tonight I was prepared for the cold with gloves, a warm coat, and a scarf, but hot chocolate seemed like an even better idea to deal with the freezing arena. "It's part of the ritual," she added.

"The ritual?"

"You always get up and dance when they play music."

"Yes, I remember from last week."

"And you always get hot chocolate. For some reason it tastes better at a hockey game."

"Maybe because they set the rink temperature to arctic conditions."

Kecia laughed. "They kind of do, don't they?"

I held up my mittened hands. "Just slightly."

Kecia looked at me. "I just want to second what Amber said—we really do miss you."

"Yeah?"

"When you just up and quit, we devoted an entire practice to discussing what to do." She paused. "You know, um, because of the circumstances."

The circumstances.

Kecia took another sip of her hot chocolate. "But you seemed to want to be left alone so we didn't pry."

"At the time I did, or thought I did," I admitted. "I guess cheerleading always seemed more about Chris and me than just me."

"It doesn't have to be," she said, and I wondered whether she was right. Chris was the reason I tried out freshman year, an excuse to be even closer to him at his games, but maybe there were other reasons for me to go back. "Anyway, you still have a spot on the squad if you want it. After all, nobody can flip like you do."

"Thanks. That's good to know," I said. It was nice to feel wanted, but I wasn't ready to commit to anything one way or the other.

The buzzer sounded, signaling that the game was about to start, and people stood for the anthem. The two teams took the ice, some players hopping straight over the wall and others passing through the narrow, low door in each of the team boxes. They circled the rink as Krupa made her way out, and this time when the players removed their helmets I was prepared to see Will. Even so, I felt butterflies.

By the time Krupa finished and reached our seats the game was already two minutes into the first period and Will had scored the first goal of the night. People were cheering wildly. "Look at you," she said as I clapped, my eyes following Will's jersey. "Miss Hockey Enthusiast."

"I'm just being a good fan."

"You should've seen Rose last week," Kecia said.

Krupa nudged me. "Can you at least tear yourself away from the ice long enough to explain to me what's going on?"

"I think I can do that," I said, trying to remember what I'd learned so far. As I alternated my attention between Krupa and the game, I did my best to explain what it meant to be offsides, what icing was, high sticking, too, and other reasons why players ended up in the penalty box. It wasn't long before Krupa was cheering as much as everyone else and wincing when there was a fight or if the players thundered into the boards.

"I'm not sure I can say I like hockey yet, but it *is* riveting," she said at the start of the first break. Kecia and a few other cheerleaders went to stand in line at the bathrooms, and once they were out of earshot she added, "Speaking of riveting, who is number six?"

I studied the metal beams crisscrossing high above us and contemplated my answer. "It's Will Doniger," I said finally.

"The landscaping guy from your house? The senior?"

"That's him."

"Huh," she said.

"Krupa," I warned—her wheels were already turning, I was certain. "Don't get ahead of yourself."

"Then help me understand the sudden interest."

I shrugged. "He helped me dig the new flower bed."

"For the peonies? And you are just telling me this now?"

"Yes, for the peonies, and calm down, it's totally minor."

"It is not, considering what it means to you. That was awfully nice of him." Out of the corner of my eye, I could see Krupa watching me, her brow furrowed.

"It's his job."

She looked smug. "Did he get paid for it?"

I made a face. "Not exactly."

"Very interesting. Did he know why you were doing it?"

"What is this, twenty questions?"

"Stop stalling."

"Oh, I don't know. Sort of. He knew my mother some, I guess. I mean, I think somewhere deep down he understood."

"He understood deep down," she repeated.

I turned to her, exasperated. "Will you stop searching for hidden meaning, please?"

"He's really good-looking," was Krupa's nonanswer. "Don't tell me you haven't noticed."

I shrugged. "You can't even see him under all that gear."

Understanding dawned on her face. "Is he the real reason we're here tonight?"

"No," I said, shaking my head even though this was more or less a lie. "We're here because you had to get your hundred bucks and because Kecia invited us and because last week was fun and I could use a little fun as you of all people keep reminding me."

"Hey, don't get all defensive on me now. I was just curious."

Thankfully, the buzzer sounded ending the break, and the players started lining up to wait for the second period to begin. When Kecia returned she didn't even bother to sit, and she didn't need to because barely thirty seconds in, Will and two other Lewis players were nearly in a fight.

"I think your new friend is about to get punished for almost killing someone," Krupa said, and I punched her shoulder. "Hey!" she protested.

"You seriously need to calm down."

"Doniger spends half the game in the penalty box," Kecia explained, giving Krupa and me a strange look before turning back to the ice. The rest of period two passed without Krupa making any other comments that might embarrass me, a fact for which I was grateful. At the beginning of the second break, once again techno blared through the arena. Everyone jumped up to dance, and like last week I sat there, frozen.

This time, Krupa came to my rescue. "Let's go somewhere."

"Great idea," I said, and we made our way across the bench, doing our best to avoid flailing arms. On the stairs, I stopped and turned back. What I saw made me feel a pang for the days before my life changed so drastically. The cheerleaders looked like they were having the time of their lives, their gloves and scarves and hats a moving rainbow of color, and for a minute I wished I was dancing alongside everyone else. Would I ever feel that carefree again? "Let's get hot chocolate," I suggested, thinking that at least there were other, simple things I could enjoy. "Apparently, it's a tradition."

"Sounds good, my treat," Krupa offered. "I'm the one getting paid to be here anyway."

"True."

We pushed through the crowd to the snack bar and inched our way up to the counter. My eyes were fixed on the cups going by, the steam rising in thin wisps through the cold air, and I sighed in anticipation.

"Thinking about number six?" Krupa asked.

"You need to stop," I said, and shot her a look of warning. "Don't go jumping to conclusions. Besides, it hasn't been that long since Chris and I broke up."

"It won't always be that way," Krupa said as we reached the front of the line.

She ordered and paid and we stepped to the side to wait. When our hot chocolates arrived I grabbed them off the counter and handed one to Krupa. The third period began and we rushed back to our seats. The score had been tied all night at 1–1 and when the timer on the board reached the game's final minute nothing had changed. The crowd was tense and, much to the Lewis fans' dismay, at the very last second a player from the opposing team slipped the puck by the Lewis goalie and we lost, 2–1, in an upset. The arena fell silent, stunned by this unexpected finish, and the Lewis players skated off in different directions, their shoulders hunched in defeat. The big padded gloves on Will's hands were up around his head, his helmet off, tossed to the side on the ice, his face hidden.

Krupa turned to Kecia and me. "That was disappointing."

"No kidding," Kecia said. "I guess there won't be any celebrating tonight."

"Do you mind if Rose and I meet you outside in about ten minutes?"

"Sure," Kecia said, and headed down the stairs with the rest of the cheerleaders.

I blocked Krupa from exiting the row. "Where are we going?"

"To wait by the locker room," she said, and pushed past me.

"Stop scheming," I begged as she yanked me along. "What has gotten into you?"

"Stop accusing me of stuff. Besides, I'm sure Will could use some consolation after losing his game."

I didn't even bother to respond.

We reached the crowd outside the locker room. Mrs. Doniger noticed me and waved. I hoped Krupa didn't see her, but then she asked, "Who's that?"

"If you must know, it's Will's mother."

"Perfect," Krupa said, and walked toward her. There was no choice but to follow.

"Hi, Mrs. Doniger," I said. "Nice to see you again. This, ah, is my friend Krupa."

"Hello, Rose. It's nice to meet you, Krupa."

"Hi," Krupa said, and launched into something entirely unexpected. "So I need to run and I was wondering—the car is kind of full, and since Will and Rose are friends . . ." Her voice trailed off.

I wanted to kill her.

"Oh, of course. I'm sure he'd be happy to give Rose a ride," Mrs. Doniger said, and smiled at me. She waited for me to say something, and I opened my mouth but no words came.

Krupa's eyes danced. "Okay, great! Gotta go, call me later, Rose," she said, and ran off before I could protest. I watched as she disappeared across the arena and when I turned around again Will was standing there.

My cheeks caught fire. "Hi," I said to him. "Sorry about the game."

He shook his head, obviously upset. "Yeah. Thanks for coming."

"Rose needs a ride home," his mother said, before I could excuse myself and escape. "You can take her, right?"

"Oh, sure. I'll drive you," he said without any hesitation.

Maybe Krupa wasn't so crazy after all.

18

I STAND CORRECTED

My second time in Will's truck turned out to be a lot less silent.

As we crossed the parking lot and Will unlocked my door, I realized I was nervous to be alone with him. It felt as if something was shifting between us. By the time I put my seat belt on, he had the engine running. The darkness made me aware of everything Will and I did, each step, each movement. His iPod was lying on the bench between us, and while the truck idled, he fiddled with the wires attached to the contraption rigged into the dashboard. His hand brushed the leg of my jeans. When the screen lit up and the sounds of Radiohead came from the speakers, I didn't even feel the urge to ask that he turn it off. Will put his arm across the seat so he could look behind him and back out. "What?" he asked, when he saw I was staring.

"Radiohead?" I asked.

"You don't like them."

"No, that's not it. I just imagined you'd have different musical tastes."

"You've been imagining my musical tastes?"

I'd left myself open for that one. "*No*. But if I took the time to predict your listening habits, Radiohead would not make the list."

"So what would?"

We waited at the light to exit the parking lot. "I don't know. Something metal probably."

He looked left before turning down the street. "You think I'm a metalhead," he said with some offense.

"I didn't say that. But . . . it's just . . . you're . . ." I stopped.

"I'm what?"

"You have this way about you," I said, immediately wanting to backtrack again. "Scratch that. It has something to do with how you play hockey."

"And how do I play hockey?" He tried to sound casual but I could hear the curiosity in his tone.

My fingers tapped the seat and I thought through what I wanted to say this time. "You're kind of brutal out there."

He laughed at this assessment. "Brutal?"

I thought about the version of Will I saw on the ice, versus what I knew of him elsewhere. "During a game you're different from how you act outside the rink. Don't get me wrong—it's a good thing. It scores you goals and wins and all that stuff."

"Not tonight."

"Well, maybe not every time," I said. "Anyway, I would've picked different music to match that feeling I get when I'm watching you play."

"You get a feeling?" A smirk appeared on Will's face as he drove and there was laughter in his voice. "What sort of feeling?"

I glared at him. "I get a feeling that you're a metalhead."

"There's some classic rock on there," he admitted, and picked up his iPod again, clicking through the menu until the sounds of Van Halen blared from the speakers.

"You're kidding me," I said. "Please."

Will grinned and turned it down. "I only listen to this stuff upon request."

"I did not request Van Halen."

"I think you did."

He tapped the outside pocket of my bag. The iPod was visible. "So what's on yours?" he asked.

I thought about it for a moment and realized at least a small part of me wanted to share it with him. "So far a lot of Nina Simone and some Ella Fitzgerald. That's all I know at this point. I haven't listened to everything yet."

"What do you mean? How do you not know what's on it?"

"It's a long story," I said. He glanced at me, his eyes a question. "Someone else uploaded the songs," I explained.

"It was a gift."

"You could say that."

"From Chris Williams," he guessed.

"Definitely not," I answered quickly. "So here's the deal: I don't listen to music. Not since April, at least."

"Not at all?"

"Well, technically we're listening right now."

"You know what I meant."

"I haven't chosen to," I clarified. "I used to be obsessed with every new band and making the perfect playlist and that sort of thing, so I'm trying to get over the aversion. And I will, I mean, I already am." I pulled out the iPod from my bag and stared at it. "It's been hard, though."

"Because of your mother," he guessed.

I nodded. "Lots of things make me sad, but music makes me really sad, and I don't want to get emotional all the time anymore so I cut it completely out of my life. But my friend Krupa has me on a recovery program of sorts. We listen to one song per day together."

Will reached for his iPod and pressed *pause*. The screen went dark so the only noise left was from the engine revving up and slowing down as we passed through stop signs. Eventually the town square came into view. It wasn't even Thanksgiving and everything was already lit up for Christmas. Long strands of tiny white lights were wrapped around lampposts and strung across the front windows of the stores and restaurants. Even the long row of bushes that circled the center green sparkled white. Despite how pretty it was, I couldn't help wishing the holidays would pass unnoticed this year. "You didn't have to do that," I said as the lights receded behind us.

"Do what?"

"Turn off your music. Besides, it's not as bad when I listen with somebody else."

"It's okay. Besides, we're here anyway," he said as he pulled up in front of my house and turned off the engine.

"Thanks for the ride," I said.

"No problem. Even though we lost, I'm glad you came to the game."

"It was fun. I think I'm officially a hockey fan."

He looked at me. "After Thanksgiving the season really picks up."

"Yeah?"

"Yeah."

I could tell he wanted to say something else and I knew I should open the door and get out. "Then I suppose I have a lot to look forward to."

Will bit his lip. He took his hands off the steering wheel and then put them back again, as if he wasn't quite sure where they were supposed to go. "Maybe I could help you listen to music again sometime, you know, on the way. If you wanted."

"On the way?"

"To my next game. Since you're officially a fan." His words hovered in the air, along with the fact that he'd just asked me out, or something like it.

"Okay," I told him.

"It's the Saturday after Thanksgiving."

"I'm free that night."

Will's eyes were fixed on the windshield. "I'll pick you up at six then."

"It's a plan," I said, and knew it was time I got out. I was feeling shy and nervous about what might happen if I stayed, so I opened the door and hopped to the ground, ready to leave, when at the last second I turned back. "So, if I don't run into you at school next week, have a good holiday."

"You, too."

"Thanks again for the ride." The groan of the door closing was loud in the quiet of the neighborhood, the trees shadowy in the moonlight. Will started up his truck and I listened to it idling as I walked up the brick path toward the house. He pulled away only after I'd turned the key in the lock and was safe inside. When the latch clicked shut I leaned against the door, closed my eyes, and sighed.

19

BOTTLE IT UP

"Who was that?" demanded a voice in the darkened house, and I almost jumped a mile. My eyes adjusted to the dim light and I could see the thin, straight outline of my grandmother.

"Grandma Madison," I exclaimed. "You're here already."

She flipped on a light. "Well, obviously," she said, annoyed. The edges of her sleeves and pants were perfectly tailored, ending at her wrists and brushing the tops of her shoes. "Are you going to answer my question or keep me in suspense all night?"

"Sorry, what did you want to know again?"

She glared. "Who dropped you off?"

"Oh. Nobody." I moved toward her. Somebody needed to make a gesture of hello to cut the awkwardness in the room. I tried to kiss her on the cheek but she stepped out of the way.

"You're telling me that was an invisible truck with no driver."

"Nice to see you, too," I said, and forced her into a hug before heading off to the kitchen. Her soft footsteps padded against the floor behind me. I opened the fridge to stare at the shelves in case anything tempted me and saw that it was stocked with food and for the first time I hadn't been the one to do it. Grandma Madison must have brought a carload of groceries. Maybe she wasn't so bad after all. "It was just a friend," I said, and took out a yogurt, kicking the door shut. "Don't worry about it."

"Do you sigh like that when all your friends leave you at the door? And don't try to tell me it was that football player," she added before I could respond. "Jim spilled the beans that you broke up."

I pulled out a kitchen drawer and grabbed a spoon, plunging it into the yogurt. "So you already know everything, then, Grandma. Stop being so nosy."

She harrumphed. "Stop being so obvious then, Rose," she said, and gave me an accusing look before walking away toward the guest room. She pulled the door shut with a forceful thud behind her, and for once I was thankful to be alone again.

Maybe Grandma Madison actually was the perfect antidote to the pain of enduring our first big holiday without Mom. She didn't tolerate sentimentality and provided a constant stream of sarcastic commentary that almost instantaneously dispelled whatever emotion was in the room.

On Monday after school as I was hovering near the oven, distracted by the delicious smells wafting into the kitchen, I became nostalgic and started to say, "I remember when Mom used to—" when Grandma immediately interrupted.

"Damnit, Rose!" she barked. "What did I tell you about leaving that meat loaf in the oven longer than fifty minutes? It will dry out!"

"Sorry, Grandma," I droned, any trace of wistfulness sucked away by her harsh attitude. I grabbed an oven mitt. "Calm down."

Then on Tuesday when I heard Jim's car pull up in the driveway I was so excited I dropped everything and ran out to hug him and help with his bags. When the two of us came inside dragging laundry and several suitcases, instead of offering to help or even greeting Jim, the only thing Grandma managed to do was yell at me for leaving the soup unattended on the stove.

And on Wednesday, when I was in the kitchen mashing the potatoes by hand, I started to tear up—Mom and I had always loved pushing the ricer down into the mixture of milk, butter, and potato, watching as lines snaked up through the waffle-patterned holes—and suddenly mashing potatoes became a sad, significant experience rather than just another dish to get through on the Thanksgiving checklist.

"Don't go snotting into the food, Rose," Grandma snapped when she noticed me sniffling over the bowl.

After that I kept my tears out of the kitchen.

On the brighter side, Grandma Madison's blunt, ongoing remarks came in handy where Dad was concerned, specifically with regard to his drinking.

"We're having a dry holiday tomorrow, James," she announced in that commanding I'm-your-mother voice she always used with him.

The four of us were sitting around the kitchen table, Jim, Dad, and me wolfing down roasted chicken and tiny hills of mashed potatoes—Grandma almost hadn't let us take any since she claimed they were the "Thanksgiving mashed potatoes" reserved for Thursday.

Dad paused, his fork midway between his mouth and plate. "What are you talking about?"

"Don't play dumb with me," Grandma said, slamming her water glass against the table, making everyone jump. "Dry, James. As in *no* alcohol. No wine. No hard liquor. None."

"Ma," he said, dropping his fork, and it clattered against the dish.

This wasn't going to end well. I got up and rushed over to the fridge to refill my glass so I was out of the way in case silverware started flying.

"James, this is not up for discussion. It just is. You take one sip of anything other than soda or water or whatever nonalcoholic beverage you want to drink this holiday weekend and you are out the door—"

Now here, Grandma impressed me. I was sure she would say *she'd* be out the door and not the other way around, that she'd be swayed by my father's reaction, but she stood her ground.

"And we'll just have our Thanksgiving without you," she finished.

"Ma—"

"Don't *Ma* me," she said, standing up and leaning forward over the table. She wasn't a big woman, but she was still intimidating. "That's it. End of story."

Dad's mouth closed. He stared at her in something like disbelief. I, on the other hand, took my seat again and studied the chicken on my plate, trying to hide the relieved smile on my face.

Thanksgiving was awkward and relatively quiet, almost silent, even though Grandma was with us. "Can you pass me the sweet potatoes?" was about the extent of the dinner conversation.

Mom's absence loomed over everything. She wasn't there to carve the turkey, or say which dishes came out the best, or to make a toast or even entertain us with funny stories about her kids. The bottom line: Mom wasn't there, and we all felt it. Occasionally, Jim tried to fill the hush with gossip from his first year at college, but even when he said, "So I met this girl in sociology class. She's really cute," nobody bit. There was only silverware clinking against plates and a single comment from Grandma Madison.

"You're not going to major in sociology, are you? You'll never get a job."

There was one bright spot, though, for which I was incredibly grateful. Grandma held Dad to her no-drinking rule. It made me wish that I, too, could have that power over Dad. But for now I'd take the help from wherever it came. While Jim and I cleared the table that night and Dad was in the kitchen with Grandma putting away the leftovers, I gave thanks for this reprieve because sometimes you have to be grateful for the little things when the big things get to be too much.

———————

The next morning Jim and I went out for breakfast, just the two of us. It was tradition, and this year, more than any other, we needed at least one holiday ritual to stay the same.

I smirked at my brother from across the table and grabbed his menu so he couldn't hide behind it. "Tell me about this girl from sociology."

Jim yanked the menu back and studied the breakfast selections even though we always ordered the same thing: blueberry pancakes with extra blueberries on top. "There isn't a girl—I made her up," he explained. "I was willing to say anything to break that awful silence yesterday."

"You mean Grandma's snide remarks don't count?"

"Let's make this a Grandma-free breakfast. From now on we won't even say her name."

"Okay," I said, and propped both elbows on the flecked Formica table, wrinkling the place mat without any fear since Grandma wasn't here to correct me. "I second that."

"Rose," a voice said from behind me, and I watched as my brother's eyes got big and then dreamy. Kecia waltzed up to our table and pulled me from the booth and into a hug. "It's so good to see you," she said.

I smiled. "It's good to see you, too. Did you have a nice Thanksgiving?"

"It was fine. You know, the usual. My family always has to make everything a big production."

Jim cleared his throat. "Rosey."

"Oh, sorry. Jim, this is Kecia, and Kecia, this is my brother, Jim. He's home from college." To Jim I explained, "Kecia and I used to cheer together."

"I know, I played football, remember?"

Kecia extended a slender, perfectly manicured hand to my brother. "But we've never officially met until now."

I worried Jim might kiss her hand, or not let go. Happily, he took it only briefly.

"Likewise," he said, his eyes glued to hers. "So you remember me?"

"I do," she admitted.

Jim smiled upon hearing this and I was sure he was about to embarrass me so I changed the subject. "Are you going to the game tomorrow?" I asked Kecia.

"Of course. Are you?"

"I am. Will you save me a seat?"

"Definitely," she said, and turned back to my brother, whose face registered joy at the attention. "I'm trying to turn Rose into a hockey fan. It's working so far."

"Rosey at a hockey game?" Jim gave me a quizzical look. "Interesting."

"She loves it—ask her," she told him. "Listen, I should go. I'm picking up takeout and my dad is waiting in the car outside." Kecia glanced out the window. "But I'll see you tomorrow night."

"Sounds good," I said.

"Bye, Rose. Bye, Jim." Kecia gave us a wave before heading up to the register.

Jim's eyes followed her the entire way.

"Oh my god," I said, but this wasn't enough to get Jim's attention. I snapped my fingers next to my brother's cheek. "Jim. Hey, Jimmy!"

"What," he said, picking up his mug of coffee, his eyes watching me from above it.

"She's not an object to ogle at," I pointed out.

He grinned. "Oh, no, she's clearly much more. I absolutely remember her, too, but I don't quite remember her looking like *that*."

"Please spare me the details running through your brain. She's my friend."

"Well, lucky you," he said, and turned away again to take in Kecia one last time as she headed toward the exit, takeout bag in hand. The chime attached to the top of the door jingled as it opened and shut and she disappeared from view. The waitress came over to take our order, then hurried away, shoving the pad and pen into the pocket of her apron. "So tell me more about hockey."

"It's nothing. Just something to do."

"But it's a new thing, right? I mean, I'm glad you're going out and doing stuff, especially if it involves her." Jim wiggled his eyebrows and I rolled my eyes.

"Stop being creepy," I said.

I waited for him to go on, but instead he said, "I guess everyone wants pancakes this morning," and got up from our booth. "Chris, great to see you."

My pulse quickened, and out of the corner of my eye I saw Chris Williams and my brother shake hands.

"Hey, Jim," he said. "We've missed you this year out on the field."

"Yeah, well, my body doesn't miss it."

"I bet."

I felt Chris's gaze.

"Hi, Rose," he said.

I looked up, expecting to feel the usual mixture of pain, regret, and hope that came with seeing Chris since our breakup, but what I felt instead was nothing much at all. Maybe I *was* getting over him. "Hi, Chris," I said, and managed a smile. "Happy Thanksgiving."

"I thought about you guys a lot yesterday. You know, first big holiday without your mom." Chris's eyes never left my face.

"Thanks," Jim said. "That means a lot."

"It does," I said, and tried to read the expression in Chris's eyes. It looked as though he wanted to say something else, but our waitress arrived at the table with a series of plates balanced up her arm. She placed a stack of pancakes in front of me and another in front of my brother.

"Well, I guess I'll see you later," he said with some hesitation, and strolled off toward the booth in back that the diner kept reserved for Lewis football players.

Jim stared at me through the steam rising between us from the pancakes. "I still can't believe you guys broke up."

I began cutting a section of my pancakes into bite-size pieces. "Well, we did."

"But he's obviously still into you."

I stabbed my fork onto my plate and raised a wedge to my mouth. "If he was, don't you think he'd tell me?"

"Would you get back together if he wanted to?"

At first I responded without thinking and said, "Yes," but a second later, I changed my mind. "Actually, *no*, I don't think I would," I said, and took a bite full of blueberries.

"I liked your first answer better."

"Well, the second one stands."

Jim poured syrup into a pool at the side of his plate. "Rosey, come on, let me talk to him. Maybe I could help."

His concern was so genuine and the gesture meant so much that I almost wanted to tell him yes, just to have the experience of my big brother stepping in on my behalf to try to fix my life. But I didn't need it fixed, at least not in this particular way—not anymore.

I pointed my fork at his dish. "Eat your pancakes. They're getting cold," I said, and I turned the conversation to other things.

20
PRIVATE CONVERSATION

On Saturday evening at precisely 5:55, Grandma Madison poked her head out the front door. "Are you waiting for the invisible truck with no driver?" she wanted to know.

I looked up from the chair on the porch, where I was shivering and trying to read, huddled inside my thick winter coat. "Grandma," I whined, and shooed her away. Enduring the cold for a few minutes while I waited for Will to pick me up was preferable to him ringing the bell and suffering through comments from Grandma and Jim. I'd debated for half an hour about what to wear, and I just wanted Will to arrive so we could get on with whatever lay ahead.

Grandma tapped her foot impatiently. "Get back inside or you'll get sick."

"I'm fine."

"But it's freezing."

"Really, I'm fine."

"Oh, suit yourself. It's not like I'm going to bite any of your boyfriends."

"Right," I said under my breath.

"I heard that."

"I don't have a boyfriend," I added defensively.

"Mm-hm. Just like you weren't having sex with that football player."

"Grandma," I hissed, but she had already shut the door with a loud bang.

The headlights of a truck flashed around the corner and Will pulled up in front of the house. I stuffed my book in my bag and raced down the front walk, opening the passenger door before he could turn the key and get out.

"Hey," I said, out of breath.

"Hey," he said. His hand rested on the gearshift, but he made no move to put the truck into first. He wore jeans and a thick, coal gray sweater, the edge of a black T-shirt just visible around his neck, and I could see his hockey gear in the back of the truck through the narrow window behind us. Hot air blasted from the dashboard and occasionally the gusts lifted his long bangs off to the side of his face. He shook his head and they fell into place again.

"Did you have a nice Thanksgiving?" I asked.

"As good as it could be," he said with a shrug. "My sisters liven things up."

"Ours was just okay, too." I thought back to Thursday and reconsidered. "Actually, it pretty much sucked. You know?"

He nodded. "I do."

I turned away for a moment and tried to discern if there was any movement at the front windows of the house, wondering if Grandma was watching.

"Everything okay?" Will asked.

"I think so. My grandmother can be a pain. She's probably spying on us."

Will laughed at this. I yanked off my hat and, one by one, the fingers of my gloves. I wedged everything into the small space between us and put my hands up to the vents, enjoying the warmth. Will tugged the bright green pom-pom at the top of my hat. "Nice."

"Thanks. Watching hockey is a cold profession," I said, and Will laughed again.

He took the truck out of neutral and we headed up the street. His hand nearly bumped my knee every time he shifted gears. I considered inching closer to the passenger door so we wouldn't end up in some awkward situation, but then, there wasn't much room to move over anyway.

"So I have a few questions for you," I said.

Will pulled onto the highway. "What kinds of questions?"

"The ones that explain why you spend so much time in the penalty box."

He grinned. "Oh, that kind. All I have to say is that it's never really my fault.

"I'm sure."

"No, really."

"Enough of the kidding. This time I want the truth."

"Fine, fine. How about I go over why I landed there during the last game?"

"That's a good start—though we might be here forever," I said. "Just make sure not to leave out any important, incriminating details."

Will glanced over at me. "Picky."

"Sometimes. Now get on with it already," I urged, and proceeded to grill him the rest of the way to the rink. As with the last two games, I sat with Kecia—Krupa wasn't singing tonight; she was away for the holiday. But unlike the previous weekend, Lewis won tonight. Will scored once and made two assists, so he was in a good mood when we returned to his truck for the ride home. I pulled the scarf around my neck up to my mouth to hide my smile.

"Got everything?" he asked before backing out of the space.

"All set," I said.

"Since I answered your questions on the way here, now you have to answer mine," he said.

"But—"

He interrupted my protest. "It's only fair." The truck stopped at a light and he turned to me. "Ready?"

"I guess," I reluctantly agreed.

"If you could go anywhere in the world and money was no object, where would you go?"

"Anywhere else is better than Lewis."

"That doesn't count as an answer."

I laughed. "You dodged my first question, remember?"

"True. But then I answered it."

"Yeah, yeah. Okay, so ever since I was, I don't know, maybe six? I've wanted to go to Bangalore—that's a city in India."

"You want to go to India?" He sounded intrigued.

"Krupa's family is originally from Bangalore and she and I have been talking about taking a trip for years. And don't get me started on the food we would eat."

"Do you have a favorite dish?"

"To be honest, it's hard to choose," I said, trying to decide, "but Mrs. Shakti—that's Krupa's mom—makes these lentils that are to die for."

He made an *ick* face. "Lentils?"

"I know, right? You'd change your mind if you tasted hers, I swear."

After discussing no fewer than five of my favorite Indian meals in great detail, Will changed the subject again—he could be talkative when he wanted. "This next question"—he said, and looked at me while we waited at another light—"you don't have to answer if you don't want to."

"Uh-oh," I said, bracing myself.

"Of all the songs you've listened to so far on that iPod of yours, what's your favorite?"

I thought about it. "I think I can answer that. This is going to sound random, but I think it's 'You Are My Sunshine,' that version from *O Brother, Where Art Thou?* Do you know it?"

"Actually, I do. My mother loves that sound track. She used

to sing that song to me when I was little, and then to my sisters, too."

"Do you think it's required that all parents sing that to their kids?"

"I don't know, I wouldn't be surprised," he said, and slipped right on to another, less touchy topic.

Will seemed genuinely interested to find out more about me, and I found myself offering opinions on all sorts of issues and confessing things I dreamed about doing someday. Soon I was shifting toward him instead of farther away. The more unself-conscious he became, the more he pushed his hair out of his face so he could really see me and I could see him. I became aware of how the blue of Will's eyes changed when he got excited about something, and how his face became like one big open invitation when he smiled, like right now, after we arrived at my house and I agreed to go to his game next Friday, too.

"I can't wait," I told him before I got out. When I headed up to the house, listening to the sound of Will's truck idling until I was safely inside, just like last time, after the front door closed behind me, I leaned against it and sighed.

———————

The following Monday I was at my locker when I noticed Will coming down the hall, and I wondered what would happen next, if we would just pick up where we'd left off on Saturday

night or continue to act like we didn't know each other at school.
I immediately saw how different he was. The Will from the truck
who laughed and smiled at me was replaced by a boy whose eyes
were distant, almost blank, as if he were a thousand miles away.

"I can't believe Mrs. Jantzen is giving a biology test right
after a holiday," Krupa complained as he walked right past us
with barely a glance in my direction.

My lungs exhaled with a relief I didn't realize I would feel.

"Rose? Are you listening?" Krupa waved a hand in front of
my face, her glittery nail polish catching the light.

"Yes. Sorry. Biology test today," I said.

"Did your brother go back to school already?"

"What?"

"Rose! Did Jim return to college?"

"Oh. Yeah. He'll be back again in a couple of weeks after
finishing exams," I answered distractedly, and Krupa looked at
me strangely.

That one encounter with Will was the beginning of a strange
set of interactions—or *non*interactions—between us. As November turned to December, we fell into a routine of sorts. Every
Friday and Saturday he picked me up for his game, dropped me
at the front door of the rink, and drove around back to park. I
took my seat in the stands with Kecia, Tamika, and Mary, and
eventually Krupa, too. No one asked how I got there, or why I
was so interested in watching Will on the ice, as if there was an
unspoken rule not to pry for details about whatever it was he

and I were doing. As my game count rose higher, it was difficult to believe I hadn't always done this on weekends. But during the week, Will and I barely acknowledged each other's existence; we didn't call each other or text. We didn't communicate at all.

"Rose, just talk to the boy," Krupa said one day when, yet again, he had passed in the hall without saying hello.

"I think it's better that we keep our friendship private, for now at least. It's different when we're here. *He's* different."

"And you aren't?" Krupa asked, filling her bag with books to take home.

"I don't know. Do you think I am?"

"You don't seem at ease with him like you do at the games, that's for sure. Maybe if you guys got used to hanging out here—"

"No," I interrupted. "It's just what he and I do, and it works so I don't want to mess with it."

With each ride home from the rink, Will and I stayed together longer and longer, parked out in front of my yard. Sometimes we would talk past two a.m., until both of us were yawning and our eyes were heavy with sleep. It wasn't long before I fell in love with the inside of Will's truck, the intimacy of talking for hours in that small space, watching the trees sway outside in the wind while we were inside, warm and protected, and during the occasional snowfall that turned the world around us white. The more time we spent together, the more we opened up about even the most difficult subjects.

"So, remember that iPod?" I asked him one night, when, as usual, we were parked in front of my house, with Will occasionally turning the engine on so we could blast the heat and warm up.

He nodded. "I keep waiting for you to bring it so we can listen."

"Well, it's sort of from my mom," I confessed. "Wait, not sort of," I backtracked. "She made it for me. It's like she left me a sound track for when she was gone. You know, to have after she died." The last word was like a punch in the silence. "She put together these playlists for me." I laughed a little, thinking about how I used to pester her that she needed an iPod because the best part of having one was how you could arrange your songs so that they told a story, and how you could make the perfect playlist to set a scene for your life, or to remind you of an experience you never wanted to forget. "She put a playlist on it of all her favorite songs. Then there's another of holiday music—I haven't touched that one yet. There's one called 'Happy Rose,' filled with the cheesy dance music I used to listen to that drove her crazy. It must have taken her forever to make all of them." I trailed off.

"What an amazing thing to have given you. To have *made* for you."

"I know," I whispered, my words two short breaths in the quiet. I was relieved Will understood the importance of the iPod and so I decided to confess something else, something I couldn't stop thinking about. "One of the playlists on it, it's called 'TBD by Rose.' To be determined, I guess. It's blank."

"Not a single song?"

"Not one. Not yet," I added.

"So she wants you to make a new playlist. That's intense."

"I know," I said, feeling the weight of this task. "Sometimes it's overwhelming to have this big open space that I'm supposed to fill, when it's still difficult to listen to anything at all, never mind the picking and choosing through songs to get a playlist just right—to get *this* one just right. I used to be so obsessive about them. I don't even know how to begin." I stared down the road ahead of us, watching the bare branches of the trees dip down toward the windshield in the wind. "The closer we get to Christmas, the harder it is to think about ever filling it in. God, I'm dreading Christmas this year." I fidgeted, pulling on the fingers of my gloves. I leaned my head back against the seat, wondering how to interpret Will's silence. "Was that too much information?"

"No," he said. "Not at all."

"Okay. Good. Because you could tell me."

"Really, it's okay. I was just thinking about your TBD playlist and what you might want to put on it, or maybe what I'd put on it if my dad had left me something similar."

"Oh," I said, surprised by this sweet, vulnerable response. "Any suggestions?" I asked, almost wishing he would give me a song to start things off.

"I think I'll leave that to you. You'll figure it out. You did manage to plant peonies and that was well out of your skill set."

That comment lightened up the mood and I nudged his arm. "Hey, I did great with the garden."

"Yeah, with my help."

"So did your dad ever give you anything? You know, for afterward?" I asked.

Will's hands tightened around the bottom of the steering wheel. "Hockey," he said.

"What do you mean?"

"My father brought me up on hockey—he played when he was my age, too. I'm grateful, but sometimes it's a bit overwhelming, like you said before. For me, it's the pressure I feel because this is his legacy. Me playing hockey, I mean. Don't get me wrong—I love the game. It's always been my favorite thing"—in the glow of the streetlight, I saw the blue of Will's eyes deepen in that familiar way—"but sometimes hockey feels like this never-ending thing I'll always owe my dad. You're lucky your mom's iPod is so tangible. So concrete."

"I guess so," I said, and thought about how the iPod was just one piece of a larger puzzle. The journey outlined by my Survival Kit was anything but tangible, and there was still so much left unanswered. Sometimes I worried I wouldn't get things right or understand what the tasks truly meant. "Your dad was right to give you hockey."

"What do you mean?"

"When I watch you play, I can tell that you love being out there."

"Not always," he said.

"Well, every time I've seen you."

"I hope you'll share the iPod with me sometime," Will said. "You said it was easier to listen with someone else. I'm here if you ever want to."

"I know," I said, and looked at the clock. It was after midnight and we'd been sitting in front of my house for almost two hours. Maybe we'd revealed enough secrets for one night. "Soon. Maybe after the holidays are over. On that note, it's probably time I go." I opened the door and cold air sliced across us. "Thanks for telling me something about you and your father."

"Rose," Will said, and stopped me from getting out by placing a hand on my arm. His palm was warm against my skin. "I'm having fun. This"—he stopped, nodding at me—"this is fun, what we're doing."

The wintry air was rushing inside, but before I jumped down to the street I looked back into his blue eyes. "I know. For me, too," I said.

Will's hand remained a moment longer and when he let go I pushed the door shut. As I walked up to the house, aware of each step that took us farther and farther apart, I felt his fingers pressed against my skin as if they were still there.

21

BLUE CHRISTMAS

I woke to snow falling outside and Christmas music blaring through the house. I recognized "The Wassail Song," one of Mom's favorite carols, and knew it was on the holiday playlist from her iPod. I hurried out of bed and grabbed the cardigan hanging over the back of my desk chair, wrapping it around me. The playlist jumped to "The Holly and the Ivy" by the time I reached the kitchen. Memories of my mother singing as she made holiday cookies flooded my mind so powerfully that I almost believed I'd find her there. But Jim's voice broke the spell. He must've arrived late last night after finishing his last exam. "You took my iPod," I yelled angrily over the music.

Jim looked up from spreading jam on toast, stopping mid-lyric. "Hey, Rosey."

"Turn. It. Off!" I screamed. Of all the music I found difficult to hear, Christmas carols were the worst.

But Jim only lowered the sound. "Calm down," he said, seeming startled by my anger. "When I saw Mom's favorites on here I couldn't resist."

"I don't want to listen," I snapped, and stomped over to the iPod dock and hit *stop*. Silence fell over us.

"It was sitting here on the counter," Jim backpedaled. "I didn't think it would be a big deal."

I bit my lip, unable to speak, and a sob rose in my throat. Just a few bars of these familiar songs and I wanted to weep.

"Aw, Rosey. Are you okay? You're not, are you?"

I shook my head.

"Are you thinking about Mom?"

I nodded.

"Me, too. I think about her all the time." His voice caught and he sighed. "You want a hug?"

I nodded again and Jim wrapped his arms around me and rested his chin on the top of my head. Tears rolled down my face. If I could go back to the day of Mom's funeral, when the whole future lay out ahead like one big nightmare, I would have prepared myself to cry at least once a day going forward, no matter how hard I tried not to. Though maybe it meant that I loved Mom more than words could express. The one thing tears were really good for was when we ran out of words.

My sobs turned to sniffles.

"Rosey?" Jim handed me a napkin to blow my nose. I saw that his eyes were red from crying, too. "Sometimes I can't believe Mom isn't going to suddenly walk in the kitchen. I keep expecting her to, you know?"

"I do," I said. "I'm sorry I lost it."

"You don't have to apologize. Why wouldn't we be losing it? It's our first Christmas without her."

"I know. It's crazy she's not here. It's like, impossible or something."

Jim pulled two slices of bread from the bag and put them in the toaster. "Sometimes I feel like Christmas won't happen if she isn't here to make it happen, which means we need to do it ourselves. I thought that waking you up to Christmas carols might be festive."

"This sounds stupid, but I hear a song, any song, and I want to sob," I confessed. "Obviously," I added.

Jim leaned over the toaster, watching the coils turn red. "When 'Have Yourself a Merry Little Christmas' came on before you got up, I cried hard."

"You did?"

"Yes." The toast popped up and Jim caught the two pieces and placed them on a plate for me. He pushed the jar of jam closer and handed me a knife. "Music sometimes . . . I don't know. This may sound strange but it almost—"

"—brings Mom back to life," I finished.

"Yes."

"I know just what you mean." Talking to my brother about Mom made me feel less alone, especially since my father barely mentioned her. "Where's Dad and Grandma anyway?"

"They went out a while ago. Grandma dragged him Christmas shopping at the mall. She said he *had* to go."

"God, I haven't even thought about presents this year. I mean, the thought of not buying Mom a gift about kills me," I said. For a while, the only sounds were from Jim and me eating.

Then Jim spoke. "I think we should rise to the occasion for the holiday songs."

"I'm so tired of feeling sad, though."

"You'll get used to it. We have to start somewhere and what's Christmas without music?"

"But—"

"Rosey, come on. It would mean a lot to me."

I sighed. "Can I reserve the right to skip something if I think I can't handle it?"

"That's fair," Jim said.

"Okay, I guess."

Jim scrolled his finger around on the iPod. "Here's a good one." He looked at me for permission.

I nodded, and Jim pressed *play*.

The first few bars of Paul McCartney's "Wonderful Christmastime" floated out of the speakers, and immediately, a lump formed in my throat. But this time Jim reached over and squeezed my hand and held it until the song was over. Next was "Do You Hear What I Hear?" followed by "We Need a Little Christmas." After a while, I began to move around the kitchen, taking out mixing bowls from the cabinet along with flour, baking soda, sugar, and red and green sprinkles for cookies. I gave Jim various tasks, and together we baked while the holiday playlist scrolled from one song to another and snow fell prettily outside. Little by little, our mood became more festive. Soon there were dirty bowls and cooling racks stacked with cookies covering the counters. It was easy to tell which ones Jim made because they were oddly shaped. By the time Grandma and Dad returned from the mall my brother and I were dancing around and singing at the top of our lungs, our mouths half-full of cookie so that crumbs were flying everywhere. They didn't say a word or tell us to turn the music down or even to clean things up. They just walked through the kitchen and let us carry on.

———————————

Later on I came upon Grandma Madison with her nose pressed against a window by the front door. "There's the Doniger boy, out there shoveling snow."

Part of Will's landscaping business included plowing driveways and shoveling walks. As soon as I saw the snow this morning I knew he'd be at the house today. But I was surprised Grandma recognized him.

"You know Will? Doniger," I added quickly.

"Yes I do and so do you, I see. Your father and brother are out there with him in case you're interested." I walked over to stand beside her and we watched the three of them working their way up the front walk through the snow. "You'd better be careful," she added after a while.

I sensed her eyes on me. "Careful?"

"Your eyes give you away."

"What are you talking about?"

"Rose, if you don't already know, then you'd better do some soul-searching and figure it out."

"Okay," I said, to get her off my back.

"You know his father died of cancer—"

"Two years ago this January," I finished. "You know about Mr. Doniger, too?"

"Your mother told me when he passed away. When she first got her news about the cancer, the two of them discussed treatments and remission and"—she paused, her tone softening—"hospice. I think she wanted to be prepared."

"Oh" was all I managed to respond.

"She appreciated having someone to talk to about it." Grandma's breath fogged up a round burst against the glass as she spoke and she sounded sad. "It's written all over that boy's face."

"What is, Grandma?"

"That he's lost his father. Such a shame. You can always tell."

I looked at her. "You can?"

"Yes." Grandma stared at me like she could see right through to my deepest insides. Her eyes shone like glass, and for an instant I thought I saw loss in them. "It's all over yours, too," she said, and walked away, leaving me alone by the window to ponder whether her observation was true.

22

ARE WE FRIENDS OR LOVERS

The days before Christmas break passed quickly. Everyone was festive, exchanging Secret Santa gifts and singing holiday songs off-key in the halls. The happier people became the more I noticed my own sadness. Krupa and I didn't even decorate the outside of our locker with wrapping paper and bows. Ours looked lonely next to the others covered in sparkly tinsel and cheesy golden garlands up and down the doors.

"Do you need a ride today?" Krupa asked me. "I just got the car back from the shop so I promise you'll actually get home."

I mustered a smile. "Sure, I'd love one. Thanks."

"Then I'll see you in"—Krupa checked the time—"exactly fifty-three minutes, when they set us free for almost two entire weeks!"

"Yeah. Can't wait," I said, my voice flat. "I'll be right here, ready to go."

She looked at me with sympathy. "Soon you'll be out of here and everything will seem better. Have fun during your free period."

Krupa took off, and the halls began to empty. The last straggler disappeared and I was alone, or thought I was, until I felt someone come up behind me.

"Hi, Rose."

I leaned my forehead against the cold metal of the locker door. "Hi, Chris."

"What's going on?"

"Oh, you know, Merry Christmas and all that," I said, and forced myself to turn and face him. There he was, tall and blond and gorgeous as ever. I was surprised to see he wasn't wearing his football jacket, and almost equally surprised to realize that it didn't bother me anymore.

He looked nervous. "I'm sure it must be hard, this time of year."

"Yes, it is. I bet you're excited, though," I said. "You love Christmas."

Chris took a step toward me. Close enough that I could see the tiny curved line that always formed on his left cheek when he was about to smile, and each individual eyelash fluttering as he blinked, so blond they matched the color of his skin. "I do. And I've been doing a lot of thinking."

"Thinking about what?" I asked, worried where this was going.

"Nothing is the same without you, Rose," he began, and that curved line on his cheek deepened as his lips shifted into a smile.

My eyes widened. It was about to happen: Chris was going to tell me he wanted me back, just like I'd imagined so many times back in October when I'd hoped for this outcome so desperately. "No?"

He shook his head. He took another step closer. "I miss you."

"I miss you, too," I said automatically. After two years of dating I was used to saying this to him if he said it to me. If Chris had said "I love you," I probably would have returned the same sentiment without thinking twice. This was exactly the problem—I hadn't thought before I'd spoken. If I were smart, I would have remained silent.

"You do miss me," he said, seemingly relieved.

This time I was careful not to say anything further. I looked up into his eyes, trying to read them. His nervousness was gone, replaced by a growing confidence, and he leaned his right hand casually against the locker next to mine. "Remember Christmas your sophomore year, when I took you to Gianni's for that really nice dinner?"

I nodded. Of course I remembered. That was the night Chris and I had sex for the first time. I couldn't figure out where he was headed, but something told me to step to the side so that the wall of lockers was no longer at my back.

"Do you remember the ride there?"

The ride . . . Come on, Rose, think.

"How you loved what I'd done." He laughed and sounded happy. "You told me how sweet it was and how it made you smile and so we left it there for weeks." He reached into his bag and began to dig around. "Everything was so good between us back then." His hand reemerged and in his palm I saw green leaves and a flash of white berry.

That holiday season Chris had attached mistletoe to the roof of his SUV over the passenger seat so every time we stopped at a light he had a reason to kiss me.

He held it above my head.

Oh god, this was Chris trying to be romantic and all I could think about was Will Doniger, how I hoped he didn't come upon this scene and get the wrong idea, and how, if I was going to be honest, if I'd been standing under the mistletoe with Will my feelings about the situation would be entirely different. This thought sent color rushing to my cheeks—and apparently gave Chris the wrong idea.

"I knew you'd be happy," he said, tilting his head to the side.

"Chris, no," I said, putting my hands up and stepping away. His left arm was still outstretched, the mistletoe hanging from his fingers, leaving a me-size space below. I began to back down the hall, first one step, then another and another. "This was sweet of you, but I'm just not . . . I can't . . . I'm sorry."

His eyes turned cold and the mistletoe fell from his hand to the floor with a *shhhh*. "Is this about Doniger?"

I halted, surprised, and closed my eyes.

"It is, isn't it? I knew it."

I didn't say a word, dreading what came next.

"I heard about this thing you have going on with him. Did you think I wouldn't find out? That someone wouldn't tell me?" Chris's voice cracked and I opened my eyes again. His feet were planted slightly apart, his shoulders back, arms at his sides and hands balled into fists, huge and imposing. "Are you dating him?"

I breathed deep, searched for the right words to handle this. "No, I'm not dating Will Doniger, or anyone else for that matter."

"You're sure?"

"We're just friends." This was as close an approximation of my relationship with Will as I could offer at the moment. "Chris?" I asked nervously.

"What?" he snapped.

"Why should it matter who I've been hanging out with? You and I broke up."

Something passed over his face, maybe regret, but it was there only a moment and was gone. "But I still love you, Rose," he said, and looked away. "Don't you still love me?" he asked, these words reverberating off the lockers on either side of the empty hall. A long silence followed this question, and when I was about to respond, Chris put up a hand, stopping me. "Wait, don't answer right now. Just think about it, will you at least do that much?"

"Okay," I whispered, because I didn't want to hurt him any more than I already had. He grabbed his bag off the ground and stalked off. All I saw was his back before he rounded the corner. Feeling dejected, I gathered my things, put on my coat and scarf, and went outside into the wintry air, snowflakes floating around me from the gray clouds above. At least out here there was peace and quiet. I wanted to get away from the mess Chris and I had just made, and from the holiday spirit of people excited about break, so I started to walk. When I reached the edge of the school grounds I headed left and kept on going until I'd walked so far I was already halfway home. I wouldn't need that ride from Krupa after all.

23
FAMILY TREE

When I was almost up to the front porch steps, the door opened a crack and Grandma Madison appeared. "Rose, you're home. Good, good. Come on. We're going to get a Christmas tree. It's about time. Jim!" she yelled at the top of her lungs, making me jump. "She's here. Let's go!"

"Right now?" I exclaimed. A field trip to pick out a tree was the last thing I wanted at the moment. "Do we have to—"

"Yes, we do. Jim! Come on! She is standing *at the door!*"

Jim showed up behind Grandma, towering above her. "Hey, Rosey," he said with such cheer that I could tell it was false. By the time he shut the door and locked it, Grandma was halfway to the driveway. Jim hopped down the steps and took me with him.

"What is going on?" I asked, suspicious that they were covering up something. "You guys are acting weird."

"We didn't expect you home so soon," he said lightly. "All your presents are sitting unwrapped on the kitchen table." He smiled in such a mischievous way that I almost believed him, until I saw the look in his eyes.

"I thought we agreed we weren't buying presents this year," I said.

"I was helping Grandma wrap hers when you came home early and surprised us." He knocked on the front of the car as he circled around to the passenger side. "You sit in back," he told me.

Grandma unlocked her station wagon and doors opened and slammed as we got in. She turned the key in the ignition, her eyes visible in the rearview mirror as she backed out of the drive-way. "It wouldn't be Christmas without a tree, so we're going to get one, bring it home, string up the lights, and decorate it," she said, listing the various tasks like items to check off on a grocery list. "We should have done this weeks ago," she added.

"But Dad is the one we always go with—"

"Your father isn't interested in getting a tree this year," Grandma interrupted. "If he was, he would have already taken you two."

Jim was quiet, staring out the window, and I didn't speak the rest of the ride either. Only when we pulled into the parking lot at the Christmas tree farm did things begin to lighten up. Kids were running around with their families, excited to pick out a tree, and the smell of freshly baked pies floated our way from the nearby farm stand when we got out of the car. There was a bin filled with jingle bells, and every time someone picked them up they rang out. Jim immediately walked up to the most Charlie Brown tree in sight, with branches going every which way, the lower ones already turning brown. He touched the top and a cascade of needles fell to the ground. "How about this one?" he proposed with a grin, though his eyes became sad. "Mom would have liked it. Don't you think?"

"Yes. But she would've gotten mad if we'd actually brought it home," I said. "Come on." I grabbed his arm and dragged him farther down the center aisle while Grandma lagged behind. When she caught up to us, we were ogling a giant evergreen that would never fit in the living room.

Grandma shook her head. "No," she said. A smile played at her lips, though.

After arguing about the pros and cons of certain trees for almost an hour, we finally found one we agreed was perfect in height, size, and shape. While Grandma Madison paid for it, Jim and I got rope and strapped it to the top of the station wagon. The mood in the car on the way home was decidedly better, even lively, as Jim and I strategized about decorations and Grandma Madison added her opinion. Soon we were turning up the driveway, and I was actually excited to begin the decorating. Jim and I untied the tree, and careful not to break any branches, we followed Grandma into the garage as she directed us left, then right, so we didn't knock into anything. But the instant we walked through the kitchen I found out why Grandma and Jim hadn't wanted me to go inside earlier.

Dad was passed out in the living room, his body only half on the couch.

"Oh my god," I said when I saw him. It looked like a storm

had hit. Shattered glass lay everywhere and Mom's collection of student artwork had been knocked off the shelves onto the floor, some broken in pieces. Her African violet was tipped on its side, the dirt spilling out and most of its fuzzy green stems snapped in half. "Dad," I said with dismay. Tears filled my eyes and began to roll down my cheeks.

"Rose," Grandma barked, and put out an arm, like she might be able to protect me.

I turned to her. "You guys just left him like this?" I shouted. "What did you think would happen? That he'd clean up by the time we got back? That some sort of miracle would occur while we were gone and he'd get sober?" I looked at Jim. He was still struggling to get the tree the rest of the way into the living room. Deep down I knew it wasn't their fault, that it wasn't anyone's fault other than Dad's, but they were here and I was tired of him not getting better and of me having to be the responsible one, even with Grandma Madison and Jim around.

Grandma didn't say a word, her arms twitching at her sides, like she wanted to wrap them around me or maybe steady me, but couldn't quite make her limbs move. Jim just stared at me, holding the tree upright, so tall it cleared the top of his head by a foot.

"You guys try taking care of him when he's like this for once! You clean up this mess," I said through gritted teeth, trying not to scream. Just when it seemed like my family might be turning a corner and that things would get easier, something happened to set everything back. "Have fun putting up the tree by yourselves," I spat, and stormed off to my room. I got into bed and pulled the covers over my head to shut the world out.

———————

During the night my eyes opened and wouldn't shut again. It was only two a.m. and I was exhausted, but my body refused to cooperate. I got up to make some tea, hoping it might help me go back to sleep. I reached the hallway outside my room and heard Grandma's voice.

"Ellie never would have stood for this. Pull yourself together," she said. "Your kids need you. Rose especially. You're forcing that girl to act like a parent. You have a problem, James."

"I do not have a problem," Dad said, his voice hoarse. "Give me that bottle of ibuprofen. I have a headache."

"I bet you do." I heard the clatter of pills against the sides of a plastic container, the shake of someone spilling them into their palm. "You're hurting your children and you have to stop."

"If I'm hurting anyone, it's myself."

"Do you really think Rose wants to see you like this? Do you really believe your son wants to deal with this when he comes home from college on break? They need to be able to depend on you."

"Ellie was the one who—"

"You are still their father and not only are you coming home drunk and forcing them to witness it, but you are *driving*, James. You are *driving home drunk*."

"But—"

"No buts. You could kill someone," Grandma hissed. "You could land yourself in jail. You could kill *yourself* and then where would Rose and Jim be? Without a mother *and* without a father. Is that what you want?"

I covered my mouth in shock. Grandma was saying all the things I'd wanted to say but hadn't had the courage. But then I heard sobbing, big, heavy, uncontrollable heaves, and my chest tightened, and my throat, all the way up into my cheeks and eyes. Ever since the day of the funeral Dad had been so stoic I didn't think I would ever hear him cry again.

"I know, I know," Grandma Madison soothed.

"I can't do this, Ma," Dad wept, "I just can't."

The sobbing grew more intense and I turned around, tiptoeing to my room. I couldn't listen anymore. I closed the door softly behind me and got back into bed, pulling the blankets over my ears, closing my eyes, hoping that if I fell asleep I might forget.

The next morning we pretended like nothing had happened. I didn't know who had cleaned up the mess in the living room, but it was gone. The dirt and glass and broken pieces were wiped away as if they had never been there, and everything gleamed.

24

ALL I WANT FOR CHRISTMAS IS YOU

It wasn't until Christmas Eve that Jim and I finally began to decorate the tree. We were trying to decide on holiday music. We were getting good at not becoming overly sad. I tapped my finger against my chin, thinking. "Hmm, I know: let's listen to the only good song to ever come from Mariah Carey's lips."

"As you wish," Jim said, searching for it on the playlist.

After the incident with Dad, Jim and I had gone into a holiday frenzy, decking the halls like mad, as if this would help us forget or at least put a barrier between that night and the present.

"I don't want a lot for Christmas / there is just one thing I need," Jim sang off-key, grabbing an ornament. "I don't care about the presents / underneath the Christmas tree!" he went on as he placed the sparkly orb high up on a branch I couldn't reach.

"Your voice is awful," I shouted over the music, laughing. "Did anyone bother to mention that you are not Mariah Carey?"

"Like your voice is any better," he said, in between lyrics.

"Point taken," I said, joining in and singing extra badly on purpose to make him smile. We discovered that the best antidote to sadness was singing every lyric loudly and out of tune. We knew them all by heart, much to Grandma's dismay. "You're hurting my ears," she kept telling us, and at one point she even shouted, "You're going to get coal in your stocking if you two keep on like that," and put up her hands, stomping off to the kitchen.

"Did she really just say that?" Jim asked, shaking with laughter.

Any other year and in any other circumstance, Jim and I would never have acted this way, so unself-conscious about what we would normally consider embarrassing behavior. But if it took making idiots of ourselves and overdoing the holiday cheer to get through this Christmas then so be it. We put holly on the railings and across the shelves and mantel. We strung lights outside. Jim hung mistletoe in every doorway, which, aside from reminding me of Chris, I found amusing. "Are you hoping Kecia will visit?" I asked each time I saw him hanging another bunch.

"Maybe," he responded cryptically. "So what if I was? You laugh now."

And I did, right up until Will rang the front doorbell.

Grandma Madison answered, calling out, "Rose! The invisible truck driver is here to see you," and walked away without inviting him in, leaving Will standing on the front porch in the snow and the cold.

"Grandma, you're so rude sometimes," I hissed on my way to the door.

"So that's Grandma Madison," Will said, looking past me until she disappeared into the kitchen.

"The one and only. Don't mind her, she can't help what she says," I said, unable to hide the big smile on my face about this unexpected visit.

"Why did she call me the invisible truck driver?"

"Oh, don't worry. It's a long story."

"So I brought the wreath you wanted," Will said, holding it up.

"Thanks. Um, sorry, now I'm the one being rude, do you want to come in?" I asked, suddenly nervous.

He hesitated. "I would, but I really only have a sec. I've got to get home to Mom and my sisters. You know, Christmas Eve and all that stuff."

"Of course. I'm sorry, I wasn't thinking. Thank you for bringing this by," I said, taking the wreath. "It was really nice of you."

"I wanted to see how you were doing, too," he said.

I gestured at the front of the house. "We're doing our best, hence the crazy amount of decorations." Every inch of the porch was strung with lights—the planters, the bushes along the front, even the furniture. Jim had spent hours out here getting everything perfect. Most of the lights were white, but when he ran out of those, he broke into the old-school, multicolored strands with the giant ugly bulbs. "I think we might be overcompensating."

Will laughed and his eyes darted to the top of the door.

We were standing under mistletoe. I was going to kill Jim. "So, um, Merry Christmas, I guess," I said awkwardly.

"You, too," Will said, and I thought he was about to leave, but instead he asked, "You're coming to the New Year's tournament, right?"

"If you still want me to."

He nodded.

I rocked back and forth on my heels, feeling the weight of the giant wreath I held against my body. "Can't wait," I said, my voice shrill, as thoughts flew through my mind about the fact that, at least theoretically, Will had an excuse to kiss me. If he wanted to. Or I could kiss him, if I wanted. Did I? *We* could kiss each other. It didn't even have to mean anything. It was a tradition, just what people did when they were standing under mistletoe.

Will wore a funny look on his face. "Okay, well, Merry Christmas."

"Bye," I said, quickly closing the door right as Jim broke into hysterics. "Not funny, Jim!" I shouted, stomping after him, wreath and all, looking for something smaller with which to hit him.

"Oh, but it's so funny, Rose," he taunted, dodging me. "Though I was hoping it would be Kecia so I could shove you out of the way."

"What are you, twelve?" I said, chasing him into the living room, where he proceeded to hide behind the tree.

"Voices," Grandma called from the kitchen, sounding tired. "Please lower them."

At one point we almost knocked over the tree, which sent Grandma into a rant, but all I could think was that if Mom were here, she would be smiling and laughing and running around with us.

———————

Christmas morning arrived and we gathered around the tree. The branches were heavy with ornaments, and silver tinsel glittered from top to bottom. Dad managed to get up early with the rest of us and we sat with mugs of coffee in our hands, trying to wake up, and trying hard to forget the obvious, too. I was glad this day was finally here. It meant that soon the first Christmas without Mom would be behind us.

"Where'd you get that, Rose?" Dad asked me, standing up and coming over for a closer look. He smiled as he reached for the tiny crystal pendant dangling from my neck, taking the heart into his hands and pulling it into the light where it sparkled and sent little flecks of rainbow shining onto the ceiling.

This morning I'd decided I was ready for something new from my Survival Kit. Before the sun had a chance to peek above the horizon, I reached into the paper bag. My hand closed around the tiny crystal heart and I smiled. Surely the heart was supposed to be about love, and love seemed a good next step, especially on Christmas.

"Mom gave it to me," I said, plain and simple, letting the word *Mom* roll off my tongue and take flight. I imagined her flitting around the room like a firefly, lighting up at different moments to remind us she was there, alighting on the very top of the Christmas tree like a star. "This is the first time I've worn it."

"It's pretty," my father said, putting his arm around my back and pulling me into a hug. When he let go of the heart I caught it between my fingers and closed my eyes, almost believing that Mom had planned on giving it to me for Christmas, one last present to enjoy. This was close enough to the truth that I let myself have this wish, and on today of all days I felt I was allowed.

"I love you so much, Dad," I said, and got up on my tiptoes to kiss him on the cheek. It was wet with tears.

JANUARY & FEBRUARY

A Crystal Heart

25

THE HEART OF LIFE

On New Year's Day, when Will picked me up for his hockey tournament, the sun was high and shining against the snow. Aside from the time we'd driven out to the farm, I'd only ever been in his truck at night, and the light that brightened the cab this afternoon seemed almost strange. Colors were sharp, and suddenly I worried how I looked, so exposed in the glare. I pulled the seat belt across my body and turned to him. "It's good to see you," I said, and smiled, happy we were back in familiar territory.

But he seemed nervous and fidgety, in a black wool coat with the collar high around his neck as if he wanted to hide. "You, too," he said.

"Are you ready for this game or what?"

"Sure. Um." He wouldn't look at me. "My mother is going to invite you to dinner tonight," he said, and abruptly shifted into first, stepping on the gas. The truck lurched forward as we headed out of my neighborhood.

I waited for him to elaborate, the cab feeling smaller than usual with the two of us so close together yet unsure how to act. "And?"

"I wanted to give you a heads-up, that's all," he said.

House after house went by, Santa Claus statues, giant candy canes, and other assorted Christmas decorations still scattered across lawns. A few people were outside taking down lights from trees and bushes and dismantling their displays. "You only give someone a heads-up if you think there will be a problem, so when your mother asks, what do you want my answer to be?"

"Whatever you want," he said, and pulled onto the highway.

"Will, come on." I needed more direction. "Seriously, yes or no?"

We merged onto the interstate and picked up speed, passing two exits before he responded. "Yes. Tell her yes and come to dinner," he said, but still refused to look at me.

The heat was making me feel stifled and prickly all over so I shut the vent on my side and loosened my scarf. "Okay, so it's settled," I said. "I'll go to your house."

He nodded, his face front, staring at the road.

Neither of us spoke the rest of the ride and I hoped it was simply because we had an entire night ahead of us and for once could have our conversation elsewhere. When we arrived at the rink and I got out into the cold, snowy air, I couldn't help but wonder where elsewhere might take us.

Lewis won both of their games easily and by early evening Will and I were at his house. He went upstairs to change and his younger sisters, Emily and Jennifer, claimed one hand each and led me into the family room toward the tall sparkling tree by the windows, taking it upon themselves to entertain me. There was a doll-strewn place on the floor next to it, and the two girls began proudly showing off their spoils from Christmas.

"This is the Barbie Santa brought me," Emily explained.

Before I could respond, Jennifer was shoving Emily aside to show me her Barbie, which she assured me was better than her sister's. "Don't let Emily fool you. She doesn't believe in Santa anymore," she said, plopping down on my other side after Emily presented me with yet another doll courtesy of Santa. "In fact, she's known that for, like, three years, but she keeps pretending because she's afraid she won't get presents anymore if she admits she knows the truth." Jennifer crossed her arms, confident that she'd had the final word.

"That's not true. Dad said—"

"It doesn't matter anymore what Dad said—" Jennifer's mouth mimicked Emily's, and with the mention of their father suddenly we were in tricky territory.

"Mom!" Emily yelled.

"Rose," Mrs. Doniger appeared in the doorway. "Why don't you come spend some time with me in the kitchen?"

"Sure," I said, grateful to extricate myself from what looked to be a painful fight brewing between the sisters. Mrs. Doniger crouched down next to them and began to whisper, her voice too low for me to overhear what advice she was giving her daughters on such a touchy subject. This gave me a chance to peruse the shelves of family photos in the foyer near the kitchen. Unlike at our house, there was no dust clinging to the portraits. A number of them were of Will's mom, dad, and the kids from year to year, a few were old wedding pictures; there were photographs of Emily and Jennifer—separate ones—posed in various dance costumes, some of Will on the ice, and Will and his dad in a hockey rink, Will still in uniform, his mask off so you could see his face. I was interested to see how much Will looked like his father and that he was smiling in all of them. I studied that smile for a while—I'd never seen this version. It was big and broad and almost cocky, revealing genuine happiness and ease, the kind that's only possible when you've never known heartache or loss. I remembered what it was like to smile like that, and I wondered if Will noticed there was a difference between his before and after smiles.

"Rose, can I get you something to drink?" Mrs. Doniger asked, brushing by me into the kitchen. She opened the fridge, studying the contents inside the door. "We have just about anything you might want: water, juice, seltzer, soda—"

"Just soda, thanks."

She pulled a bottle from the shelf and reached for a glass from the cabinet. "Sorry about that with the girls. Their father's death is tied up in the holidays—it's so complicated. Emily has been hanging on to her belief in Santa ever since. Jennifer has done the opposite of Emily, of course, and wishes Christmas didn't exist at all." She sighed, handing me the glass, the soda fizzing as tiny bubbles rose to the top and burst. "How was your Christmas?"

"As good as it could be, I guess," I said, and could tell from the look in Mrs. Doniger's eyes that she understood. "It's been nice to have my brother home from college, and my grandmother has been staying with us since Thanksgiving, though she can get pretty difficult." I laughed and took a sip of my Coke. "To be honest, the weirdest part was getting through New Year's Eve. We all stayed home and went to bed early, like maybe we could just ignore it. But waking up this morning, I realized I can finally say that my mom died *last* year. Somehow it helps. It makes it feel further away." I gulped down more soda, surprised that I would reveal so much to her.

"I remember that very same moment," she said. "It's strange, isn't it? How a change of one day on the calendar can make such a difference in how we feel."

I nodded. "The seven-month anniversary is coming up on January fourth. Seven months *sounds* like a long time and I think it should *feel* like a long time, but it might as well be yesterday."

"Don't push yourself. Seven months is barely a blink, take my word for it." Mrs. Doniger opened and shut drawers, taking out cooking utensils. "It must have been hard to share your mom with so many people in our town. I bet everyone has some special memory of her they want to tell you about."

"Yes. It felt as though the entire world showed up at her

wake. I almost don't even remember that day." An image of the long, endless line snaking out the door at the funeral home flashed through my mind. "Let's change the subject. I'm sorry to bring up this stuff. It's so depressing—"

"Rose," she interrupted. "Don't worry. It's fine. It's more than fine actually. You need to talk about it. It's part of how you move through the grief."

"Thanks. Really. I appreciate it," I said. She stirred a pot on the stove and set a cutting board onto the counter. "Can I help?"

"That's all right, I've got everything under control. You relax. Besides, I'm sure my son will come down soon to steal you away until dinner's ready." She glanced behind me into the hall. "Speaking of Will."

"Hey," he said, and I turned around.

"Hey."

"Why don't you kids go upstairs—"

"Kids?" Will interrupted. "Mom, seriously?" he protested.

"Sorry, sweetie." She smiled and shrugged. "Why don't you and Rose go upstairs since Jennifer and Emily will drive you crazy if you stay down here. I'll yell when it's time for dinner."

"Okay," he said, and started back up to the second floor. "Are you coming?" he asked, turning to me.

"Ah, sure I am," I said, following him upstairs, my hand gripping the banister as if at any moment I might lose my balance. "It kind of smells like a locker room in here," Will warned when we reached the door to his room.

"Nah," I said once I was inside. I was used to Jim's room, which was filled with his football stuff. No matter how much you scrubbed everything it still had the odor of sweat. But Will's smelled like his soap, a scent I'd grown to like.

"It's the hockey gear," he explained, gesturing to his bag in the corner.

"Don't worry about it."

He looked at me with skepticism.

"Hey, if you were so worried about your room, then why'd you invite me up here?" He shrugged but didn't say anything else, so I took this as an invitation to look around and see if anything would give me further insight into what made Will, *Will*. The walls were painted blue and there were a few sports posters scattered across them. A calendar with baby animals hung in a corner, almost hidden from view, and the second my eyes landed on it, he quickly explained. "My sisters."

"I never would have guessed," I said, laughing.

The top of his dresser was packed with hockey trophies, and the plaque inscriptions said things like *Most Valuable Player, Youth Hockey Association* and *Most Goals Scored, Division A, Lewis Junior Hockey*, and on the biggest one, *All State Team, Will Doniger*, for the season when he was a freshman at Lewis. A hook next to the dresser was heavy with medals and looked as though the slightest nudge would send them crashing to the floor. "Pretty impressive," I said, after discovering yet another MVP award, the honor etched into a medal hanging from thick blue and white ribbon.

"Not really," he said.

The light in the room made it difficult to tell if Will was actually blushing. "You can't really expect to be modest with all this on display."

He put his hands in his pockets. "I don't normally have guests."

"Oh," I said. For a moment I let this sink in, that Will was giving me access to a part of himself he didn't usually share. Not sure what else to do, I returned to studying the trophies and medals, and noticed they all stopped after Will's first year of high school. "So what happened?" I asked him.

"What do you mean?"

"Why did you stop playing? I heard you were injured."

"Yeah. I was," he said, running a hand through his hair.

"Well, what did you do? Get in a fight? Knock your head too hard into the boards and get a concussion?"

"No, nothing that simple."

"A concussion is simple?"

"Well, the truth is complicated."

"I've got time," I said, sitting down on the bed. I felt the crystal heart bounce against my chest, underneath my shirt. I'd worn it every day since Christmas. "So?"

"The short answer is, it was bad enough that I stopped playing for a long time."

"And the long answer?"

Will stood by the window and stared outside. The Donigers'

holiday lights were on, the trees outside his room woven through-out with tiny white twinkling strands. I waited for him to say something more but he didn't.

"I didn't mean to upset you," I said.

"I know." After a while he came over and sat down next to me, leaving about a foot of space between us, and I was sud-denly aware that we were hanging out *on his bed*. I had never been near a boy's bed that wasn't Chris's or my brother's. Will took a long breath before he started to speak. "I guess you could say my mind was injured and that's why I didn't play."

This was not what I had expected. "What do you mean?"

He fell back against the bed and covered his eyes, his legs dangling off the sides. "The reason I stopped playing hockey was because of my dad—I was too sad." He crossed his arms and stared up at the ceiling. "I couldn't handle being on the ice anymore."

This was a reaction I understood. I waited for him to go on.

"Before my father got sick he never missed a game. He was always telling me I was good enough to go pro someday, and how playing varsity at Lewis was like a stepping-stone to a col-lege scholarship and then the NHL. He believed in me like nobody else ever has." Will stopped and the only sound left in the room was from our breathing. "It never occurred to me that my father wouldn't get better, that the last game he'd gone to of mine was his last ever. And then he got sicker and sicker and then—" Will stopped. "And then he died."

Silence gathered around us again, like the wind swirling the cold air. Slowly, I lay back against the bed, until Will and I were side by side. "So that game in November, was that the first time you'd played since, you know, your dad?"

"No. I tried once before at the beginning of sophomore year."

"What happened?"

"I got kicked off the ice and ejected from the game for fighting within two minutes of the ref dropping the puck. I had my gloves off and the guy's jersey pulled halfway over his head and everything."

"That's intense." I knew by now that when fights got really bad, a player tried to get his opponent's jersey up his arms to trap him in a vulnerable position. It was the cardinal sin of hockey.

"Yeah, slightly. Anyway, I couldn't bring myself to go back again afterward. Every time I got on the ice all I felt was rage, so I took some time off. At first Coach thought I'd only need a couple of weeks but then it turned into a couple of years. He redshirted me to save my spot on the team."

"That was nice of him."

"He was pretty understanding. And it means I get to play an extra year to try to get the college scouts' interest back. I have a lot of coursework to make up, anyway."

"Really," I stated. Will and I had never talked about whether he was planning on going to college after he graduated. Lots of people in Lewis didn't, and then, I hadn't let myself think that far ahead, even though occasionally I wondered if Will would disappear from my life almost as suddenly as he'd become a part of it.

"Last year Coach started pestering me to come back, and I practiced with the team here and there. It wasn't until this fall that I felt ready to try again."

"Huh."

"Huh, what?"

"I thought I was the only one who avoided stuff that reminds me of painful subjects."

"These last couple of years, I've learned just how good I am at avoiding things."

"Yeah?"

"Oh, yeah."

"What made you decide you were ready?"

He laughed a little, but it was a sad laugh. "My dad."

"What do you mean?"

"I realized if there was anything that would upset him, it would be finding out I'd quit hockey because of him."

I turned to face Will, the comforter soft against my cheek. "I'm sure he would be happy to know you went back."

Will looked at me, his eyes shining in the darkness. "I'm glad I did. It was the right thing, and if I hadn't, I don't think you and I would have started hanging out."

My breath stopped at these words and my face grew warm. I shifted my attention to the ceiling and suddenly I saw stars.

I waited for them to fade, but instead they only became clearer, until I realized there were entire constellations taking up every inch of space. "Wow, you've got Orion's Belt up there," I gasped. "And the Great Bear." They reminded me of the star that awaited me in my Survival Kit.

"They've been there since my dad and I put them up after a trip to the planetarium when I was six," he explained, and the two of us stared at his makeshift night sky for a long while without saying anything. "So what do you avoid?" he asked eventually.

"Everything," I said at first, even though this wasn't a real answer. "Music, as you already know. Basically, anything that reminds me of my mother, which is a lot. And I try to avoid having feelings."

"That's impossible, you know that, right? It forces you to shut people out altogether."

"I've gotten good at it."

"Which part?"

"All of it."

"Is that why you and Chris broke up?"

I was a little surprised by such a forward question. "Probably," I answered after some thought. "It was at least part of the reason. Or most of it."

"My girlfriend and I broke up when my dad got sick," Will said, and I half sat up, caught unawares by this new piece of information about his past. "I couldn't deal with being in a relationship anymore either."

"Your *girlfriend*." The word choked out of me.

"Is it that hard to believe I would have a girlfriend?"

"Um, no. It's just that—" I said, and stopped. I'd never al-lowed myself to think about it. "I don't know. It's not hard to believe at all. So who was it?"

"No one you'd know. She was from another school."

I felt strangely relieved by this. "Interesting." I wanted to ask more about her, to find out what she looked like, to get a handle on the kind of girl he would date, but I resisted.

"Enough about my past," he said. "New topic."

"Okay," I said, tapping my fingers against the comforter. My left hand was so close to his I had to consciously make sure we didn't touch. "Hmmm. Oh, I know." I got up from the bed and waited for my eyes to adjust to the dark so I could find my bag. I fumbled around and pulled out the iPod, scrolling my finger around the menu so it lit up. It became the only glow in the room aside from the stars. "On the topic of things we avoid." I sat down again and held it out to him. "Here. As promised."

"Wow, the iPod."

"You said you'd listen with me," I reminded him.

"I did," he said, and took it from my hand, searching through the playlists. He got up from the bed and placed it in his speaker dock. John Mayer's "The Heart of Life" began playing and he lay down next to me again. I could feel his eyes on me as we listened.

"I went through a John Mayer–obsessed phase," I explained,

when another of his songs came on. The iPod was like a time capsule of music I'd listened to when Mom was still alive.

"How's the TBD list going?"

"Nowhere at this point. But soon, I think. I'm getting there."

"You want to know the name of the playlist I chose?" he asked, and I could hear the smile in his voice.

I breathed deep. "Sure," I said, even though I already knew what it was.

"Moody Rose. I was curious to know what was on it."

"John Mayer, obviously."

"A bunch of pretty make-out songs," he said, and laughed. From the sound of his voice, I could tell he was grinning.

"Yeah, hilarious. Well, I don't have much use for this playlist since I'm done with romantic entanglements. Way too many feelings involved."

"You sound certain about that."

"I am," I said, turning to look at him even as regret began to pulse through me.

Will stared at me hard. "That's too bad," he said.

My gut told me to switch topics before one of us said something we couldn't take back, but I couldn't help myself. "What's that supposed to mean?"

"I'm not sure. But I can understand why you feel that way."

"Really?"

"I told you. I went through it myself."

"I know," I said, but couldn't decide if Will being so

understanding all the time was a good thing or not. I knew he'd let it go, whatever *it* was. But for a second, a moment that went by so quickly I almost missed it, I wished he would push me beyond this place where I'd stalled out. As we listened through the playlist, I played with the heart at my chest and thought about how the items from my Survival Kit were beginning to intertwine, one merging into the other. Will had helped me with the peonies and now with the iPod. Was I supposed to fall in love with him, too?

"Will? Rose?" his mother called out to us. "Dinner is ready."

We got up and both of us stretched. When he turned on the light, which seemed extra bright after all this time in the dark, I wondered what would have happened if his family wasn't waiting for us right now, whether we might have stayed here, in his room, listening to music all night.

If maybe, just maybe, we would have kissed.

I thought if we had, it would have been perfect.

26

HARD TO EXPLAIN

The first day at school after break was filled with heavy reluctance as the long haul of winter set in. Aside from one long weekend, there weren't any vacations scheduled until March, and the best to hope for was a snow day now and then. I was by my locker, thinking about this depressing reality, when I saw Will walking toward me in the hallway. We hadn't yet spoken since all that talk in the dark at his house. I assumed we would continue as always, barely acknowledging each other, but I was wrong. The moment he noticed me his face broke into a smile.

And suddenly, our private friendship became public.

Will leaned his shoulder against the locker next to mine. We usually spent so much time in his truck that I sometimes forgot how tall he was. "Hi, Rose, nice to see you again," he said, his voice full of confidence.

I bit my lip, nervous about this change in behavior.

"I had fun the other night," he went on. Suddenly the Will from the photographs, the one whose smile was happy and sure, was standing in front of me. "Did you?" he asked.

I returned the smile. "I did."

We stood there, grinning, not saying anything else, like we held some delicious secret between us. The minute bell warned that we needed to get to class but neither of us moved.

"See you later?" he said.

"Yes," I answered. "Soon."

As the cold days of January passed, some of them heavy with snow, dark and short as if the sun couldn't bear to see us, something changed and I started to feel as if spring was upon us instead. Each morning a little of the weight my heart had been carrying was lifted. I smiled and laughed more easily and the world and everyone in it seemed to glow. Something invisible inside my chest was working overtime to mend the biggest wounds from the last year and the smaller scrapes and cuts everywhere else, too. Even as the seams were stitched and beginning to heal, my still-tender heart strained against these threads and expanded until I thought it might burst.

Each day before I left for school I took the crystal heart from a tiny dish on my bedside table and clasped the chain around my neck, careful to keep it hidden under the shirts and sweaters I bundled on to stave off the icy air. I carried both hearts, my own, filled with growing feelings for Will, and my mother's gift, like secrets.

Will and I began to hang out at school all the time—in the hallway by our lockers, at lunch, during free periods in the library. So much that people were starting to talk. Not Krupa or Kecia, who accepted Will's presence as if he had always been there, but there were lots of others who huddled and whispered when we walked by. After the third time Will came to my house to hang out after school, my family began to have questions, too. The night before Jim went back to college for spring semester and Grandma Madison was scheduled to go home, I was ambushed at dinner.

"So, Rose," Grandma said, "I take it you're over that football player."

Across the table, Jim shook his head before shoveling another forkful of meat loaf and mashed potatoes into his mouth. Grandma had made our favorite dish, enough so we'd have plenty of leftovers after she was gone to give me a little reprieve before I'd be the only cook in the house again.

Dad looked at me, waiting for my answer.

But I wasn't sure what to say. I'd become spoiled by the willingness of Krupa and Kecia to remain mum on this subject, and had thought I would escape this sort of grilling here, too. "Chris and I have been broken up a long time now."

"That's not what I meant and you know it," Grandma said, and picked up her glass of soda between two French-manicured fingers. We now drank only soda, water, or juice in the house, as per Grandma's orders. Grandma had Dad on a tight leash, and I was impressed by his improvement—he hadn't come home drunk in weeks and I wondered if this would last after she left. Grandma gave me an uncharacteristically genuine smile. "I'm glad. I like the Doniger boy and I think he's been good for you."

I opened my mouth in surprise.

"I agree," Dad said, chuckling, before he returned to his meat loaf.

"Will and I aren't dating. We're just friends."

Grandma sniffed. "Right," she said. "I may be old but I'm not senile."

Jim watched me as he chewed and swallowed. "Well, I don't know how I feel about it. You're never going to find anyone better than Chris. Seriously."

"Can you stop hanging on to this idea that Chris and I are going to get back together, please?" I said. "Why do you even care?"

"I want you to be happy," he said.

"She is happy," Grandma said, and glared at him. "Can't you tell? I wouldn't be leaving otherwise," she added gently. She placed a hand over mine, her rings cool against my skin. "I wouldn't go if I thought you weren't okay, Rose. I love you so very much."

A lump formed in my throat. I was so accustomed to Grandma's jagged edges that this revelation of why she felt it was okay to leave, that she wasn't here only to take care of Dad or help with the meals and the house with Jim home—that she'd been watching out for me especially—made me unsure how to respond. So I didn't say anything, not then, and eventually we finished our dinner without the subject of Will coming up again. But the next morning after we said our goodbyes to Jim and the three of us watched him drive away, his car packed with folded laundry and books and food, I stopped Grandma Madison just as she was unlocking the door to her station wagon.

"Grandma, wait," I said, my voice hoarse. I ran down the driveway.

"If you delay me and I hit traffic I'm going to blame you," she said, the sarcasm I was so accustomed to back in her voice.

But this time I didn't buy it. "So I wanted to tell you—"

She jangled her keys with impatience. "Can we do this over the phone? I know you prefer all communication to go through your brother, but you could try me once in a while. You have my number after all, and that fancy cell of yours," she said, which was Grandma's strange, coarse way of telling me that she was there for me.

"Yes, I do. And I will call you more. But this is not for the phone," I said. Before I could chicken out, I walked up to Grandma and wrapped my arms around her in a big hug. She felt so fragile, so thin and breakable, when everything about her personality was so strong and harsh. She hugged me back and her keys clinked when they fell to the ground. "I love you, too, Grandma," I whispered, finally answering what she had said to me last night at dinner. "And thank you." When we let go, I retrieved her keys from the driveway and handed them back. "You don't want to hit traffic." I did my best to smile through the sadness, watching as she got inside, fixed mirrors, and let the car warm up. Before she backed out, she rolled down her window.

Her cheeks were stained with tears.

"Call me, Rose," she said.

"I will."

I stood there, waving, until she disappeared up the street.

27

COLORFUL

Memories of my mother began to emerge from the places I'd buried them, gingerly stepping out into the light again. Unlike before, now I sat with them, allowing myself to remember a conversation between us that was especially important, or the way she smiled at me when I came home from school full of news to report. These were just little things and they still made me sad, but I became better at being in the sadness and at resisting the urge to chase it away. One memory in particular, a much bigger grief than the others, found its way into the front of my mind. For a while, I let it sit untouched, refusing to acknowledge it, even though more and more each day I was aware of its presence. On February 4, the eight-month anniversary, I decided I was ready to face it.

Krupa and I were at our locker before our last class. "I have a favor to ask you," I said.

She checked her reflection in the mirror. "Anything for you, my dear," she said, distracted, patting her hair, trying to flatten it. She made a pout and began to apply lip gloss.

"Do you have any plans right now—I mean, other than chemistry?" I asked.

"Not if you need me for something." Krupa looked at me. "Don't worry, there isn't a test today or anything. Tell me what you want to do—ooh wait! Does it have to do with Will?" she asked.

I blushed. "No, not at all."

"Oh well, I figured I'd ask anyway. So what is it?"

I fiddled with the crystal heart at my neck, hidden from view just beneath the opening in my shirt. Playing with it had become a near constant habit, as if it were my own heart and I needed to keep checking that it was still there. "I want to walk over to the elementary school."

"Oh." She was quiet a moment. "Today is February 4."

I nodded. "Eight months."

"Are you sure you don't want to wait for Will?"

"Yes. This is something I want to do with just you," I said.

"Okay, let's go right now. I'm ready." Krupa shoved one arm, then the other into the sleeves of her puffy red down jacket. She grabbed my stuff from the second hook and pushed it toward me. My heart expanded with gratitude for my best friend. "Come on," she said, and headed toward the school exit. I followed, pulling on my coat and wrapping a scarf around my neck on the way. Once outside, our breath puffed little white clouds into the cold air and we did our best to navigate the slippery walks, our footsteps crunching on the thin layer of snow that the shovels hadn't removed. On either side of us were steep drifts.

"So why today?" she asked. "Is it because of the anniversary?"

I thought about her question. "That's part of it," I said. "But it's more that I know exactly what Mom would be doing right now with her kids if she was still teaching. I want to see if they kept the tradition."

Krupa nodded, looping her arm through mine like we were two rings on a paper chain, and we turned down the path between the high school and the elementary school. I hadn't been here since the day of my mother's memorial, but it was time to let myself remember, to go back through one of the saddest memories, so maybe one day I'd be able to go forward again and maybe even move on. When the playground came into view, though, my breath caught in my throat.

———

My mother's death wasn't a shock only to us, it stunned the entire town. Everyone, her fellow teachers, her kids, their parents, her former parents, all of them expected her to make a full recovery from cancer. She'd done it once, when I was in eighth grade, so why not a second time? Back then she went through the surgery and chemo and the sickness with a smile on her face and cheerfulness in her voice. One day I even returned home to find my mother waiting for me in the kitchen after some of her friends had taken her shopping. "I've always wanted to fit into a size two," she exclaimed. She'd lost so much weight that her clothes were big and loose and she was eager to show off her new look.

My mother never lost sight of the silver lining in her situation. She read books she'd always wanted to read, watched movies, and let us wait on her for once. She missed a full year of school, but her colleagues pooled their sick days so she didn't run out—they were as determined as Mom that she would be teaching at the beginning of the next school year. And she was, like she'd never been sick.

The doctors called Mom a miracle.

But they warned us, too. I'd never forget that part. Dad, Jim, and I were talking to her oncologist after her very last treatment—I was about to start as a freshman at the high school. We were eager to hear her say the cancer was gone, *every last bit.* "So she's totally better, right? You got it *all* out?" I asked her.

Dad and Jim nodded, as if this would help make it true.

Dr. Stellar sighed and leaned forward in her chair. "There is *no cure* for cancer," she told us, emphasizing *no* and *cure.* "Your wife," she said to Dad, then turned to Jim and me, "your mother will *always* have cancer."

This wasn't exactly new information. Everyone knows there isn't a cure—your brain absorbs this unconsciously from ads you see on television and all those races for the cure that people sponsor. But when someone you love is diagnosed, all rationality disappears. You think there *has* to be exceptions to this rule, and I wanted Dr. Stellar to tell us that Mom was one of these.

"The good news is that your mother is in remission, and hopefully she will be in remission for years. So no more treatments for now," she said with a smile, but she wasn't finished yet. "You should know, though, that when the cancer comes back, and chances are it *will* come back"—Dr. Stellar paused to let this sink in, preparing us—"the kind of cancer she has is virulent. It's aggressive. *When* it comes back, it's very likely that this will be it." She stopped, looking at each of us, one by one, straight in the eyes. She wanted us to understand the full meaning of her words.

We didn't say anything. We were so happy about Mom's recovery that we didn't let ourselves truly hear this last part. We convinced ourselves that Mom was too full of life to ever let cancer win. But Dr. Stellar was right in the end, and *when* it happened we weren't prepared.

When my mother got sick again last April everyone assumed she would be okay. The teachers were ready to donate their sick days again, and the kids at school made get well cards and art to decorate her hospital room. Mobiles hung from the ceiling and bright construction-paper flowers lined the walls around all those blinking and beeping machines. It was a rainbow everywhere you looked.

But the beginning of June, just before the school year ended, Mom died.

Having a teacher die was complicated, we found out, especially for kids as young as my mother's students. They were confused about where she went and why she didn't come back, so the elementary school was left with a dilemma: how to help Mom's kids cope, even as they tried to process this unexpected loss themselves. They decided to hold a memorial service a few days after Mom's funeral. They invited my family and we went, of course—we felt we had to even though the last thing we wanted was to go to another event centered around Mom's death.

It was gorgeous that day, the sun high in the sky. "Just drive around back," one of the administrators told Dad as she directed cars to the parking lot next to the nursery school playground. Children were everywhere, milling around with their parents and other teachers, everyone with markers and pens and crayons and little scraps of paper—they were so busy drawing and scribbling. One of Mom's colleagues asked if we wanted to join in and I just shook my head no and stood there frozen.

They'd brought in a tree—a birch, Mom's favorite—and planted it on the playground. Kids were patting the dirt around the bottom like this was a game or just another one of Mom's projects. Then, Mrs. Delaney, my third-grade teacher, gathered everyone in a circle around the tree and led them in a song.

My father, brother, and I hung back, watching from afar.

When I heard the children's voices, so high and sweet, I just about lost it. I held my breath, pressed my palms against my cheeks, telling myself it would be over soon, the song and the memorial, too. These were three- and four-year-olds after all and their attention spans almost didn't exist. When the singing came to an end, I got ready to leave—I thought it was over and we could finally, thankfully, go home again.

But there was one more thing on their agenda and we found out what everyone had been writing earlier on: notes to my mother, colorful letters of goodbye and best wishes and we miss you. With the help of the parents, her kids began attaching these to kites, of all things.

Kites. Real ones.

My chest tightened and I twisted my body away, pushing my fist against my mouth, elbows digging into my sides. Did they really expect my family to endure this? Kites were suddenly everywhere I turned, beautiful, colorful ones, the simple diamond-shaped kind, striped, polka-dotted, rainbow, all of them grasped in the children's hands with their parents helping to hold on.

When the children were ready, they let them up.

The blue sky filled with bright swaths of color, the letters to Mom on lined notebook paper and stationery flapping in the wind. It was a perfect day for this. Mothers and fathers ran with their kids across the playground, helping them let the string out and pull it back to keep the kites high and dancing in the wind.

She would have loved it—I could almost hear Mom's voice, filled with joy at the sight and clapping her hands, staring up at the spectacle of it all.

"Wave goodbye to Miss Ellie," Mrs. Delaney called out, as

we stood there, our eyes turned toward the heavens watching those kites, listening as the kids chorused their loud farewells to my mother, waving their hands above their heads as if they could really see her floating up there, somewhere.

I rushed inside the school, seeking relief in the darkened hallways, only to find that entire walls were packed with finger paintings my mother's kids had made of her. I sank to the floor and curled into a ball, my head tucked into my knees. I would never come back here again. Ever.

I hadn't stepped foot near the elementary school since.

———————————

"I don't want to go in," I explained when Krupa headed for the entrance.

"No? But I thought—"

"Let's go around back."

"Okay."

We turned down a path, and when we reached the end of the brick building and rounded the corner, we stopped. "Here, right?" She looked at me, her eyes asking for permission to go farther.

I nodded.

The nursery school playground showed signs of kids recently playing in the snow. Three short snowmen rose up like thick, rounded stumps, and a snow fort, maybe an igloo, was apparent from the big mound in the corner. My eyes landed on my mother's birch tree along the back edge of the fence, its bark peeled white and rippled with brown, its branches edged in ice as if it was covered in crystal, just like the heart Mom gave me.

Krupa walked straight up to the tree. "It's so pretty in the snow." With a mittened hand she ran her fingers along the smooth, glassy surface on the lowest branch. "Rose." She beckoned.

I shook my head, and instead I walked toward the window to my mother's classroom, my feet sinking into the snow, the drifts that became deeper with each step.

Please don't let it all be gone.

When I reached the window I stopped and closed my eyes, preparing myself. "Oh," I hiccuped as I peered through the glass. Krupa's footsteps crunched up behind me and together we stared inside. The kids were already gone, but hanging from the ceiling, from all different heights, were hundreds of snowflakes, the kind you make by folding a piece of paper again and again, using scissors to cut out tiny triangles and squares, or, if you feel ambitious, stars and hearts and other shapes, too. You might cover them in glitter or sparkles or sequins, or maybe leave them plain and beautiful all on their own. Every year, Mom's kids began making snowflakes on the day of the first snow and from then on throughout winter so that eventually the classroom's ceiling would look like a perpetual snowfall. Some were sparkly, others gigantic, and still others miniature, like tiny masterpieces.

"Rose," Krupa said, putting both hands on the brick ledge along the bottom of the window, standing on her toes for a better view. "They didn't forget."

I nodded because I couldn't quite speak. It felt as though my mother was still here, still a part of this place.

"Look at that one," Krupa said, and laughed, pointing at a snowflake so big and heavy with decorations it crinkled from the glue and swayed heavily on its string. "And that glittery one over there," she said, about another, and then another, until eventually I joined her.

I thought about love as we stood there, the day turning to dusk and the temperature dropping, and my heart, the one inside of me, became fuller.

Silently Krupa and I made our way back through the snow on the playground and down the path across the school grounds. It started to flurry, soft snowflakes falling from the sky onto our cheeks and noses. They swirled around us like magic.

"Thank you," I whispered to Krupa when we were ready to say our goodbyes.

"Of course," she said, and turned one way, toward her house, as I turned the other, toward mine, slowly moving forward, one foot in front of the other.

28

ARE YOU GONNA BE MY GIRL

Valentine's Day arrived and by late morning I was carrying a dozen red roses. Well, almost—there were eleven so far. As I came down the corridor toward our locker, Krupa eyed the bouquet with suspicion. "I know those aren't from Will—he's not the showy type."

I shook my head.

"Please tell me they aren't from Chris. Tell me that he's not still trying to get back together with you after that mistletoe debacle."

"I'm as surprised as you and a bit overwhelmed. I thought he'd given up."

A worried look came over her face. "You're not going to consider—"

"Definitely not."

"So it's settled: you will give them back."

The fragrance of the flowers was almost overpowering. "Krupa, I'm not going to be mean about it, and besides, I haven't even seen him yet."

She slid one rose from the bunch and mashed the crimson petals against her nose so hard a few fell onto the carpet. She made a face. "Then how did you get these?"

"You don't even want to know," I said.

Krupa began to pluck the petals on the rose she held. "You love him, you love him not, you love him . . ." she said, watching them fall softly to the ground. She plucked the last. "You love him *not*." She rolled her fingers across its velvety red surface and smiled. "I guess that decision's made."

"Hilarious."

She slumped against the wall and sighed. "All right, tell me how he did it."

"He orchestrated some crazy, football-style 'Rose and Roses' blitz—that's what Tony told me when I demanded an explanation. Eleven different football players have walked up to me today, one after the other, each one handing me a single rose." I gestured toward the little white tags around the stems. "Take a look."

She grabbed the paper and read. "Oh my god, you are kidding me: 'For my one and only Rose.' How cheesy!"

I dropped my arm so the bouquet swished toward the floor, the petals rustling in the air. "I know, but that's Chris."

"Just promise me you won't fall under his spell again."

"We're over, okay?"

"Good," she said.

I offered her the bouquet. "Please take them."

She made a face. "*I* don't want them."

"I don't either."

"Why don't I toss them?" Krupa suggested with a grin.

"You never liked him, did you?"

She just shrugged.

"How about this? You give them to a freshman who looks forlorn and lonely today. Or eleven different freshmen. You decide."

Krupa's eyes lit up and she grabbed the bunch from me. "Ooh, I like the idea of playing Cupid. And, Rose, make sure you look inside our locker before you go to class. There's something there for you and it's way better than these," she said, shaking the bouquet so hard that dark red petals rained onto the floor. "Anyway!" She skipped off leaving a trail behind her.

"Remember to take the tags off first," I called after her, and dropped my bag to the ground. When I unlocked the door and saw what was there, I gasped.

A single red gerbera daisy was on the very top shelf.

Its black center was surrounded by row upon row of red, radiating outward. The petals were long and thin, the color vibrant. I brought it close to my face and smiled, the silky feel of the flower tickling my chin. My heart beat so quick and hard I thought my pendant must be pulsing against my chest. I thought back to that morning in September and the flower I'd picked, remembering how Will had been there in the yard, working. Spinning the stem in my hand like a pinwheel, I watched the blur of the red twirl.

What a sweet gesture. So thoughtful, so special.

So *Will*.

I had to find him.

Before I could go anywhere, before I could even get away from my locker, Chris found me. I saw him turn the corner and come down the hall, smiling. His blond hair looking like he'd just gotten it cut, wearing a tight short-sleeved T-shirt that made him seem even more imposing than usual. He carried a single red rose in his hand to complete the dozen. When he saw that I didn't have any roses, but instead a single daisy, his smile twisted in confusion. He stopped short and waited for me to explain.

I didn't, though. I just turned and walked the other way, certain that Chris and I were truly and finally over. Maybe someday in the future we could find a way to be friends.

———————

That weekend, Kecia had a party and I was excited to go. Instead of the prepackaged fantasy high school life I'd had with Chris, I was beginning to have one of my own making. When Kecia opened the front door, Krupa and I found ourselves looking up into three stories of airy, open space with only a sparkling crystal chandelier to fill it.

"So, your house is kind of nice," I said.

Kecia laughed. "Ostentatious, you mean." She beckoned us to follow her upstairs. "I love your outfit," she said to Krupa, whose shirt, made from sari material, was a burst of swirling pink and silver threads.

"My mother made it."

Kecia seemed surprised to hear this. "I wish my mom was that talented."

Tamika appeared, leaning over the banister. The top of her cheeks shimmered, iridescent blush giving her skin a subtle shine, and she'd twisted her long, thick, nearly permanent braids away from her face into an updo. "Hi, guys!"

"You look amazing," I said.

"Thanks! Hurry up. People are going to start arriving." She turned and stalked off, the sound of her four-inch heels muffled by the thick carpet.

"Tamika gets bossy when we throw a party," Kecia explained, and led us down a long hall to the back of the house. We turned right into the bathroom, which was palatial. The floors and countertops were marble, the fixtures crystal, and there was a giant hot tub below the windows. Fluffy towels were piled everywhere and five sinks lined one wall, each with its own set of mirrors, where Mary and Tamika were fixing their makeup.

"I guess we don't have to fight for space," I said.

Kecia shrugged. "My parents are over the top. Pick any spot you want."

"I don't need one," I said. "I came here ready."

Tamika turned. "Rose Madison, you are not going to our party dressed like that."

I looked down at my sweater, jeans, and boots. "Why not?"

"I have the perfect thing for you," Kecia said, and ran out of the bathroom, returning with a long, red, frilly top dangling from her fingers by spaghetti straps. She held it out to me.

"Um, that's nice," I said, when inside I was thinking there was no way I was wearing something that flimsy. "But isn't it kind of summery?"

"The party is indoors," Mary said.

"But—"

"Just try it," Krupa urged. "If it doesn't work, you can wear what you have on."

"Or something else from my closet," Kecia said quickly. "Rose, trust me. It will look amazing."

"Fine." I held out one finger and she let the satiny straps, thin as threads, slide onto it. "As long as I can keep the jeans." I slipped inside the changing area and pulled my sweater and T-shirt over my head. I stared at the fancy tank top—it looked so tiny and not at all warm.

"I can't wear a bra with this, can I?" I called.

"You don't need one. It's tight," Kecia explained.

"All right, all right." Off came my bra and I shimmied the shirt down over my torso. I was already tempted to throw a sweater over it, but then I saw my reflection in the mirror. Each short layer of red chiffon cascaded from one to the other. It reminded me of a 1920s flapper dress. And it was the very same color as the daisy Will had given me. "Okay," I said, thinking that maybe this wasn't such a bad idea after all. "You guys were right. I kind of like it." I peeked my head out from behind the door.

"Show us," Kecia prompted, and I stepped outside.

"Oooh," everyone gushed.

"That heart pendant is perfect," Krupa said, and reached for it to get a closer look. "I've noticed you wearing it lately, but this outfit really shows it off. It's beautiful." She looked hard at me. Maybe she thought it was a gift from Will. "Perfect for a V-Day party," she added, just as the doorbell rang, announcing the arrival of the first guests.

One after the other we headed downstairs, a train of five girls—five friends—ready for a party. Happiness coursed through me. For a long time I'd thought this part of high school was over for good, that I'd never want to do things like be at a party or fuss over an outfit with friends, that after my mother died it just wouldn't seem right. But here I was, doing just these things, and with each step the crystal heart bounced against my bare skin. Tonight I was wearing my heart on the outside, in plain view, for anyone to see.

————————

Krupa joined me on the soft white couch, where I'd been sitting for the last half hour, my eyes focused on the sliver of front door I could see from here. People milled around the room, cups of beer from the keg in their hands. A group of girls nearby were whispering, and a burst of deep laughter came from some guys in the corner. Krupa laid her head on my shoulder, her long, thick black hair cascading down my arm. Her wide eyes blinked up at me. "Who are you watching for? Hmmm?" she asked.

"Like you really need to ask." I shrugged her off me. "He isn't here yet and maybe he won't come at all." The longer the party went on without Will's appearance, the more disappointed I became.

"Why don't you text him and see where he is?"

"Will and I don't communicate like that."

Krupa looked at me. "What do you mean?"

"We always settle everything in person. When we see each other we make a plan for next time and that's it—nothing happens in between. It's sort of this weird, unspoken rule we have. I'm not sure why."

"But half the fun is in the constant messaging."

"What? You mean the waiting around to see if he texted or didn't, and then what he said if he did, and then what to say back, and blah, blah, blah to infinity? Honestly, it's kind of nice, having a friendship without all that extra drama to worry about."

Krupa scoffed. "Friendship? Please. Admit it, you are completely in love."

"Shhhh," I hissed. "Nothing has happened—" I began.

A mischievous look crossed Krupa's face and she lowered her

voice to a whisper. "Well, I'd better go refill this drink," she said, and popped up from the couch, grabbing her glass off the coffee table.

"But we were—"

"Back in a while," she said, and disappeared into the next room.

When I turned back, I saw Will on the far side of the room, looking uncomfortable, his thumbs hooked into his jeans pockets, something I knew by now that he did when he was nervous. His expression was blank, closed off, even as people said hello. Sometimes he mustered a small smile that would disappear the instant they moved on. But when our eyes met he smiled for real and started making his way through the crowd toward me.

Butterflies took flight inside me. "You're here," I said, returning his smile with an even bigger one. It was becoming difficult to hide how I felt.

"We're all here," he said, and sank down into the cushions next to me, leaving quite a bit of space between us.

I considered shifting toward him but stayed put. "We?"

"The hockey team. We almost never get to go to parties during the season so everyone jumped at the chance to go to this one. Though, soon all of my weekend nights will be free," he added, looking at me with curiosity. Next weekend the play-offs for the state hockey championship would begin, marking the end of the season. Maybe Will was nervous about what would happen between us once our regular routine was gone.

"I think it's a good thing," I said, staring right back. "Won't it be nice, to be able to do whatever you want again? Whenever you want?"

"It's not like I go to parties much anyway. I haven't been to one in . . ."—he paused, counting—"over two years."

"Seriously?" I asked, though I shouldn't have been surprised since I didn't ever remember seeing him at one.

"When was the last time *you* went to one?" he countered.

The answer was last March, almost a year ago, but before I could respond a bunch of hockey players rushed by us. "Will's got a girl," one of them said, and punched him in the shoulder. Will tried to grab his arm but his teammate was too quick and was already on his way into the next room. When he turned to me again there were two red spots on his cheeks. "Don't mind them," he began, but was interrupted again.

"Will, Will, Will," Tim Godfrey, a senior I'd seen after games but had never formally met, was chanting Will's name over and over like a fan at a game. He squeezed onto the couch between us and put an arm around Will's neck, in a friendly sort of headlock—if a headlock could ever be considered friendly. Tim grinned at me. "Rose Madison, I don't believe we've ever had the pleasure. Will doesn't like to share."

I tried to hide my smile. When I went to shake Tim's hand, he brought mine to his lips and kissed it. "Nice to meet you," I said, and laughed.

"Come on," Will said to him. "Don't you have other people to harass?"

"Don't you just love this man?" Tim asked me, a goofy look on his face.

"Quit it," Will said, and punched him in the shoulder. To me he mouthed "Sorry" and "He's really drunk."

Tim was undeterred. "Let me give you some advice about Will," he went on. "He is very shy and sometimes he just needs a little push." He pressed a single finger on Will's upper arm to demonstrate.

"Ah, I think I get it," I said.

"Will." He leaned closer, like he was going to tell him a secret. "Girls like it when you ask them to dance," he whispered, but loud enough so I could hear. "Many other men have done the same with ladies in the next room." He stood up and yanked Will with him, who looked like he might die on the spot. Tim turned to me. "Rose, you'd love to dance with Will, wouldn't you?"

If he wasn't acting so clearly out of affection, I might have felt more embarrassed, but the intent was obvious: to give Will that little push. Something I knew all about myself. Maybe we both needed this. "I would love to," I said, and stood up. Tim took my hand and passed it to Will. Our fingers automatically wove together, like we'd held hands a million times before. The noise and lights and people around us disappeared and all I knew was the feeling of his palm against mine and the tingling of skin touching skin.

Tim patted our backs, like Will and I were little boats he

wanted to send floating across the water. Still holding hands, we headed into the next room, where one slow song after another had been playing all night. Without looking at me Will said, "You don't have to do this, you know. They were just playing around. They like to—"

"I want to," I said, not letting him finish, "dance with you, I mean."

"Okay," he said, seeming relieved and beginning to relax. The two of us moved toward the crowd of couples swaying under a ceiling of white twinkle lights. Will stopped. "Middle or edge?" he asked, surveying the floor.

"Middle-to-edge," I decided, and led him into the crush of people.

"At least here maybe the guys will leave us alone." Will shrugged his shoulders, his smile sheepish. "Tim meant well."

"I got that much," I said, and put my arms around his neck.

Will hesitated a moment, but then I felt his arms slide around my waist. As we swayed, turning slowly, I breathed in the scent of his skin. Occasionally my attention was caught by the fact that we weren't alone in the room, when I noticed Kecia smiling at us and when Mary passed by and whispered "Nice" in my ear.

"I've been meaning to thank you," I told him after a while.

"Thank me?" He pulled back a little, to look at me.

"For the flower. On Valentine's Day."

"Oh. That. It was just a little—"

"I know what it was. It was perfect," I said, drawing him close again. "I loved it."

"I'm glad," he said. "I hoped you would."

I rested my head on Will's shoulder, enjoying the feel of his sweater against my cheek and his hands on my back. The only thing that mattered was where I was and who I was with now, and when Will's arms tightened around me I knew I was right where I needed to be all along.

29
MY HEART

The day for game one of the hockey championships arrived and everyone at school was excited. First thing in the morning I caught up with Will in the hall at school. "You didn't tell me I needed to plan for this! I heard it's impossible now to get tickets for tonight."

His blue eyes widened. "Do you really think I would leave you out? That I wouldn't make sure that you could go?" He leaned against the wall of lockers, and slid his hand into mine. Our faces were inches apart, close enough to kiss. I forgot that we were at school, that we weren't alone, that I should be breathing. "Rose?" he pressed.

I snapped back to reality. "Sorry. The tickets. So you have one for me?"

"It helps if you know a player. We get a block."

I tried to count how many I'd need in my head—Krupa, Kecia, Tamika, Mary—but became distracted again by the fact that we were holding hands and publicly so. "Um, so how many can you spare?"

"How many do you need?" he asked, and I did my best to go down the list.

———————

Later that night when we arrived at the rink, people were streaming in the doors, past scalpers outside selling tickets. A light snow was falling, and the weather report predicted it would become heavy and continue through tomorrow. The approaching storm only intensified the anticipation all around us.

Fans cheered louder than ever as the players shot out of the team boxes onto the ice at the start of the first period, skating in circles while the refs conferred in the corner of the rink. When Krupa joined Kecia and me a few minutes into the game, she nudged me. "Why aren't you watching?"

I was covering my eyes, so I widened my fingers to peer at her through the gaps. "I'm nervous," I admitted. "If they lose, it will be awful."

Krupa drew my hands away from my face. "Will you just admit that you are in love with him already?"

"It's pretty obvious," Kecia said from my other side.

I didn't respond.

"And it's obvious the feeling is mutual," Krupa added.

Will skated to the penalty box, hoisting himself over the boards to wait out his three minutes, and the clock began counting down. "You don't know that."

"Have you considered asking him if he wants to be more than friends?"

"No. I can't."

Krupa sighed and we sat in silence for a while. The last seconds on Will's penalty disappeared and he was back on the ice in a flash. The crowd jumped to their feet, and between wool-covered fingers I watched as the Lewis players passed the puck between them, the opponents checking them into the boards so hard it made me wince. When they neared the goal the cheers intensified. After no one scored, everyone let out a collective breath, and the teams raced to the other end of the rink. As the tension eased I put my hands in my lap, but the relief didn't last long. Soon the crowd was up again as two Lewis players, one of them Will, passed the puck back and forth, gliding in between the opposing players like they weren't there, and Will's stick came down like lightning to slap it into the goal.

The score went to Lewis 1, Jackson 0.

I jumped to my feet with the rest of the crowd. As Will extricated himself from the pile of teammates hitting him on the back in congratulations, he skated a quick lap around the rink and when he was right below our spot in the stands he stopped. Even through his face mask, I could tell he was searching the crowd. When he saw me, he nodded ever so slightly, then skated away.

My cheeks burned red.

"Oh. My. God. Rose!" Krupa squealed. "Did you see that!"

"I think I'm going to cry, that was so cute," Kecia said on my other side.

"Right, like he's not in love with you," Krupa said.

For the rest of the game I endured smirks from my friends, but I didn't really care, and when, in between periods two and three, the techno music blared like always and everybody got up to dance, for the first time all year I danced along with them.

By the time we left the arena snow was falling heavily and several inches had piled up. The weather report was now predicting at least a foot, so the celebrations for Lewis's win would have to wait. Will drove me straight home, his eyes glued to the road. When we arrived at my house, there wasn't any sitting and talking in his truck because he was immediately heading out to plow the driveways Doniger Landscaping was responsible for during winter.

It was difficult to hide my disappointment when we said our quick goodbyes.

But later that night, Will surprised me with a text.

I'd been asleep and when my cell first buzzed I grabbed it off the bedside table, annoyed. Then I saw that it was Will, and I sank back into the soft pillows on my bed. *The entire world looks like the inside of a snow globe,* I read, smiling dreamily in the silent darkness. Minutes later he sent another text, and then another, and I drifted in and out of sleep between them.

Mr. D'Angelo's pine tree looks like the abominable snowman, Will wrote, and sent a photo.

There are snow angels in the park. Again, a picture, three winged figures already disappearing beneath a cover of white.

Maybe they will cancel school on Monday. The school entrance was obscured by a drift so high it reached the top of the door.

The next time my phone buzzed Will's message was different. *Come outside. Wear boots. Bring an extra scarf. And maybe a corncob pipe.* The photo was of Will, one hand reaching away from his body to take the picture. He stood next to the beginnings of a snowman, and a tall black lamppost rose up nearby, outlining him in light.

He was here. In the front yard.

My heart pounded out the words *Will is outside, Will is at my house* and I scrambled to get up, hunting my room for snow gear, but came up with nothing.

Then I remembered Mom's teacher closet.

I grabbed the crystal heart from the dresser and tiptoed through the living room and the kitchen. The floor of the mudroom was slick with water from the snow that Dad and I trekked in earlier that night and I did my best to avoid the puddles. I took a deep breath and opened the closet door. Among Mom's paint smocks and aprons I found what I was looking for: puffy snow pants, her sky blue down jacket, and her bright yellow boots, the outfit she wore to play with her kids in the snow at school. I pulled the pants up over my pajamas and put on Mom's jacket, stuffing the heart deep into its left pocket. I took an extra scarf and hat from the shelf and ran into the kitchen to grab a carrot from the fridge. After shoving my feet into my boots, I trudged to the door, wrapping a scarf around my neck and pulling on mittens as I went. The second I was outside I stopped.

The snow came up above my knees.

The world was completely silent under a thick white blanket glowing as if it were made of light. The soft wet flakes came to rest on my nose and lips, and my breath caught. It was beautiful. In the middle of this moment of awe, a fat, wet, icy snowball landed splat across my cheek, and it took all the restraint in me not to scream.

"Hey, Rose," Will called out as I wiped my face. Shielded by my arm from another attack, I turned in his direction. He stood a good twenty feet away, too far for me to fight back, grinning wide.

"You look awfully proud of yourself," I said. "When you said to come outside, you didn't mention the part about offering myself up for target practice."

Another snowball hurtled toward me and I lurched to avoid it and almost face-planted in the steep drifts, but it hit me in the back. Moving through such deep snow was like trying to run through the ocean. "Truce," I yelled.

"All bets are off in a blizzard," he said, lobbing another snowball at me.

This one I dodged. Frantically, I began packing snow into my mittened hands, watching Will approach out of the corner of my eye. I launched a fat snowball in his direction that shattered into a million icy sparkles midway between us, not even close to hitting him.

"Come on, Rose. You can do better than that."

"Hey," I protested, already packing more snow. "You lured me out here with the promise of building a snowman. I even brought a carrot."

"You would've come out regardless," he taunted.

"You think?" I swiveled around so the snowball left my hands like a shot put, and this time it smacked into Will's chest. I threw my hands up in victory.

"I do," he said, and pitched another back at me.

"You're dreaming if you believe I would have left my comfy bed for this."

He smiled. "I'm not dreaming. You're standing right here."

"Don't you have other driveways to plow or something?"

He looked up into the sky, the storm thick and white above us, tiny specks of snow pouring down. "Not for a few hours. I saved your house for last."

"So you could pelt me with snowballs on your time off? How sweet."

His eyes sparkled. "So you think I'm sweet?" He took a swipe at the snow, sending an arc my way, and I shifted in time to avoid most of it.

"That's not what I meant," I said, and pitched another snowball like I was throwing a strike past a batter at home plate. It went wide and missed Will entirely. I immediately scooped more to form another. I took a step. "Careful, Mr. Hockey Star."

"So the truth is finally out: you think I'm a hockey star." He took a step closer. "Interesting."

"You know you're proving my point, right?"

He laughed. "You're the one who said I was sweet."

"Since when did you get so forward, Will Doniger?"

He shrugged and waded toward the beginnings of the snowman rising up from the steep drifts.

I waded after him, calling out, "Maybe it's the blizzard. It's acting like alcohol or something. Making you say things you wouldn't normally."

He began pushing armfuls of snow onto the base. "I thought you wanted to build a snowman," he said.

"I did. I mean, I do."

"So get over here."

We watched each other through the snowfall, icy flecks drifting down around us. I didn't move.

"I promise I won't use you for target practice anymore. Truce," he said.

"Okay," I relented, and made my way toward him, slowly, each step an effort.

Will and I began packing snow higher and higher, until our snowman reached up to my chin. Occasionally we broke the silence with a word or a laugh, but for the most part we were quiet, concentrating on our icy masterpiece, and I was reminded of that day when we dug the peony bed, back when we hardly knew each other. Now here we were in the middle of the night enjoying this magical landscape and building a snowman of all things.

"What are you smiling about?" Will asked.

"I didn't know I was."

He smoothed the head with his hands. "Tell me."

I took the carrot from my pocket, broke off the end, and gave the snowman a nose. "First you become forward, then you get demanding," I said, and removed the extra scarf from my pocket, walking it around the snowman's neck, careful not to twist Will into it. It was blue-and-white striped, our school's colors. "Look at that. She's a Lewis fan. Maybe she's one of your groupies." I grinned, pulling the two ends through the loop I'd made, and took out the hat, plopping it on the snowman's head. I arranged the pom-pom so it would fall forward in a fashionable sort of way. "We need something for the eyes."

Will turned and took off in the other direction. "Hey, where are you going?" I called out.

"You'll see." He walked until he reached the edge of one of the gardens, disappearing behind a high snowbank. Only a few bushes were tall enough to clear the drifts. When he returned, his jacket and jeans were dusted with white. He opened his hand and in his palm were two wood chips.

"What do you think?" He looked at me for approval.

"Perfect," I said, and he pushed them into the face just above the nose, wide enough apart for the eyes. Snowflakes were already scattered across the hat and scarf and I wondered if our snowman would be gone by morning, buried in the storm, all evidence of this dream erased. I didn't know if it was the snowflake that came to rest on Will's cheek, the part that rounded up from his smile, or the way his eyes shone blue in the reflection of the snow, but I reached up to brush that flake away with my mitten.

And then I kissed him.

I leaned toward Will until our lips were barely an inch apart, put my hand on the back of his neck, and pulled him close until there we were, kissing in the middle of a snowstorm, his lips soft against mine, arms wrapped around my waist and his hands on my back. "Hey," he whispered after a while. His warm breath felt like heaven in the cold air.

"Hey," I whispered back.

"I thought—"

"I know—"

"Are we—?"

I wasn't sure what this meant or what would happen tomorrow. All I knew was that right now, kissing Will was the best idea in the world.

So I kissed him again.

The snow fell around us like a dream and it didn't feel real, spending this night with Will, a boy I'd barely known less than a year ago, who had since become someone I couldn't imagine life without. He took my hand and pulled me along through another drift and I thought about the crystal heart. When he stopped and drew me close again, I took it from the pocket of my jacket and slipped it into his, wondering if he'd find it later and know it was mine. He put his arms around my waist and I wrapped mine high around his neck, pressing my lips against his in another kiss, and I was utterly and perfectly happy.

———————

After Will left, I went back to bed. I couldn't sleep and for the first hour I lay there, curled up under my down comforter, eyes closed, going over every single kiss, wanting to pinch myself. Between the snow and the quiet and the dark and the beauty and the surprise it felt like maybe I'd imagined everything.

I fell asleep smiling.

When I woke, the sky bright with morning light and the snow tapering off, there was one more text from Will waiting for me. It was a photo he'd snapped of us. My arms were wrapped around his waist, his left arm pulling me close and the other holding the phone out to take the picture. Even then his eyes were on me, and I wasn't looking at the camera at all. I was gazing up at him because I couldn't tear myself away, which seemed about 100 percent right.

I looked like a girl in love.

I thought about how I'd given the crystal heart away to Will and knew with every fiber of my being that this was the right thing to do. My heart, the real one at the center of my living, breathing body, belonged to him.

30

LAST NITE

In the morning, when I entered the kitchen, Dad was working on his laptop at the table. The white light of snow against the glass door shone down on my father. He looked up from typing. "What's the big smile for?"

I poured myself a cup of coffee, surprised Dad had made a pot on his own. "Oh, I don't know, it might be the snow." I felt giddy, so happy I might burst, and I was starving. "Do you want some breakfast?"

"Sure."

"How about pancakes?"

"Whatever you'd like."

I went in search of ingredients and came across a bag of chocolate chips in the cupboard. "Hmmm, we can have chocolate chip pancakes. There's nothing like dessert for breakfast," I said, and my father laughed. I took out a bowl, poured in the flour, and added a teaspoon of baking soda and some salt, and mixed everything together.

"You get more like your mother every day," Dad said, shaking his head. "Chocolate chip pancakes after a snowstorm."

I savored this compliment as I whisked the egg in a separate bowl, measured the buttermilk, and folded everything together, trying to smooth the flour into the mixture. With one hand I dribbled chocolate chips into the batter and began to ladle little round pancakes on the griddle.

"Did something happen, sweetheart? Something good?"

I stared at the round splotches of batter as they bubbled up from the heat. "Game two of the state championships is tonight and I'm going," I said, and poked underneath a pancake to see if it was brown enough to turn.

Dad grinned. "So who'd you bribe for tickets?" he teased.

I rolled my eyes. "Will Doniger, like you didn't already know."

"I remember when I was your age and Lewis was playing in the championships. Those games were a lot of fun. I remember how your mother loved it when they got in fights. I'd have to pull her back down into her seat."

"You and Mom went to hockey games?"

"Everyone in Lewis goes to hockey games, but your mother and I starting going to them our senior year, right around the time I was trying to convince her to date me." He sat back in his chair, suddenly lost in thought. I waited for him to say something else about Mom, but he didn't. One by one I flipped the pancakes. "You know," Dad said after a while, "Will is having a phenomenal season. He's been all over the sports section. That kid is good enough to go pro, I think."

With the syrup and butter balanced in one hand, I brought a

plate piled high with pancakes over to the table. "Yeah. I've heard that, too," I said with a smile. Then, Dad and I ate breakfast together like a normal family for the first time in almost a year.

———————

When Will came to pick me up for the final game I was nervous.

"Hi," we said together, our faces pressed close inside his truck. Quickly, we both looked away and laughed. I stole another glance at him, but his eyes were on the windshield. He was smiling.

"Ready?" he asked.

"Uh-huh," I said.

We took off, the wheels of the truck sending snow into the air as Will navigated the icy roads. When we arrived at the arena, I broke the silence. "I can't believe this is the last time we'll do this."

"Me neither," he said, and pulled into the parking lot. He stopped in front of the entrance to let me out.

"See you on the ice," I said, and was about to hop down to the pavement, but before I could lose my nerve, I leaned over and planted a kiss on Will's lips. At first he looked surprised but then he smiled. "Good luck," I added, and left before he could respond, focusing on the sound of my boots crunching in the snow, my face bright red. I couldn't stop grinning.

When the game was about to start and Will took off his helmet for the national anthem, there was a grin on his face, too.

All night, as the players crashed into the boards, my eyes followed Lewis jersey number six on the ice. The score stayed zero-zero for most of the night, until well into the third period when Will checked another player hard and took off behind the puck. The crowd got to its feet as he raced toward the opposing team's goal, then slapped the puck to a teammate who passed it right back. Will was almost on top of the goalie, both of them wrestling with the puck, shoving each other, their skates and legs and arms clashing hard. Then Will hit the puck straight into the back of the net and thousands of hands went high into the air, screaming and whistling and cheering and stomping.

Krupa squeezed my arm. "That was amazing."

"I know," I said, and wished with all my heart that I could bottle this happiness so I would be sure not to lose it again. I didn't need the crystal heart around my neck any longer to remind me what it felt like to be in love.

———————

Lewis ended their season as state champions.

Krupa, Kecia, and everyone else went ahead to the after-party while I waited for Will with his family. Celebration was in the air and I couldn't stand still. Will's sister Emily was twirling around in circles. I focused my excess energy on braiding Jennifer's long brown hair, weaving it so the locks that shone a lighter brown would stand out.

"Beautiful," I told her as I twisted a rubber band around the end. This left me again with fidgeting hands and I grasped at the wooden lip along the boards, picking at the peeling red paint.

"You seem happy," Mrs. Doniger remarked.

I smiled. "They won."

"Will's happy lately, too."

I was trying to think of how to respond when Will emerged from the locker room. A part of me wanted to dash through the waiting parents and his teammates to see him.

Mrs. Doniger rushed forward. "I'm so proud of you," she said to her son, and threw her arms around him. "Your father would be, too."

He rested his chin on her head and blinked a few times. "Thanks, Mom."

Mrs. Doniger pulled back, her eyes shining, and Jennifer and Emily squeezed between them. As much as this win must feel great, I also knew it must be bittersweet, too, to have played a season like Will had and not have his father there to witness it. After whispering something to his mother, Will came over to say hello.

"Congratulations," I said.

"Thanks." He shifted from one foot to the other. A puck lay on the ground between us and he kicked it against the boards, where it made a hollow thud. "So, you want to get out of here?"

"Are you sure? I mean, you should enjoy this. Take your time."

"Well, if you want to stick around—"

"No," I said quickly. "I'm ready if you are."

"Then let's go." He turned and headed toward the back exit, only stopping to pick up his gear.

I followed, my heart pounding. "That could be worth money, you know." I gestured at the hockey stick in Will's left hand, and he gave me a curious look. "It won the state championship," I said, and he laughed. Outside the air was cold and crisp and snowflakes floated lightly to the ground. Will's keys jangled as we neared his truck, and the moment we disappeared around the passenger side he pulled me into a kiss. When we stopped to catch our breath, I noticed how he'd parked in a corner against a concrete wall. "You chose this spot on purpose, didn't you?" I accused, but drew him toward me again before he could answer.

"Maybe," he said after another while.

"That was smart thinking."

"Yeah?"

"I've barely been able to think about anything else."

"Other than . . ." He waited for me to finish.

"Kissing you, dummy," I said.

"Really?"

"You shouldn't be that surprised," I said.

He grinned. "I'm just glad to know we're on the same page."

"You, too?" I asked, and shivered.

He wrapped his arms tighter around me. "You're cold."

"I don't think it's the cold."

"We should warm up inside the truck, and besides, we have to meet up with the team at the party."

"I know," I said reluctantly. Really, I didn't care about the wintry cold or going to a party or anything else. I leaned in to kiss him again but he shifted away. "Hey," I protested. "Where are you going?"

"We should get in. If I keep kissing you we'll never get out of the parking lot."

"I am liking this parking lot."

"Me, too. But," he said, practically picking me up and moving me to the side so he could open the passenger door. "Come on. We can continue this—"

"Conversation?" I finished, trying to be helpful.

"Yes, we can continue this conversation later. I promise."

"Can you believe," I said, "that you and I used to not even talk to each other?"

"Rose—"

"Seriously, we used to ignore each other. If I had known then what I know now . . ." I trailed off.

This stopped him a moment and he looked at me. "And what exactly do you know now?"

"Oh, all kinds of things." I grinned.

"Tell me."

"We should get in the truck, remember?"

Will made a frustrated, choking sound at my lack of an answer as I climbed up into the cab, careful not to touch him. Only about ten seconds passed after he got into the driver's side before we were kissing again. We didn't even pull apart when a group of his teammates passed by, whistling and yelling and banging on the back of the truck. Will waved them away through the cab's back window, but this only sent them howling louder. "You're like a drug or something," Will said long after they were gone.

"So are you."

He took a deep breath.

"I wish I could bottle this," I whispered.

"And drink it every morning."

"And every day at lunch, and then again at dinner, and before bed."

"You'd get sick of it," he said.

I shook my head. "Never."

"Seriously," he said. "I want to freeze this moment."

"Good thing you don't need to."

"No?"

"Will Doniger, there is nothing in the entire universe that could make me stop wanting to be with you. And so on and so forth ad infinitum."

"Really."

"Cross my heart," I said. I thought about the sparkling crystal heart that I'd left in his jacket pocket and wondered if he had found it yet.

"We should go," he said. "Shouldn't we?"

I sighed. "I suppose so."

The two of us sat back against the seats. Will placed both hands on the steering wheel and kept them there, and I gripped the bottom of the seat, my fingers curling around the edge. Finally, after several deep breaths, we were on our way.

31

FALLING SLOWLY

By the beginning of March, Will and I were officially a couple and we finally started acting like one, too. Every day he picked me up for school and drove me home afterward, we walked down the hallways together holding hands, I visited him at his locker and he at mine. Krupa and Kecia got used to having him around, and his teammates got used to me, too. We ate out in big groups at the diner, went to the movies, hung out at each other's houses.

Everything was perfect.

I began to believe there was life beyond my mother, beyond grief and sadness, and I almost forgot about the items that remained in my Survival Kit. The silver star, the box of crayons, the tiny, handmade kite. Will and I had yet to discuss the crystal heart, though I didn't give it much thought.

One morning after another heavy snowfall, maybe the last one of winter, Will drove me to school as usual. Slowly, carefully, he turned into the parking lot and inched along the back row, the road covered in a sheet of ice. When we reached the farthest corner, I directed him toward a spot. "Let's park here," I said.

He gave me a funny look. "Isn't this kind of far away from the entrance?"

"Hmmm, maybe so."

"Is something wrong?" he asked.

"Why would anything be wrong? Nothing is wrong. Trust me."

"Okay," he said with a shrug and swung into the space. A forest of snow-covered trees met us through the windshield, beads of ice along the thinnest limbs, the branches so heavy they almost brushed the front end of the truck. Will's hand went straight to the door handle.

"Wait," I stopped him.

"What?"

"Where are you going?"

"Same place as you. I think."

"Don't you have first period free?"

"Yes. Why?"

"Well, so do I."

Will's hand retracted from the door handle. "What does that mean?"

"Let's see, not a soul is around, we have a beautiful view." I gestured outside at the branches, swaying in the wind, the occasional ray of sunlight dancing off the ice. "Neither one of us has to go to class at the moment."

This got a smile out of him. "Oh."

"Yeah, *oh*."

He reached over and took my hand, playing with my fingers.

"Your cheeks are red," I observed.

"Nah," he said, glancing out the window.

"It's extremely cute."

"Cute? I'm not sure I want to be cute. People say my sisters are cute."

"Hot then."

"You think I'm hot?" A grin tugged at his lips as he stared out the front of the truck, but the red only deepened.

"Maybe," I said. "Hey, where does forward-Will go when we get to school? It's like, kissing me on school grounds is against the rules or something."

He laughed. "I guess I feel different when we're at my house. Or really, anywhere outside of here. School, I mean. I'm more, I don't know . . . *me* when we're alone or in other places."

"You mean, you become Mr. I-don't-care-who-sees-me-kissing-Rose-Madison?"

"Is that how I am?" He actually sounded surprised.

"Um, yes. I like that version of you."

He laughed nervously. "Yeah?"

"Mm-hm."

"I'm not very"—he paused, thinking—"*public* when I'm at school. I never have been. I keep a low profile."

"Yes, I know. You kept such a low profile I barely knew you existed for two years."

"Come on, I worked at your house."

"But you never talked to me. Ever."

"I'm not like you, the center of attention."

I blinked, surprised he thought this about me. "To be honest, I'm not sure that was ever really me either. And I was never the center. I was only nearby."

"Well, as far as I'm concerned," he said, and paused as if to brace himself, "I don't like to flaunt what's going on in my personal life in front of everyone at Lewis. I hope that's okay." He glanced at me sideways.

"I think I'll live. Besides, I also like shy Will."

"Oh, great. Now I'm shy Will."

"Yes, at this particular moment you are, but back to more pressing matters," I said, checking the time. "We have exactly thirty-five minutes before we even need to enter the building." I scooted across the seat, closer. "Tons of privacy, no one around to worry about. Just you, me, the truck, and some trees."

"You're not shy at all, are you?"

"Careful, or I might kiss you at your locker between classes today in front of everyone."

"Maybe that wouldn't be so horrible."

I put my arms around his neck. "Let's start with the school parking lot and go from there."

"Sounds like a reasonable compromise."

"I'm glad we could come to an agreement," I said, and those were the last words spoken between us until we had to go inside.

———

The call came during sixth period. I was hanging around the library, searching the shelves for something to read. The photograph of a beautiful girl on the cover of a book caught my attention so I picked it up. Happiness hummed through me as I flipped through it, enjoying the promise of the day's end and seeing Will again. I closed my eyes and leaned against the tall bookshelf, remembering this morning.

A sigh came from the end of the row.

"So you couldn't wait," I said without looking up, assuming it was Will. He knew I was here and I was hoping he would figure a way out of history so we could meet. I'd imagined a make-out session in some remote corner of the stacks.

There was another intake of breath. Then a woman's voice, "Rose Madison?"

I opened my eyes. Suddenly I could feel what was coming next, ominous, like the whisper of a candle blown out. The school librarian approached me, already halfway down the aisle. "What's wrong?" I whispered when I saw the look on her face.

"The principal is looking for you. Have you checked your cell phone?" She hesitated a moment. "The hospital has been trying to reach you. It's your father."

The blood drained from my body, starting at the top of my head straight down through my face and torso to my legs and feet, everything gone cold. I reached out to grip the edge of the hard metal shelf and tried to steady myself, my fingers slamming against the coarse spines of old books. Thoughts raced through my mind like a ticker at the bottom of a news channel. *Is my father dead? Dying? How did it happen? Was he drinking? I lost Mom and now I'm going to lose Dad, too. I'm going to lose my dad, my father.*

I pushed past the librarian but she stopped me. Her hand felt warm and reassuring through my shirt and I wished she could make that feeling radiate all the way to my fingertips. "I should go," I said.

"Do you need a ride? Is there someone I can call?"

I shook my head. "I've got to go," I repeated, and began to walk, then run toward the exit. I had to find Will. He would know what to do, how to handle this. The library door was heavy, resisting my body like it didn't want to let me out. I pushed through and immediately bent in half, both hands gripping my knees, my lungs heaving, everything a blur, like the world spun out of control. I had to pull myself together, so I forced myself up and began to stumble through the corridors, winding my way around the halls until I was outside Will's classroom. Hands cupped against the window, I peered in, needing him to see me, my breaths short and ragged. It felt like forever before Will noticed I was there. When he came out I stepped to the side, gripping the nearby wall of lockers for support. He shut the door softly behind him, the short click of the latch the only noise.

"What's wrong?" he asked, his voice a hush in the empty corridor.

I started to cry, I couldn't hold the tears back any longer.

"Something happened," I said between sobs. "Something bad. My father is in the hospital and I'm so scared." I buried my face in my hands and waited for him to put his arms around me, to move my body in the direction it needed to go, to be strong for me, to take me to see my father and tell me everything would be all right, that we would handle this. But his hands never reached for me and the reassurance never came, so I wiped my eyes with my palms and looked up. Will watched me from a distance, his arms glued to his sides, with an expression on his face that I couldn't read.

"Will? Can you—"

"Rose, I'm sorry," he said before I could finish.

"But, I need—can you take me? To the hospital?" I stuttered, wondering why I even needed to ask.

"I'm so sorry," he repeated, and I began to panic.

What was he sorry for, exactly? And why wasn't he doing anything, just standing there, frozen? Before I could pose any of these questions, I heard another voice in the hall, loud and deep.

"Rose," it said. "Rose," I heard, closer now.

I turned and saw Chris Williams standing there.

"Are you okay? What's the matter?" These words fell from his lips and suddenly it was nine months ago and he was asking these same questions but because of my mother. Chris was suddenly at my side, someone that I could grab hold of, cling to, and all I had to do was reach out.

But I wanted it to be Will.

MARCH

A Box of Crayons

32

BEEN A LONG DAY

That familiar hospital smell hit me like a wave and I staggered back a few steps, but I knew I had to keep going, to face whatever waited inside. "Rose," someone said as the force lessened, and I made myself step into the hall. The voice beckoned again. "Honey, come here."

"Anna," I said, turning toward the desk where she stood, her arms out, waiting for me—Anna had been my mother's nurse. "Hi," I choked out. She hugged me and the hospital smell disappeared, replaced by the sweet scent of her perfume and the feel of her soft curls against my cheek. During the two months Mom was here, Anna had witnessed everything, the highs and the unbelievable lows, until the very end when my mother's pulse dropped all the way to zero and stopped forever.

She let me go after a while. "I'm going to put you somewhere private while you wait for the doctor."

"But my dad. Can't I? Shouldn't I go see him? Now. You know?" I stuttered.

The springy rubber soles of Anna's shoes squeaked as she

pivoted me around until I was facing an office I knew well, the one reserved for discussions the doctors didn't want to have in front of the other people in the waiting room, the same office where I'd learned the news about Mom.

Anna guided me inside and shut the door behind me.

———————

I slouched into the armchair where I'd sat less than a year ago, tilting my head back against the smooth, cool leather. Memories I'd tried so hard to erase crept back into my consciousness, first in dribs and drabs—the last day I saw my mother truly alive, standing on the front porch, where she waved at me as I left for school and called out that she loved me. The final few minutes of her life when I'd held her hand, how my fingers clasped hers, how I felt their warmth, and took in the sound of her heart on the machine, ever slower, watching her face until I kissed her on the cheek, her skin so thin and tired, my fingers slipping from hers, one by one, never forgetting for a second that I would never touch or see her again. The sadness that I'd mistakenly believed had receded for good was like a tide at the beach, gone out for a few hours, till at the turn of the day it rushed back, reminding me it was still there.

The beginning of the end for my mother came on her favorite kind of day, on a bright, sunny afternoon in April, the kind that gives you spring fever, where you want to throw on a tank top and skirt and expose as much skin as possible to the warmth and the light. I was down on the track that circled the football field at cheer practice, and in between dances and stunts, basket tosses and plain old cheers, my teammates and I spread out sweat-shirts on the springy burnt orange surface so we could lie in the sun. We stretched our arms out, trying to soak up as much vita-min D as our bodies had lost over the dark, wintry months. How happy I felt that day, so much energy pulsing through me, my blood racing, everything inside me rejoicing because the warm weather was here and summer was around the corner.

During one of these breaks my dad called. "Your mother isn't feeling well," he said, his voice laced with worry. "I think I'm going to take her to the hospital."

"Well, what does *she* say?" I asked, unconcerned, peeling off yet another layer, loving the feel of the heat on my body. "Is she even willing to go?" My mother had always called the shots when it came to her cancer and I could just imagine her protests against Dad making a decision on her behalf.

"I'm not sure I care what she wants," he said. "She's in pain."

Even this didn't faze me much. She had endured all kinds of agony last time around, proving she could handle anything. She'd beaten a type and stage of cancer almost nobody lived through and everybody called her a walking miracle, even her doctors.

"I'm going to take her," Dad said, desperation creeping into his voice.

Rebecca, our captain at the time, waved me over because practice was going to start again. "Sure," I said to my father, distracted. "Whatever you want. Just call to let me know what happens."

"I will," he said, and I heard the sound of car doors opening and slamming through the phone.

"Tell Mom I love her."

"Okay," I heard my father say, and then there was a click.

The cheerleaders were already setting up to run through our most difficult pyramid, three tiers of girls with one at the top—me.

"Rose, are you ready to join us or what?" Rebecca wanted to know.

"I'm coming," I said, and pushed away thoughts of my parents on the way to the hospital as we practiced the formation again and again. Kecia, Tamika, and Mary were responsible for popping me high in the air so I could land on the second tier of teammates.

"Ready?" they said as usual, on maybe our eighth try that day.

"Ready!" I responded, preparing myself to fly.

"Down-up!" Kecia commanded.

I can hear it now, clear as day.

I remember traveling up, up, up, my muscles tight, my toes pointed, my body straight like a shot, riding the momentum until the very last second, when I started to come back down and landed square on the shoulders of two girls, who grabbed my legs immediately, anchoring me. Once I was steady, I punched my arm straight toward the hot sun and smiled at the imaginary crowd in the stands. This time when I looked out, my eyes met Jim's and I laughed with surprise. For almost two years I'd pestered my brother to visit me at practice. "Hey, Jimmy!" I called out, my voice echoing through the empty stadium. I waved but he didn't smile, and that's when I knew something was wrong.

"Kecia!" I yelled. "I need to come down. Now." Anxiety rolled through my already tense muscles. After a few moments of organizing on the ground that stretched on forever, I heard her voice.

"Ready?"

"Ready," I called back, everything about me becoming unsteady.

"Down-up!" the girls directly under me shouted, and again I felt the momentum of traveling up in the air until my body began its descent, Kecia, Mary, and Tamika cradling my back and legs before I could reach the ground and popping me back onto the track. The second I landed I ran over to Jim.

"Rose," he croaked, his eyes pooling with tears.

I suddenly felt desperate. "What? What! Tell me."

"Dad's been trying to reach you, but you didn't pick up. It's Mom. Something happened right after they got to the hospital. We've got to go. Now." Turning on his heel, he hurried away, and I followed, already numb, without a single glance behind me to my teammates. I even left my stuff sitting there. When I got into Jim's car, I checked the time. Only thirty minutes had elapsed between Dad's phone call and now. I hadn't even asked to talk to Mom on the phone when I'd had the chance.

"I should've taken her sooner," Dad said when we ran into the waiting room, his head in his hands, looking hunched and broken in a chair. "I shouldn't have listened to her. She was in so much pain."

"It's going to be okay," Jim said, putting a hand on Dad's back.

But we hadn't seen Mom yet so we didn't know.

The door to the office opened a crack. My head was down, eyes glued to the table in the office. "Rose?" I looked up as Anna peeked her head inside. "Five more minutes and the doctor will be here."

A heavy sigh burst from my lungs as if I'd been holding my breath. I nodded to let her know that I'd heard. Without thinking, my fingers felt for the crystal heart pendant, but then I remembered it was gone and I wished for it, for anything that might provide comfort. I could hardly believe I'd left something so precious in Will's jacket pocket, a last gift from my mother, and he might not even know it was there. What if it got lost? My mind wandered back to this morning, when Will and I were in his truck, and it already felt so far away, like it had been another Rose there, another girl he'd been kissing. With

Will I'd slowly worked my way toward the Rose of before, who laughed often, who felt things so deeply, who could move through the world brimming with feeling and emotion. But now she was gone, all over again, *that* Rose. Somewhere deep inside I think I'd known she wouldn't last for long.

"Don't assume the worst," Anna said, opening the door farther, a triangle-shaped sliver of harsh fluorescent light cutting into the room. "It's not as bad as you think." The brightness clashed with the soft incandescent bulbs illuminating the office. "If it weren't true, I wouldn't say it. You know I'm always honest, even if the truth is not what a family wants to hear."

"I know," I managed after a short silence, my voice hoarse. "I remember," I said, sinking again into my memories of my mother, because they wanted to come back and I didn't have the strength to force them away anymore.

———

The worst moments we endured in this hospital were the times when Mom woke up from her coma. On three separate occasions she returned to us, each one more hopeful than the last. The first time we'd expected it. We were certain it marked the beginning of her recovery, that Mom would magically transform from a limp body on a respirator to her vibrant, talkative self once again.

"Your mother's awake!" my father said, excited, running into the waiting room where Jim and I had been sitting for weeks, barely leaving even for school. We did all sorts of things to pass the time: playing cards, doing the homework that piled higher each day. When Dad appeared I was painting my toenails a hot pink color, and the bottle nearly tipped as I scrambled to my feet. I raced after my father and brother, down the wide white hallway, the nail polish glistening wet and three of my toes still unpainted. I don't know what I'd expected, but "awake" turned out to be something altogether different than I'd imagined.

"Mom," Jim and I said at once, before we'd even had a chance to step into the room and get close enough to see her.

Mom's eyes were definitely open, but only halfway, her mouth showing two rows of teeth, her jaw slack. The worst were her legs and left arm—they would spasm and skitter across the bed, then fall off the side and dangle there until the nurse would put them back under the blanket, only to have them bounce across and down once more.

"I love you," we took turns saying in case she could hear us, in case she could understand. The woman who lay there, occasionally blinking her eyes at us, unable to speak and control her limbs, was not the mother I knew. Within hours she was gone again.

A few weeks later, she woke a second time, but in much the same way. There was the initial flurry of excitement from us, the promise, the hope of recovery, the possibility of taking away tubes and unhooking machines, and then the accompanying shock and disappointment when she slipped away. The only thing that changed was how hard we bottomed out when we lost her.

But the third time she woke was different from before.

"Mom is conscious," Dad said, pulling Jim and me up from the waiting room chairs. His change in description—from *awake* to *conscious*—was notable, and I wondered if he'd intended the difference, if we would see the real Mom in that room or still the empty-eyed woman whose only resemblance was that they shared the same body. "Ellie," Dad said as we raced in to see her, his voice full of emotion.

Mom turned her head toward the door.

She didn't speak, but it was clear she *saw* us, she *recognized* us. Mom was *alive*.

To us, this meant her recovery was imminent, that she would fight the cancer with courage and hope just like last time and she would *win* again. I knew it, we all did. We were so sure.

"Your kids made you these," I said to her, pointing out the patch of construction-paper tulips taped across one wall of the room. With Mom watching, Jim and I alternated, taking her on a tour of the cards and homemade decorations and mobiles hanging from the ceiling—who they were from, what grade, which teachers, and when they had arrived. We took turns getting into bed with her, making sure to do so on the side where her legs and arm kept falling off, our bodies there to be close to her as much as to prevent her from noticing she no longer could control her movements. Dad, Jim, and I talked over each other, filling in the silence that she couldn't, telling her everything we could think of from the weeks when she'd been asleep, trying to make her laugh, doing our best to occupy her attention, telling her she was going to get better, that we loved her and were so happy to see her. Her hospital room became the site of a family party.

We stayed long past visiting hours that day.

Finally, Anna came in to shoo us out. "Hey there, beautiful," she said to Mom—she always called her that, even when Mom was unconscious, and I loved that Anna did this. She checked the tubes and monitors measuring Mom's heart rate, her breathing, and other vital signs, her voice cheerful. "These people need to give you some rest."

"We'll be back first thing in the morning," Dad said quickly.

"The second we're allowed to be here," Jim added.

We were so happy, so excited, that we didn't mind Anna's directive to go home. Tonight, we were leaving with real hope in our hearts, with the future in mind, with faith in my mother's recovery.

Just before I slid off the hospital bed I felt the soft grip of a hand on my arm.

My mother's hand.

"Mom?" A thrill flew through me. "Dad! Jim!" I called out to get their attention and they gathered behind me, looking at Mom, waiting. She hadn't yet said a word since she'd woken up, just watched us and listened and spent time being aware.

Being alive.

This time she was struggling to communicate with something more than her eyes. A clear mask covered her mouth, but we could see her lips working as she tried them out. After a long wait and with tremendous effort, she managed to mouth three words.

"I." Her mouth opened wide and stopped. Then, "Love." And then, "You," she said, her lips closing after this last word. She was careful to look at each one of us in the eyes, Dad, Jim, and then me.

"Oh, Mom!" we were shouting. "We love you, too. We love you so much! You are going to be okay!"

That's when I noticed the tears rolling down her face to the pillow.

I brushed them away, my fingers gentle along her cheek.

By the next morning, she'd slipped away again, this time for good.

The office door opened and I lifted my mind from these painful memories. The doctor walked inside and pulled up a chair next to me, setting her clipboard on the smooth wood surface of a side table. For a moment I wanted to reach out and touch the beautiful braids cascading past her shoulders, wondering how long it would take to weave so many and wishing we could discuss this instead. But she started speaking and I had to focus on why we were here.

"I'm Dr. Stone," she began.

"I'm Rose Madison," I said, a reflex.

"I know." Her voice was firm, but somehow reassuring. "Your brother isn't here yet?"

"I called him. He's at college. I don't know when he'll arrive, though. Maybe in another hour." If I kept babbling maybe I might hold off whatever came next. "Jim said he was already getting in the car when I was on the phone with him—"

Dr. Stone placed a hand on my arm, as if hitting an invisible *pause* button. "Let's talk about your dad," she said.

"Okay," I whispered, the word barely audible even in the quiet room.

All that wanted to come out of my mouth was a string of questions: Was he drunk? Is that why this happened? Did he hurt anyone else? Did he kill someone else? Is he going to die? Is he going to die, too, like Mom died?

Dr. Stone looked at me, her brown eyes steady. "What you need to know first, and what you need to remember while we discuss the details, is that your dad is going to be okay. He'll need recovery time but he will get better."

"Really?" Hope found its way into my voice.

"Yes," Dr. Stone replied. "But now we're going to talk about the circumstances. Okay?"

It felt as if she was leading me down a rocky path in the middle of a brook, little by little, guiding me through each step, waiting, patient, making sure I was ready to place my foot onto the next slippery surface. "Okay," I agreed.

"Your father's car hit a tree off the side of the highway," she began.

———————

Time at a hospital goes by differently, as if on its own clock. A few minutes can sometimes feel like days and vice versa. A week can pass without you realizing it. I had no idea how long I was in that office, maybe hours. When I came out and returned to the waiting room, my eyes narrowed to a squint in the bright hallway, the white flickering glare intense after the soft darkness of the private room.

"Rose." I heard my name, said by many people at once, and Krupa's arms wrapped around my waist and her hair, long and soft, pressed against my shoulder.

"I want to go home," I told her.

"What about your dad?" She watched for my reaction. "Is he okay?"

"There's nothing to do but wait."

"Oh, Rose—"

"No." My voice was quiet and steady. "I don't want to talk about it."

"Rose?" Kecia came toward us, her heels, normally so loud clicking against the floor, silent now, like soft slippers. "Can I do anything?"

"Thanks for coming." I forced myself to see her, to look beyond Krupa, noticing that Mary and Tamika sat in a nearby row of waiting room chairs. Chris was still here, too. He'd not only waited, he'd called my friends. Will was missing from this group, though. He hadn't come, hadn't changed his mind. This thought flashed quickly and was gone. "Has anyone heard from Jim?" The loud sound of my voice cut across the quiet of the waiting room.

Krupa looked at the clock on the wall. "He left around two, and it's after five so he should be here soon, depending on traffic."

I sat down in the open seat between Chris and Tamika. Kecia and Krupa took seats in the row across from us.

"Are you hanging in there?" Chris asked, and I stared as if he might be a stranger, his perfect bone structure, his almond-shaped eyes, his face so beautiful. For the first time all afternoon I began to wonder why he was really here, if this was another strange attempt to get me to consider going out with him again. I shrugged in answer to his question since I didn't know what to say. Regardless of his intentions, I was grateful. I needed someone and he was there for me.

As if he could read my mind, he said, "Just let me be a friend. That's all I want—I swear—to be here as your friend."

"Really?" I asked.

Chris nodded, his eyes sad, but I could tell he meant it. Within moments, with just a few words, we resolved six months of uncertainty and hurt and missed connections. I was so unbelievably relieved to have this sudden consolation of closure.

The second hand on the clock ticked in circles, around and around, time passing slowly. All my energy was given over to willing Jim to walk through the door, and that Will, too, would suddenly appear. I needed him to explain how what happened earlier at school had been a mistake, a misunderstanding, that he was ready to be there for me and wouldn't leave my side, whatever happened next. But my attention was soon drawn from these wishes by the welcome sound of my brother's voice.

"Rosey!" Jim called from across the waiting room, rushing toward me, and I felt myself being pulled up from the chair, my brother's arms around me, holding me tight to his chest. It felt so much like home that I started to cry. All day I'd done so well holding back the tears, but now that Jim was here I couldn't stop them. He let me sob into his sweatshirt for a long time, never lessening his grip. Eventually, when I calmed down enough to speak, I told him what I had decided during those hours in that tiny office. "You need to deal with Dad," I said. "I can't any longer. It's your turn."

Jim looked at me with confusion.

But I knew this was what I had to do.

Before Jim could say anything I spoke again. "Here is the deal: Dad is going to be fine." I stopped, making my voice even while I told him this news, as if I was giving him a list of items to pick up at the store and not discussing our father's fate. "But he has broken bones and a concussion and is undergoing some sort of surgery. They are keeping him"—I paused, gathering the words—"*unconscious*, but for just a few days, so his body can rest. He'll come home probably in a few weeks. Maybe three. Maybe four. We have to wait and see." I needed to backtrack. "No, *you'll* have to wait and see. I don't want to. I can't. I can't see him on one of those machines like Mom was. I just *can't*." Tears spilled down my cheeks and I sniffled, wiping my face with my sleeve.

"Rosey." Jim sounded shocked. "You're not going to stay? Seriously?"

"I'm not." I stepped away, as if proximity might chain me here. There was a long silence before he spoke again.

"Was he . . . had he been . . . ?" Jim couldn't even say the word.

So I said it for him. "Drinking?" I had lost my ability to care whether other people heard or knew. "I don't know. The doctor didn't say anything. But from the sound of it, my guess is yes. Probably. He didn't hit anyone else, though, just a tree," I added, like this was good news, and in a way I suppose it was.

"Oh god. Oh god." Jim put both hands up to his head. "What should we do? What are we going to do?"

Gently, I touched my brother's shoulder. "The question is: what are *you* going to do?" On this last line, my voice cracked and I turned to my friends, the tears streaming down my cheeks, one after the other. "Would someone take me home? I need to go home. Now. Please," I said, and without looking back I began to walk away, down the hall toward the exit, listening to the footsteps of the others behind me, alternately clicking and padding and shuffling against the shiny, tiled floor of the hospital corridor. I was doing the right thing for me, but maybe it was the right thing for Dad, too. Maybe leaving him here, refusing to see him, would finally make that message sink in, about how if he kept drinking, not only did he put himself at risk, but he risked losing me, his daughter, too. Jim could handle this on his own, at least for now. He'd have to, just like I'd done. Today, though, I wouldn't be the one to bear this responsibility. Anybody else but me, I thought, as the wintry air rushed right through my sweater as if it was thin as a spider's web, taking that familiar sour hospital smell with it.

33

NOT YOUR YEAR

A week passed and then another, and the rainy gloom of March matched my gray mood. I kept my word about my father and refused to see him. The daily messages he left on my cell I erased before I even listened to them. Aside from the occasional word exchanged with my brother or Grandma Madison, who had come back to stay for the duration, I spoke to no one. I didn't go to school. Instead, I sealed myself in my room, shades pulled tight to avoid the dreary view of old snow, melting and turning into brown muddy slush, the trees still bare of leaves. Grandma Madison hovered, made remarks about the scraggly state of my hair and my disheveled appearance, but she couldn't hide the worry knotted through her voice. Krupa called, Kecia called, and I watched the screen of my cell light up with their pictures and turn black again when it rang through to voice mail.

The one person I hoped would call didn't.

It was as if Will vanished from my life as suddenly as he'd appeared in it. He hadn't come by once to see me, to explain, to ask if I was okay, or even to check if my father was recovering. I kept going over the day of the accident, how paralyzed Will had seemed, that closed-off look in his eyes, and how he'd let me leave school with Chris. The more days that passed without any sign from him, the more it felt like I must have dreamed everything between us, the nights in his truck and his room, the snowstorm and all that followed afterward. An impossible distance opened between us, one I didn't intend or create.

I felt helpless.

Jim traveled to and from the hospital with updates on Dad's condition, whether I wanted them or not. I learned that my father was on the mend, that he would be home in April, but even this news didn't help me to feel anything. His accident had robbed me of what little joy and security I'd managed to regain. If he hadn't kept drinking, if he had listened to my pleas, to Jim's, to Grandma's, none of this would have happened.

I'd still have Will.

Life was fragile and love was, too. At any moment, even our happiest ones, our world could shatter and we wouldn't see it coming. There was only more loss ahead, showing its ugly face when we least expected it. The Rose I became when my mother died, the girl who didn't want to see people, who couldn't have fun, who didn't want to be touched, who refused her friends' help—the Rose I was before Will—was pulling me down again, an anchor tied to my legs, permanent and unforgiving, denying any effort I made to get away. I thought I had lost her, but I was mistaken.

This was the lesson my father's accident forced on me.

———————

Then one afternoon the doorbell rang, and after a while it rang again. I was lying in bed reading a book, and I yelled for Jim to answer, then for Grandma. The sun peeked through the waning March clouds, brightening the gap between the shades of my room. When the bell sounded a third time, I concluded I was home alone and waited for silence to tell me the visitors had given up and left.

They were persistent.

Eventually the chimes became too much so I got up. I was still in my pajamas, barefoot, my hair in a sloppy ponytail, strands falling around my face and trailing down my back. When I opened the door, Krupa, Kecia, Tamika, and Mary were standing on the front porch.

"We've missed you," Krupa said, walking past me without waiting for an invitation.

"We won't take no for an answer," Kecia said as Mary and Tamika followed her inside. I watched them disappear around the corner into the kitchen. Then I shut the door and went to join them, feeling like a zombie. Chairs scraped against the tiled floor and a flurry of activity ensued, opening and unpacking and whispering. Dangling from Kecia's fingertips was a giant bag of chocolate bars, and Tamika poured the contents of her bulky purse onto the kitchen table. Eye shadows, eyeliners, compacts, bottles of nail polish and remover, lipsticks, and hair clips spilled across the wooden surface, clacking as they spread out and rolled to a stop. Mary took out a series of old, battered DVD cases. They looked at me, waiting for my reaction, but I didn't have the heart for this today. A tear rolled down my cheek and then another. I opened my mouth to protest, but Krupa spoke before I could tell them to go.

"We'll only stay an hour," she said. "Today is just getting out of bed and sitting with friends in your house, nothing more."

I knew they were right, that I had to start somewhere. "Okay," I said after a long silence. "For just a little while." I let them lead me into the living room, where they consoled me with chocolate, lipstick, movies, and most of all, their friendship.

Every afternoon that followed, my house filled with friends. I was surrounded by people and activity, but still I felt lost. My father would be coming home soon, and I wasn't sure how to begin again or who was at fault anymore—him for being so reckless, or me for my refusal to forgive. With the end of March came warmer weather. Tiny green buds began to dot the bare branches of the trees, the ground began its spring thaw, and the plants in my mother's gardens poked up from the soil, drinking the sun and stretching toward the sky. Every morning I watched from the windows to see if Will had returned to work—I knew it would happen eventually and I wanted to make sure I didn't miss him.

Then one day he appeared in the yard.

He was out back, next to the peony bed, tearing open a bag of compost. My breath stopped when I saw him through the living room windows, my heart quickened and I put a hand out to steady myself on the sill. I wanted him to turn my way, but he didn't, as if he purposely avoided looking at the house. Now was my chance to thaw this frost between us, to go outside and meet Will at the very spot where he and I began and where little red shoots were about to push up from the soil, soon to be the peonies that he'd promised me would grow. He crouched down for a moment, studying the bed, then suddenly he turned and looked at the exact spot where I stood at the window.

Our eyes met.

Quickly, I turned away.

Krupa was standing behind me. "You should go and talk to him."

"I miss him," I whispered. "But he just dropped me without a word, or any explanation."

"Why don't you ask him what happened? His reasons may not even be about you."

More than anything, I wanted my mother back. I wanted her to take care of me, to tell me what to do about Will, to show me how to fix everything with my father. I wanted her to take away this endless grief and complication and more emotion than I knew how to handle. Without consulting my brain, my feet began to move, carrying my body across the house, past Krupa and everyone else in the kitchen until I reached a door I hadn't opened in almost a year, and grasping the knob, I turned it, went inside, and closed it behind me.

I was in my mother's office.

Stacks of construction paper were piled high on the shelves, sparkly pipe cleaners poked up from mugs like pencils, mobiles hung from the ceiling, and paintings by Mom's kids covered every inch of available wall space. Bright markers and scissors and colored cotton balls were strewn across the desk, as if Mom was still here, working on a project she was planning to teach tomorrow. Her office had always been like a miniature version of her classroom. The experience of taking in these possessions that were once my mother's evoked the memory of another, similar moment, when I'd gone into Mom's closet after the funeral and discovered the Survival Kit she had left for me.

I'd let myself off the hook for too long, ignoring the tasks that remained. I remembered the box of crayons, and suddenly I knew what came next. From Mom's shelves, I gathered as many pairs of scissors as I could fit in one hand, wedged a thick stack of construction paper under my arm, grabbed a mug of pipe cleaners, and brought everything out to the kitchen. I went back and forth shuttling the things from Mom's office, setting up piles on the table and the countertops: markers, pipe cleaners, glitter glue and finger paint, colored pencils, tissue paper and silvery, metallic paper and paper plates, and about a dozen other things.

Plus an enormous stack of brown paper lunch bags.

Because crayons, of course, were meant to be shared.

I'd kept the Survival Kit a secret long enough.

34

BETTER

I gathered everyone into the kitchen. Krupa, Kecia, Tamika, and Mary. Grandma Madison, too. "First of all, I wanted to say that I know I haven't been the best company lately, or the best friend or the best granddaughter," I began, "but I really appreciate you guys sticking by me. I hope I can make up for how I've been acting, at least a little bit." I held up my Survival Kit, the thin blue ribbon dangling from my fingers, the side with my name in my mother's hand facing out. "I think you already know about my mother's Survival Kits—the ones she made for the parents of her children at school. On the day of her funeral, I found this waiting for me. I think it was my mother's way of offering wisdom for how I might"—I stopped, taking my time and another deep breath—"for how I might begin to figure out life without her in it."

Krupa's eyes widened.

"With my dad coming home from the hospital," I went on, "I thought a Survival Kit might do him some good, and maybe help us mend fences, so I brought out these materials from

Mom's office to make him one. Since you are here, I thought you might want to make a Survival Kit of your own for someone in your life or even for yourself. I suppose most of us could use one at some point in our lives," I said with a small laugh, and once the words were out I knew they were true. "Take whatever you want," I said, pointing to the materials I'd set up everywhere. "Mom wouldn't have wanted all this fun stuff to go to waste. She loved her projects and I'm sure she'd be happy to share."

"Oh, Rose," Grandma said, breaking the silence that followed. A tear spilled down her cheek. "What a special thing for Ellie to give you."

I nodded. "I know. It is."

Kecia picked up a pair of scissors and waited for others to follow suit. "Rose, I love this idea. I already know who I want to make a Survival Kit for."

I smiled. This had been the right thing to do.

"I'm going to begin mine, too," Tamika said, and went straight for a piece of shiny gold paper.

The mood in the room—the mood in the entire house—began to lift. It felt like the sun peeking just over the horizon to begin a new day after a long, endless night. Everyone got to work. Scissors scraped along construction paper, pipe cleaners quivered in the air as they were plucked from the table, glitter shimmered from its vials onto puffy lines of glue, shiny flecks drifting away onto the table and the floor. The kitchen filled with life and chatter and chaos, but this time I was the one who had invited it in.

The Survival Kit, *my* Survival Kit, sat at the center of the kitchen table. No one asked to look inside or pressed me about its contents, a fact for which I was grateful. I leaned between Mary and Tamika to grab the bag and take it back to my room, but when I turned the corner from the kitchen I froze.

Jim was standing there, staring at the Survival Kit in my hand, his face drained of color. "Mom made this for you?" His voice cracked, his tone was disbelieving. "You didn't even bother to tell me?"

My mouth opened wide and I stared at him, not knowing what to say. All the good feeling that had begun to rise up inside me dissolved in an instant. I hadn't even known he was home. I felt terrible. Horrible. I was an awful sister.

"Answer me, Rosey," he whispered.

"I don't know what to say. It occurred to me, but—"

"What occurred to you? That I would be upset? Jealous? That Mom cared about you more than me? That she worried about what would happen to you but not me? That's what? She thought I would somehow handle her death better than you so she left me with nothing."

"You know that's not true—"

"What if it is, though? You're not the only one who's sad about Mom. You're not the only one who's having a difficult year. You're not the only one who got stuck taking care of Dad."

"But—"

"Oh, and I love how you're making one for *Dad* after not talking to him for a month. You're *so* virtuous and *so* thoughtful, Rose. What a *great* idea, Rose. How sweet of you."

"I didn't even think—" I kept trying but Jim wouldn't let me finish.

"Exactly. That's exactly it. You didn't *think*. You didn't *think* to involve *me*. You didn't *think* I would care that you went through Mom's office *without* me, that you decided to give her things away. You didn't *think* that maybe *I* wasn't ready to see Mom's stuff all over the kitchen. And you didn't *think* that maybe Mom making you something so special, Mom choosing *you* to have a Survival Kit and not me, would hurt me. It didn't occur to you because you're so wrapped up in your own dramas that you haven't even gotten a glimpse of mine."

"Please, Jim"—I took a step toward him, reached out, and he responded by taking a step back—"maybe she *did* make you one," I tried. "Maybe you just haven't found it yet," I said, but my words fell on emptiness. Jim turned away and stormed out the front door and slammed it shut behind him. The sound of a car engine roared in the driveway, rattled there for a moment, and then was gone.

I hung my head. I'd been so thoughtless. How stupid to keep something like this from my brother, and careless to allow him to find out by overhearing me tell other people. Dejected, I placed the Survival Kit on the coffee table in the living room and sank into the couch.

Quietly, Krupa approached and sat down next to me. "Let him go, Rose. He needs some time." She put a hand on my arm. "I bet it took a lot of courage for your mom to plan that Survival Kit. She wanted to be there for you even after she was gone."

"I know," I whispered. "I'm sorry I kept it from you. I didn't mean to hurt Jim, or anyone, I just . . ." My fingers pinched folds in the afghan draped over the armrest. "I wasn't ready to share."

"It's okay with me," she said. "I hope you realize that. I can't imagine what it's been like to go through what you've dealt with this year. The thing with Jim, though," she trailed off. "That's going to be more complicated."

"God." I shifted so I could lie back. "The worst part is, I thought about this exact possibility. I actually wondered at different points if Mom had made one for Jim, but then I never said anything to him about it because I was afraid she hadn't. How am I going to fix this?"

Krupa sighed. "I don't know. But he'll calm down eventually and then you guys will just have to talk it through." The expression on her face said she was debating something.

"What? Tell me what you are thinking."

She reached out, her hand hovering above the Survival Kit. "Can I see it?" she asked in a small voice, then immediately retracted her arm. "Maybe I shouldn't have asked. Actually, forget it. You don't have to show me—"

"No, it's okay. I'm ready. I wouldn't have told everyone about it otherwise." I picked it up and placed it between us on the couch.

"So where did you find it?"

"My mother's closet," I explained. "With her favorite dress."

Krupa gasped. "The dress made of night—I remember how you always begged her to wear it."

"She knew I'd go looking for it and find the Survival Kit there." I emptied the bag's remaining contents onto the cushion: the box of crayons, the shiny paper star, and the kite. Then I ran to my room to retrieve the photograph of the peonies and the iPod. When I returned, the silver star was resting delicately in Krupa's palm. I added the two remaining items to the others.

The only thing missing was the crystal heart.

Krupa looked at each one, picked it up, turned it over, examining it from different angles. "The peonies in the backyard," she said with a knowing smile when she saw the photograph. "This wasn't your mother's," she exclaimed when she scrolled through the songs on the iPod. "She made it for you," she said, and I nodded. "And the crayons?" she asked, the slim box held out in her hand.

"Are for sharing with others. Like, sharing the Survival Kit with you guys," I explained. "You know my mother—I mean, you *knew* her—how she was about this kind of stuff. I thought that maybe, even though she's gone, that some of the traditions she had started could, well, maybe, continue on through other people."

Krupa's eyes were sad but she smiled. "Your mother would have loved seeing us here at the house, making Survival Kits, just like you guys did as a family every year."

"Except for the part where I forgot my brother," I said with regret.

There was one item Krupa hadn't yet touched. "What about the kite?"

"I'm nowhere near ready to deal with it," I said. "To be honest, I can't even imagine when I will." I picked up the star, turning it over in my hand. "Next is the star, I think."

"What is the star for?"

"I don't know yet," I admitted.

"Is this everything?"

I shook my head. "There was a crystal heart, too."

Understanding dawned on Krupa's face. "From the Valentine's party—it's so pretty! Why isn't it here?"

"Will has it," I answered simply.

"Oh," Krupa said, but didn't press me further about it. Then she went on. "You know, you said your mom left your Survival Kit with her dress."

"The ribbon was tied to the hanger."

"She obviously wanted you to wear it, Rose," she said softly. "You always wanted to. And now it's yours."

"Really?" It wasn't that wearing the dress hadn't crossed my mind, but more that I hadn't let myself think ahead to a moment when I might have a reason to.

"You'll know when the occasion is right," she added.

My throat tightened as my eyes welled. I knew what Krupa said was true, that there would come a time when I would slip that beautiful gown over my body and wear it just like my mother had once worn it. Somewhere deep I'd known this all along, that there would be a night that was special enough.

Because I was finally old enough.

It wasn't until after dinner that I managed an audience with Jim. I noticed his car was back in the driveway and I found him in his room lying on his bed, staring at the ceiling.

"Mom made you a Survival Kit, too. I'm sure of it," I said from the doorway.

He stirred and raised his head from the pillow. "No, she didn't and I don't want to talk about it. Or to you."

But I wasn't going away that easily. I walked over and sat down. "She made them for both of us. She did, I promise."

Jim rubbed his eyes and propped himself up on his elbows once he realized I wasn't going anywhere. He glared at me. "Rosey, just *stop*. You're making me feel worse than I already do."

"Listen, it's not like Mom handed the Survival Kit to me. She hid it in the house where she knew I'd find it, with that dress I was always bothering her about. We just need to figure out where she left yours."

The expression on Jim's face was sad and vulnerable. "Rosey, if it's not true, if you're not right, I don't want to be disappointed." Hope entered his voice like a scared child, and he sat up so that both our legs hung off the side of the bed, except that his reached all the way to the floor.

"You won't be." I was trusting in my mother that he wouldn't.

"You've really had it since the funeral? All this time?"

I nodded, avoiding his eyes, choosing instead to focus on the rhododendron outside pushing its leaves against the bottom half of the window. "I'm sorry I didn't tell you, I really am."

Jim drummed his thumbs against his knees. "So let's assume you're right for a minute," he said, his fingers tapping away. "If Mom left yours with the dress . . ." Suddenly, he sprang from the bed, grabbed a sweatshirt from a chair, and pulled it over his head. "Then mine has to be somewhere in the house." He began pacing back and forth. "Where would she have put it?" Jim darted from one corner of his room to the other, digging under piles of clothing, opening and shutting his closet door, tearing into everything. "Rosey, what if she made me one and I never find it?" He left the room but returned not more than thirty seconds later. He opened his mouth to say something, then disappeared again without a word.

"Jim," I called out, trying to coax him back so we could talk this through and maybe jog his memory to give him a solid clue.

Five minutes passed before I heard "I know where it is" from the doorway. "Will you come with me to get it?"

With my heart pounding, I got up and followed him to the basement door. He opened it and we started to descend, his sneakers slamming the steps, the wooden slats groaning with our weight. He walked toward the open metal shelves lining the back wall. They were packed with boxes, some marked "Christmas" on the side, and others "Supplies/Nursery." There were about ten that said "JIM" in block letters six inches tall, and "Do Not Throw Out." All in Mom's handwriting. One of the shelves was lined entirely with Jim's books from when he was a kid. He started pulling them off the shelf, one after the other, until he came to one that was face out and stopped. *The Mouse and the Motorcycle* by Beverly Cleary. "Mom and I read this together about a thousand times," he said, and picked it up.

There it was, behind the book.

A brown paper lunch bag, with JIM'S SURVIVAL KIT written in big capital letters on the front. An old Lewis High School blue sneaker lace was tied in a bow through the hole punched in the fold. Jim stared at it in awe, like he didn't believe it was really there. "She did make me one."

"Are you going to open it?" I asked, my voice quiet.

Jim shook his head. "Not yet. I'm going to wait."

Gently, I touched his arm. "You should wait as long as you need to. I waited for months before I opened mine. An entire summer."

"I'm just not ready," he said.

My brother burst into tears, heaving sobs, the kind I hadn't seen from him since Mom died. My hand automatically re-tracted from his arm and I took a step back. A few months ago I would have remained anchored to this spot, unable to comfort him—I'd learned from experience that hugging someone only encouraged the person to cry even harder and I always wanted the tears to stop. But I was beginning to understand that there would always be sadness when it came to our mother. A layer of sorrow was now knit through us so certain moments, memo-ries, even new experiences, would tap it, and this was one of those moments. So instead of leaving Jim alone until the tears dried up and disappeared, I mustered the courage to reach out and wrap my arms around him, and when I did, he bent down and cried even harder into my shoulder.

I was willing to be his shoulder as long as he needed me to be.

This was how we survived, I was learning.

———————

During the days that remained before my father was to come home from the hospital, the kitchen table, the counters, the cof-fee table in the living room, were strewn with every conceivable color of crayon along with things like scissors that cut in zigzags and tiny pots of water-soluble paints and discarded scraps of con-struction paper. My friends came and went, toting special items to add to their Survival Kits and finding open spaces to make something new.

It made me happy to have the house so full of life again.

I thought about how, if Jim had changed after Mom died and I had become a different girl, I had to allow for the possibility that Dad would be different, too. Maybe he needed help to move forward just like we did.

Together, Jim and I worked on our own Survival Kit for Dad. Inside the bag we included a photo of a pizza we'd cut from a magazine—Sunday nights in our house used to be pizza nights, a tradition we lost with Mom. We added a miniature leather baseball on a key chain to remind Dad how he loved spending summer nights outside watching minor league games. We made a small collage of photographs of our family and slid it inside a homemade frame—we wanted Dad to remember that he still had us. Then, to hint that we shouldn't let another summer go by without a visit to the ocean, Jim filled a tiny clear bag with some beach sand.

Last, of course, we put in a kite.

———————

Jim's hand rested on top of the wheel of Grandma's car as he drove. Signs for Lewis County Hospital appeared. "It's going to be okay, Rose. You can do this," he said.

Each word made me wince. "I hope so," I said, nervous about seeing our father for the first time in almost a month.

"Dad looks great and I think his attitude is changing. This

accident really jarred him in a way that you and I never could have." He turned into the parking lot and began to drive up and down the rows looking for a space.

"Stop doing that to yourselves," Grandma Madison said from the backseat. "Your father's relationship to drinking was never your responsibility to fix."

"But you've tried, too, Grandma." I turned around to look at her. Her long thin arms were crossed, her gray hair pulled back into a severe knot on top of her head. "Jim and I are both grateful for your help. With *everything.*"

"Well, unlike you, James is my responsibility. I am his mother. It's my job to make sure he gets his head back on straight."

"Grandma, this next part is up to Dad," I said, nervous to contradict her.

Her dark eyes softened. "Oh, Rose, Jim, it's difficult to stop trying with someone you love. You always hope that this next time might work, might change everything for the better. After all, take a good look at what you two brought for your father today and then tell me you've given up on him."

The Survival Kit, its brown paper bag with big green capital letters printed on one side, was sitting in my lap and I thought of all the hope we had attached to this project, through the items that we chose to include. "Yes, but how Dad interprets what's inside is up to him. All we can do is offer it and hope he takes it from there."

———

I hovered in the doorway to Dad's hospital room, and the moment I saw him my anger at his stupidity, his recklessness, evaporated. He was sitting on the bed going through the contents of his duffel bag, his legs dangling off the side, one of them in a thick pasty cast from the knee down, his left arm in a sling. "Rose," he said when he noticed me standing there. "Honey." His eyes were pleading. "I'm so happy to see you."

"Hi, Dad," I said, my voice small.

"I'm so sorry, sweetheart," he said. "I've missed you so much. I can't bear to lose you. Ever. I know I have a long way to go before I can win back your trust, but let me try. Please forgive me." Tears rolled down my father's face. "I want a second chance to do this better."

I turned away, covering my face with my hands. Seeing my father cry was so painful, but I wanted to be fair, too, even if it hurt to watch.

"Rose?"

I nodded to let him know I was still listening.

He reached out his good arm, palm open, facing upward. "Can you come here and give your dad a hug?"

At first I didn't move. But then I rushed toward him, climbing up onto the foot of the bed and sitting on my knees, so I was close enough to squeeze him tight. "I love you, Dad," I whispered.

"I love you, too. So much." He looked at me, really looked me in the eyes, and said, "I know you miss Mom." Dad had hardly mentioned Mom out loud since Christmas. "And nothing, *no one* could ever replace your mother"—I opened my mouth to say something, but Dad's hand went up, stopping me—"but I am your dad, I will never stop being your dad, and I am here for you," he said again.

I bit my lip hard, my eyes glassy with tears that I tried to blink away.

"I'm not going anywhere," he said. "I promise."

"You don't know that," I blurted.

A pained expression crossed his face. "No, you're right. I don't. None of us knows what's around the corner. But I'm going to do the very best I can from here on out and for as long as you want me to."

"I always want you to be here," I said.

His arm drew me closer. "Come on, kid. You know sometimes you don't want your old dad around."

"Yes, I do. Always," I whispered.

A smile worked its way onto his face. "I can remember more than a few times when you scolded me for embarrassing you in front of your friends."

I was opening my mouth to protest when I heard Jim's voice from the hallway. "Is it safe to come in?"

"Yes," I called out, and Jim entered with Grandma Madison close behind.

"Hi, Dad," he said.

Grandma nodded. "James."

"I'm about ready," Dad said, reaching for his things when Jim stopped him. "Wait," he said, and looked at me, nodding. It was time.

"So, Dad," I began, remembering what I had rehearsed, willing myself to get this out. "Every August, when Mom was still alive, we used to sit around the kitchen table as a family and help her make Survival Kits—"

Dad's face lit up, like he suddenly remembered something. "You found them!" he said with excitement, looking from Jim to me and back to Jim again. "You found the Survival Kits your mother left for you."

"You knew about them?" My voice was high.

"Your mother told me right after she decided to make them and I thought it was a wonderful idea. She showed me where she planned to leave them. I was supposed to tell you on the one-year anniversary."

"I've had mine since the funeral," I said.

Dad nodded. "Oh. That long." His head bobbed up and down.

"I just found mine last week. With Rose's help," Jim said.

"I'm so glad. She loved you both so much."

My throat was almost too tight to speak, but then I remembered my speech. "Well, Jim and I decided that maybe dads need a Survival Kit, too." My voice cracked. "So we made you one. Kind of a homecoming present."

Jim revealed the bag from behind his back, presenting it to Dad.

"Parent slash Dad Survival Kit," my father read aloud, wiping at the corners of his eyes. He laughed softly. "This is wonderful. Thank you."

"It's to help you figure out life, you know, now that Mom is gone," Jim said.

Dad held it in front of him, staring at it, and he was smiling.

"You don't have to open it now," I said quickly. "Whenever you are ready."

"Okay," Dad said. "I really appreciate this. What an incredible gift to receive from my children."

"We love you," I said, leaning over to kiss Dad on the cheek.

"Yeah, we love you, Dad," Jim said.

"All right-y," Grandma Madison said loudly, getting up from the chair in the corner—I'd almost forgotten she was there. "Let's get out of here. Hospitals are so unpleasant."

I laughed. "What would we do without Grandma? We'd probably cry all day."

"You probably would," she tsked, grabbing her purse. "Come on."

Together, Jim, Grandma, Dad, and I headed home. As a family. While we were walking away from the hospital, I remembered the words in the note Mom left in my Survival Kit about using my imagination. Finally, after all this time, I felt its wheels begin to turn again, slowly at first, as if they were rusty, then with more confidence, as if someone had flipped on a switch. In the light of this awareness, I began to have faith that my mother was still with me, embedded and woven into this part of me I'd tried so hard to bury, the part that was most like her: my imagination. Even though she wasn't here anymore, not literally, I could suddenly feel her everywhere, see her presence in everything, in the memories she created and left for us, in the hope she had for our survival as a family, and that she'd packed into a series of brown paper lunch bags with big capital letters on the side.

APRIL & MAY

Wishing on Stars

35

EVERYBODY

The first days of April passed, one into the other, and I devised a list of things I needed to accomplish, all of them related to the Survival Kit and my mother. I was no longer going in any particular order or interpreting my tasks so literally and narrowly. They took on a life of their own, a life that I was giving them now.

On my To Do list, among other things, was the following:

Get over my fear of entering the football stadium
Make music a part of my life again for real
Take care of the peonies—they are due to bloom soon
Ask Will for my crystal heart back

This last task required me to speak to Will, of course, and I had plenty of opportunity—he was outside in the gardens each morning and afternoon. Each time I saw him I felt butterflies and my heart hammered like mad, but I wasn't sure I could forgive him for abandoning me when I'd needed him most, for dropping me like it meant nothing, like it was the easiest thing in the world to let me go. When I left the house and headed down the walk to wait for Krupa and Kecia to pick me up for school, he pretended I wasn't there.

He avoided me and I allowed him to.

For now.

"Rose, say you'll change your mind," Tamika said one day at lunch.

"About what?" I asked. Kecia, Tamika, Mary, Krupa, and I sat at one end of a cafeteria table with a number of other cheerleaders at the other.

"Cheerleading," Mary said, nudging me.

"We don't have the strength to go on without you, and I mean that literally." Before I could get the word *no* out of my mouth, Tamika spoke again. "But what if I asked you to do it for Kecia?"

Kecia was deep in conversation with Krupa, but when she heard her name she turned to us. "Who needs to do what for me?"

Tamika and Mary smiled at each other like they had a secret. "We have a little surprise," Mary said.

Tamika set her giant purse on the table and dug through it. "The squad officially voted you captain last night."

Kecia gasped. "Really?"

"That's so perfect," I said, and meant it. "Congratulations."

"Come on," Mary said to Kecia. "You saw that coming."

"I didn't. Really," she protested. "I swear. But I'm honored. I accept."

From the depths of her purse, Tamika removed a familiar-looking brown lunch bag, neatly folded at the top, and placed it on the table. "Good. Because Mary and I worked hard on this. It's your very own Lewis Cheerleading Captain's Survival Kit."

I laughed as Kecia jumped up from her chair and ran around the table to hug Tamika and Mary.

"Congratulations, Kecia," Krupa said.

"What's inside?" Kecia asked.

"Look for yourself," Mary said. "That's why we made it."

Kecia pulled out a photograph of the team and studied it. She leaned toward me. "See, Rose," she said, holding it out to me. "You are essential to my survival."

I stared at the picture and saw myself standing high at the top of a pyramid. I felt a pang, remembering the commitment I'd made to go back to the football stadium. "We'll see," I said.

Kecia placed a hand on my arm. "Whenever you're ready."

That afternoon I made my decision. When I reached out to unlatch the gate, a wave of anxiety rushed through me and I hesitated—but then I opened the door and went inside the football stadium for the first time since last year. The sun was out and the cheerleaders were warming up on the track and I could almost feel what it was like to stretch out on cooler days, when the sun heated the surface so that it felt like a hot blanket against the back of my legs.

"Hey, Rose," Kecia called when she noticed me in the front row of the stands. She ran over and stopped in front of my spot just below the riser.

"It's a nice day for practice," I said, approaching the railing.

"Don't worry, I'm not going to ask you again about rejoining the squad, but I was wondering something."

"Oh, no. What?" I could sense a dare coming.

"Do you think you can still do a fifty-yard dash?"

During my two years on the squad, I used to travel fifty yards down the length of track in front of the stands by doing back-flips. It started at practice one day when a senior cheerleader asked me how far I could flip. I told her I had no idea, but to find out I turned around, stood at the line for the fifty-yard dash, and backflipped my way to the finish. By the end, my teammates were whooping in appreciation. When I started doing it at games the crowd really got into it, and soon it became this *thing*. The fans would quiet down when they saw me walk to the starting place. Then they counted every last flip. Usually it took about thirty or so to make it the full fifty yards, and the crowd would get louder and louder as I neared the finish. I loved doing it and feeling my body flying down the track.

"Maybe another day," I told her. "Besides, I have on tight jeans and boots—not good backflip wear."

"I've got some clothes you can borrow," she said. The rest of the squad had gathered to listen and was waiting to see what I'd do.

"I told you, I'm not—" I said, but Kecia interrupted.

"It's not a commitment to come back. Just do it for fun."

Mary walked over to us and held up a tank top and shorts. "Take it," she said. "Come on."

"Okay. Fine," I agreed, and grabbed the stuff out of Mary's hand, heading to the locker room to change and stretch. When I came out again I walked straight to the line. Before I could lose my nerve, I turned around, bounced up on my toes a bit, concentrating. I stretched both arms straight in front of me, ready to swing them over my head for the first flip, my eyes on my fingers—and then, I did it. I flung my body up and back, arching so that my hands landed just right, my legs whipping around so I could immediately throw myself into another one, and then another, and the next. The moment my feet hit the track the squad began to count, just like they used to, as I continued to flip, my momentum growing as I neared the finish, and until I landed the very last one—number twenty-nine. My face was red, my breath coming in pants, but I began to laugh. I'd forgotten how I could make my body long and limber and flexible, and how much fun this was.

Kecia ran up and gave me a hug. "I knew you still had it in you."

"Well, I didn't," I said, my lungs still heaving. "Thanks for pushing me."

"Sure," she answered, and I smiled.

It felt wonderful.

———————

When I got home I went straight to my closet. There, next to my mother's dress, was a letter jacket. Bright blue and white, leather sleeves and everything. *My* letter jacket, with *my* name stitched on one side, *Rose Madison*, and *Cheerleading* on the other, and *Lewis High School* in a big arc across the back. Anyone on a varsity team was eligible for one and Mom and Dad had bought it for me at the end of my freshman year as a surprise.

"Congratulations!" Mom said that day when I came home from school. She held it out so I could see. "Now you have your very own."

Dad was beaming. "I'm so proud of you," he said.

At the time, I couldn't have cared less. I already had Chris Williams's jacket, star football player, so why would I want another? "Um, thanks," I said.

Mom handed it to me. "Try it on."

But I didn't. "Later," I told her, and headed off to my room, where I promptly buried it among my other long-forgotten clothes. There it remained ever since. I'd never tried it on, not even once. Remembering this made me wish I could go back and change things, react differently on that day, put it on for my mother. Sometimes she used to ask about it, and one day she even said to me in frustration, "Rose, there is no good reason to be wearing a boy's letter jacket when you've earned your own."

I trailed my fingers along the leather and slid it from the hanger, holding it up in front of my body, inspecting the bright white cursive writing, thousands of tiny stitches that together made my name stand out against the blue wool. I unsnapped the buttons and shrugged my arms into the sleeves, staring at my reflection in the mirror.

It was so much smaller than Chris's.

Because this one was made especially for *me*.

I wished so badly that I could call out "Mom!" at the top of my lungs so she'd come running to my room. She'd be so pleased to see it. But before I could chicken out, instead I yelled, "Hey, Dad! Come here! I need to show you something," and then waited, listening as his uneven footsteps and crutches thudded against the wood floors, getting closer until he appeared at my door.

"Is everything okay?" he asked, his voice tired. When he entered the room his footsteps became quieter, his socks making soft swishing sounds as he hobbled toward me. "Oh, Rose," he said. "Your jacket! It fits perfectly."

"I know," I said. Regardless of whether I went back to cheerleading, I'd earned this jacket, it was mine to wear, and it said so right on the front. "I'm glad you and Mom got it for me," I told him, finally showing this long overdue gratitude.

"Well, you worked hard for it, sweetheart," he said, his face proud.

"Thank you. Really," I said, and this time I meant it.

36

KIND AND GENEROUS

The next day was beautiful and the sun shone bright through the sliding glass doors of the kitchen. I went out, basking in the heat that burned through my tank top, the scratchy cement stairs warming the soles of my feet. Slowly, I wove along the paths in my mother's gardens and only stopped when I reached the peony bed, where thick red stems streaked with a muddy green were already poking up a foot and a half from the ground. Branches shot out in every direction, already heavy with leaves. Soon they would be full of blooms.

Peonies.

I couldn't help but smile. Will had been right, of course. It was the perfect spot to plant them and I would have flowers this spring after all. I thought about how he had been out here almost every day this month, caring for my mother's gardens as always, but tending to the peony bed, too.

I missed him so much it hurt.

Later that afternoon when I was sitting on the front porch, lost in a novel, I heard footsteps scrape against the slate and stop next to me. I looked up and a million different thoughts flooded my mind. Will was standing there, and a lump filled my throat when I saw what he held in his hand. The crystal heart swung back and forth from his fingers.

"Take it," he said, shaking it a little so it bounced on the end of the chain. He stared at me, eyes steady. "I found it in the pocket of my jacket and I know it's yours. I wanted to give it back. I figured you might want it."

I couldn't speak so I put out my hand and he dropped it into my palm, the chain slinking against my skin, where it caught the light and glittered. Like always when I saw Will, my heart hammered inside my chest. I waited for him to say more, to explain his absence, to tell me what in the world had happened to make him go away, but instead he turned around.

Anger surged through me. "You're just going to leave? Just like that?" I shouted after him, and at this he stopped. Questions began to pour out of my mouth, each one louder than the other. "Where have you been? Why haven't you talked to me? How could you just disappear like that? Don't you even miss me?" He faced me again with that unwavering gaze, his blue eyes bottomless. "You've been at my house every single day," I went on. "Near my windows. Crossing the lawn. Forcing me to see how much you don't care anymore."

"I'm sorry," he said, his voice flat.

"You're sorry? That's it?"

Pain flashed across his face, the first sign of feeling in so many weeks. "I'm sorry I wasn't there for you."

"You say that as if it's in the past," I said in a smaller voice. "But you're not here for me now, either," I pleaded, my voice trailing off.

"I'm glad Chris was able to help when I couldn't."

"I wanted it to be you, not him."

He shook his head. "You don't get it, do you? When you came to me that day to tell me your father was in the hospital, I just, I just shut down. The last time I was at that hospital was when *my* father died, and even though I knew you needed me, even though I *wanted* to be there for you, there was no way I could face that place again. Not even for you."

"But it's been over two years," I whispered, then immediately wished I hadn't. I knew better than this.

"God, of all people I thought you would understand," he snapped, and I was startled. I wasn't used to witnessing his anger off the ice. "Didn't we have an entire conversation about the things we avoid? Two years, three years, some things just don't get any easier. When I think of that hospital it might as well be yesterday that my father died."

"We could've dealt with it together—"

"Come on, Rose. The last thing you needed was my baggage on top of everything else."

"You would never be a burden—"

He put out a hand to stop me. "Don't think it hasn't killed me, either, the fact that after everything you've gone through with your mother and your father, that I failed you, too. But what's done is done. Just leave it alone. It's over, okay? I was wrong for you from the very beginning. I almost never date anyone, especially not a girl like you. I'm just not *that* guy, I've *never* been that guy, Rose. I'm not good at letting people in and I don't know what I was thinking letting myself get close to you." His words echoed in my ears, and I didn't know what to say. Sadness and hurt and frustration coursed through me, and I wished I could travel all the way back to that day at the beginning of March, to redo our initial encounter in the hallway, the tremor that unleashed this avalanche of mistakes. He opened his backpack and pulled out a brown paper lunch bag, the top crumpled in his fist. "Did you know about this?" he asked.

I stared at it in amazement, recognizing Krupa's writing on the outside. She'd made a Survival Kit for Will. "Krupa gave that to you?"

He nodded.

Then I shrugged, feeling defeated because it didn't seem to matter what I said at this point. "You know, this all started, you and me, because my mother made me one of those"—I pointed to the bag in his hand—"for after she was gone. She was the one who wanted me to plant the peonies." I picked up the crystal heart and let it swing from my fingers before setting it down again. "She gave me this heart. Actually, almost everything inside my Survival Kit keeps leading me back to you. The iPod was in it, too."

"Well, it steered you wrong," he said.

I stood up from my chair, stretched my arms wide in

frustration, my palms facing up toward the sky. "No, I don't believe that. I really don't." I waited for him to respond but he didn't. "What did Krupa give you anyway?"

"It doesn't matter, because you just have to let me go. Your friends do, too. It's over." He let this word fall between us on the porch, heavy and thick. His voice was hoarse, his eyes sad. I knew that I should stop this from going any further, that I should walk up to Will, put my arms around his neck, tell him that we would figure everything out, and pull his lips toward mine. He needed to know, to believe that he and I could still be, that love could still happen despite everything in our past and the wall we'd suddenly hit. That we could fix this.

But I waited too long.

Before I took a single step, Will left. His truck door opened and slammed and the engine rumbled to life in the driveway. I watched from the porch as he drove up the street and then was gone.

I tried to get back into my novel, to enjoy the sun, the warmth on my skin, the beautiful day, to pretend Will and I weren't really over, but nothing helped and the tears wouldn't stay away any longer.

As I stood there crying, something unexpected happened.

I began to think of songs I wanted to put on a playlist for this particular moment, these particular feelings, this particular event in my life—just like I used to. The odd part of it was, I didn't have to force myself; I wanted to do it. Music hadn't always deepened my grief. For most of my sixteen years, it had healed my hurts, soothed them, given me a way to remember and the strength to move on.

Suddenly I couldn't stand its absence any longer. I went to my room, opened my laptop, and plugged in the iPod from my Survival Kit, scrolling through the menu until I found the playlist "TBD by Rose." I clicked on the folder filled with the music I'd amassed all the years of my life and began to search through it, highlighting songs and dragging them over to the blank playlist. Then I began to order them, starting with the day of my mother's funeral.

The first song on the list was "Can't Go Back Now" by the Weepies. "About a Girl" by The Academy Is . . . came next. Then "My Best Friend" by Weezer, followed by "How to Save a Life" by the Fray, and on and on.

Soon, I had set all the important events of the last year to music, even the times that made my heart ache. I promised myself that I would keep adding to this playlist for each and every new experience that warranted a song until June 4, the anniversary of my mother's death. These songs would tell the story of everything that had happened to me since I'd said goodbye to her.

The last song was the one I decided was right for this day, this moment, the one that kept running through my mind again and again. It would help me to remember how extraordinary a gift my mother's Survival Kit was, how far she had managed to lead me forward with all the things she'd put inside. I chose it not only because of my mother, but my friends, too, and especially because of Will. Without him I wouldn't have gotten here, to this place. I wouldn't be this strong. And I was grateful.

So I added "Kind and Generous" by Natalie Merchant.

When I was finished, I closed my laptop and got out my Survival Kit. I had one more thing to do before the day was over, and with the silver star in my hand I went out the front door and began to run.

37

STARS

Flip-flops dangling from one hand, I sprinted across lawns and through the neighborhoods that stood between my house and Will's, strides fast, legs stretching farther and farther. When I arrived on his front steps I was heaving and I gripped my knees, my body bent in half while I tried to catch my breath. I immediately regretted the ratty old jeans, slung too low across my hips, and the too-small tank top that left a strip of skin across my middle exposed. Once my breathing slowed, I straightened up and rang the bell.

"Rose, what a surprise," Mrs. Doniger said when she appeared in the doorway. She wore a flowing light green sundress speckled with tiny white flowers, perfect for a warm evening like tonight, her eyes the same deep blue oceans as Will's. She looked young and beautiful.

"Hi, Mrs. Doniger," I said.

"You look like you've been running. Can I get you something to drink?" Mrs. Doniger asked. "Some water?"

"Can I come in?" I almost expected she would send me away.

"Of course." She turned and I followed her inside.

My body sank against the wall near the family portraits. There was the sound of a cabinet opening and closing in the kitchen, a glass being set on the counter, and the clink of ice at the bottom. Mrs. Doniger appeared again and handed me the water, bright disks of sunny lemon floating on its surface. I put the glass to my lips and drained it, but before Mrs. Doniger could go back into the kitchen to get me another I stopped her. "Is he here?"

She nodded. "Upstairs. Go ahead. Go and see him," she encouraged.

"He might not—" I began, but she interrupted.

"I think it would be good for him and for you. He was never happier than when you were spending time together. I could tell the minute you stopped."

"Oh." I paused, trying to gather my courage. "Thanks, Mrs. Doniger," I said, and turned to leave the kitchen, hoping that I would figure out how to close the distance that had grown between Will and me once and for all.

———————

I pushed open the door of Will's room with one hand and watched as it swung wide to reveal him, listening to music, sitting on the floor at the foot of his bed. The light was fading as the sun dipped low in the sky, outlining his body in dark shadows. He removed his earbuds when he saw me standing in the doorway. "Hey," he said, and that was all.

"Can I come in?" I asked.

He nodded but his expression told me nothing. He could be happy, angry, or indifferent and I wouldn't know, and I worried that the Will I'd first met, the one who was slow to trust, who wouldn't let anyone past the guard he put up, had returned for good. I took a step forward and my chest pounded. Will made no move to get up or invite me to sit.

"You're wearing the heart," he said.

This comment was invitation enough so I kicked my flip-flops off to the side and sat down facing him, cross-legged, one of my knees close enough to brush against the right leg of his jeans. He reached out to touch the crystal heart at my neck, the soft pad of his fingertips brushing my skin as he lifted it away, and my breath stopped. He held the heart in his palm, studying it, as though if he gazed at it long enough it might reveal insights into the real hearts we carried inside our bodies. Eventually he let it go and the heart fell back against my chest, a soft, small thud against my skin.

"Why are you here?" he asked, watching me, his face still unreadable.

"I shouldn't have let you leave my house," I began, my eyes scanning the floor, the windows, the walls, running away from his stare. "I wanted to tell you that I understand why you did what you did, why you went away, I mean. Why you avoided me after what happened with my father," I said. "I might've done the same thing if it had been the other way around. But no matter what you say, you and I are far from over. You're not protecting me by avoiding me, you're just hurting both of us. You know it, too, even if you won't admit it to yourself. Or to me." My hand went to the back pocket of my jeans and I slid out the silver star, displaying it across my open palm, shiny and wrinkled. "This is one of the last items from my Survival Kit." I tilted my hand a bit, so the star flashed light. "You've been with me for every part of this journey my mother mapped out. It's almost uncanny." I placed the star on the floor between us and shifted so my back was against the foot of Will's bed, our legs stretched out next to each other. "And tonight, after you left, I remembered something."

"What?" This one word from him was a whisper.

I pointed upward at the constellations on his ceiling, bright now as the darkness began seeping into his room. "Sometimes, when I close my eyes before I go to sleep, I think of that night in January when everything between us seemed to shift and how we spent all that time gazing up at the stars." A breeze fluttered through the open windows and the crickets chirped their evening song. My left hand was so close to Will's we were almost touching. "So I came here tonight to make a wish." I picked up the star again and closed my eyes a moment. The connection was so obvious once I had thought of it, that stars and wishing go hand in hand. When I opened them again, I said, "I wish that we could try this again. I miss you."

There was pain in Will's eyes. "But I let you down."

"I'm not going to lie, it was hard not having you to help me

through the stuff with my dad," I said. "But I'm not perfect either. And it's not like you didn't have a good reason. I just didn't
see it at first and I'm sorry. It should have occurred to me why
you couldn't go to the hospital that day. You shouldn't have had
to explain."

He took the star from my hand and held it up between his
fingers, staring at it for a moment. Then he placed it on the knee
of my jeans and shifted his gaze to the ceiling. My eyes followed
his and I leaned my head back against the bed. "So what are you
saying?" he asked.

"That we'd be crazy if we don't try again. That you *are* good for
me, Will Doniger. You've proven it again and again."

He hesitated before he turned to me, words hovering on his
lips.

"Tell me," I said. "What are you thinking?"

"That I love you, Rose. I have for a while."

I stopped breathing. "Me, too. I love you, too," I said. Then,
slowly, I leaned forward until our lips touched, tentative at first,
as if neither of us was ready for this, because we didn't know, we
hadn't prepared for this possible outcome of this particular moment. But then, sometimes we forget our bodies have memories,
too, that they help us summon what our minds try so hard to
forget. Feeling rushed through me to the very tips of my fingers
and toes, emotion swelled and I opened myself up to it, all of it.
When I felt Will's arms slide around me, his hands making their
way up my back, his fingers weaving themselves into my hair,

together we shifted from this tentative hovering of lips to giving ourselves over to the kiss we really wanted, like the very first one that night in the snow. When we finally pulled apart again, both of us out of breath, I laughed, thinking I was right back where I started when I arrived at Will's front steps tonight, that kissing him made my body race like I'd sprinted all the way from my house to his.

"Wow" was all he said, and he leaned back against the bed, like he might be dizzy and needed the support. I stood up, feeling a rush, as if my body wasn't quite ready for movement either. The star slid down my leg and skittered into the folds of his T-shirt and he picked it up again, holding it in his hand. I stretched my arms high, every muscle in my body lengthening, reaching, went up on my toes as if I could touch the stars above us in the darkness of Will's room. "I should go," I said, though I wanted to stay. I felt giddy.

"You should?" Will asked. "Now?"

"I really should."

"Stay," he said, and reached out his hand to grasp mine, the star between our palms.

I smiled. "It's just for now. Not forever."

Before I could say anything else or move to go, Will stopped me with a confession. "I saw you the other day. I was by the track at the football field."

"You were?" I was surprised.

"I watched you do about a million backflips."

"Oh. The cheerleaders kind of dared me to do that," I said, feeling a little embarrassed, slipping my feet back into my flip-flops, trying to seem nonchalant. I headed toward the door, not wanting to go but knowing I should. Before I disappeared into the hallway he called out to me and I turned. "The way you flew down the track, Rose." He shook his head, like he was impressed. "You were amazing out there, you know."

I smiled, remembering how I'd said these very same words to Will once, a long time ago, that first night I'd seen him play hockey.

"Thanks," I said.

Will sighed. "You really have to go?"

"It's getting late," I said, but a big grin crept onto my face.

"Fine. I get it. I'll see you tomorrow before school."

"Bye, Will," I said, and this time I left, floating down the stairs and out of his house. On my way home I took my time, no longer in a rush. I wanted to savor the remains of this unexpectedly beautiful spring evening, a night I hadn't been prepared for, a night of big stuff that life sent my way, but the good kind.

The very best kind. The most amazing kind of all.

38

MIDNIGHT BLUE

"That dress is practically made of stars," Will said.

We were lying on our backs on a blanket, staring at the blue sky above. Two glasses, half-full of champagne, were within reach. The prom was later on tonight but we weren't going, despite Krupa's pleas and Kecia's protests. Will and I had other things to celebrate—it was our anniversary of sorts. On this day seven months ago, Will and I had planted a bed of peony roots on a warm, sun-drenched afternoon. Now, next to us, a new flower garden was bursting with life, pink and white peonies blooming across plants that had grown and flourished this spring. Earlier, when I'd gone into my closet searching for just the right thing to wear for this special occasion of our own, I knew immediately that I'd wear the dress.

That dress.

I smiled and turned to Will, our faces close enough to kiss.

"You're gorgeous, Rose," he said simply, as if this were obvious, and my cheeks flushed.

"I've always called this the dress made of night. It was my mother's."

"A dress made of night. That's really beautiful. Thank you for wearing it."

"I only needed the right occasion."

Will took a sip of champagne. "I think I have another name for it."

"For what? The dress?"

"Mm–hm," he said between sips, then put the flute down. He gathered a handful of the soft chiffon, shifting it slightly, watching as it glimmered in the afternoon sunlight. "Maybe it's a wishing dress."

I sat up farther. "I like that," I said, and thought about my mother, who would have loved the idea. "It goes well with the star in my Survival Kit."

Will began to count, his fingers moving along the dress.

I laughed as I watched him. "What are you doing?"

"Counting potential wishes," he said.

"That's a lot of wishes. It would be difficult to think of that many."

"I can think of a few already. Easily." Will paused his count to grin and leaned toward me, kissing my lips. "There goes one," he said after pulling back.

"If all your wishes are for a kiss, you've probably gotten enough for at least half the stars on this dress in the last few weeks."

"But what about the other half?" Will asked, and kissed me again. When we stopped for breath, out of my mouth came a wish I hadn't anticipated, one that a few months ago I never would have dared say out loud.

"I wish," I began, then looked away, thinking a moment. "I wish that my mother could see us. I wish she had lived to see me wear her favorite dress, just once. And I wish, most of all, that she would know I'm okay."

Will took my other hand. "I wish for that, too, Rose. For you and your mom. For me and my dad." He smiled a sad, far-away smile.

"Maybe they do know," I said.

"Maybe," Will said, running his fingertip up my bare arm to my shoulder and sending a shiver up my spine. "I'm glad *I* get to see you in your dress," he whispered, his finger tracing the line along my jaw.

"Me, too," I said, wondering if he was going to kiss me again.

Will stopped, his mouth inches away from mine.

"What?"

"Nothing."

"Tell me."

"I don't know if I should." His voice shifted from serious to playful.

"You always should," I said, playing with his fingers, a happy smile working its way back onto my face.

"You know how you thought all my wishes were for a kiss?"

"Yes," I said, wanting him to continue, curious what he was about to say.

"Well, one of my wishes may have been for something other than a kiss."

"Really."

"Really," he said.

"Okay. So . . . tell me. I'm listening."

Will was silent at first, making me wait. Then he blurted, "Do you want to go to the prom?"

"You're asking me now? It's barely a couple of hours away!"

"Yes," he said, and smiled all the way to his eyes.

"You're serious."

"I am. And if you're still in the mood to grant wishes . . ." He trailed off, his eyes so blue they matched the sky.

"*You* want to go to *the prom*?" I asked, as if I hadn't heard it the first or second time. "We don't even have tickets."

"Actually . . ." Will reached into his pocket and pulled out two slender tickets, silver calligraphy shining across them. "Krupa may have thought ahead—"

"Krupa?"

"—these were in the Survival Kit she gave me." He placed them on the blanket.

"Oh, Krupa. Of course, Krupa would do that."

"Listen, you're already dressed for it." He stood up and walked over to the garden, bent down, surveying the peonies. Then he carefully snapped a flower from the bottom of its stem. "And now you have flowers. Sorry, one flower, but it's a beauty. And I can always pick a few more." He held it out to me, endless layers of silky white petals edged in bright pink curled up into a delicate bowl filled with even more petals. I took it from his hand, stared into its center, so big and full and perfect it didn't seem real.

"I don't know," I said, hesitant.

"Come on. All our friends are going. Tamika is going with Joe, Mary with Tim, and by some miracle Krupa is going with that linebacker you like so much—what's his name?"

"Tony."

"So your best friend Krupa is going with linebacker Tony, which I know makes you happy because you said as much, and your brother"—Will let these two syllables hang in the air a moment, to let them sink in—"is going with Kecia."

"I know," I said with lingering disbelief.

"It's practically the oldest story in the book."

"What is?"

"You know, the cheerleader and the hockey player, they date, fall in love, go to prom. It's classic high school, you and me."

I took another peony from Will's hand, gathering it together with the others he kept handing to me. "I think you're a little mixed up. The cheerleader, sure, but she dates and falls in love with the football player. It's never the hockey player. When have you ever seen a movie or read a book where it's a cheerleader and a hockey player?" My grin begged for a response. "Besides, I'm not a cheerleader anymore."

"Well, in my version of this classic high school story, the cheerleader—sorry, the former cheerleader—is named Rose Madison, and she does not end up with the quarterback. She falls in love with the right wing forward on the hockey team, whose name happens to be Will Doniger." He brought me another flower.

I studied the bouquet in my hands, hundreds of delicate petals spilling into other ones, lines of pink streaking across white, red melting into fuchsia, and when I looked at Will again I asked, "They fall in love, do they?"

He nodded ever so slightly. "So what do you say, Rose?"

Now it was my turn to go into the garden and search for another flower, this time a smaller one, a thick bud, all white edged with only the green of the stem at the bottom. Carefully, I snapped it with my fingers. "This one is for you," I said, and walked over to Will, who was waiting for my answer. I threaded the stem into the buttonhole of his shirt.

Will stared at me. "Do I get an official answer or only a vague one?"

"Yes, I'll go to the prom with you. I have to, right? Apparently, it's the oldest story in the book. The former cheerleader and the hockey player. You know the one I'm talking about," I said, and took Will's hand and led him toward the house.

39

DREAMS

"Oh, Rose, stop being coy," Grandma Madison said, shaking her head.

Jim, Kecia, Will, and I were discussing prom logistics while Grandma, Dad, and Mrs. Doniger cornered us with cameras in the backyard among the gardens. "You drove your mother crazy about wearing that dress, and now that you are in it we are going to get a picture."

I rolled my eyes.

Will squeezed my hand. "Come on. Make everybody happy and smile."

"Now, you," Grandma barked at him. "Yes, you, the invisible truck driver," she added, giving me a wicked grin. "Go stand next to Rose over there by the stone bench and smile like you mean it."

"Yes, ma'am," Will said.

"I am not to be called ma'am. My name is Maggie," she crabbed.

"Well, I also have a name. It's Will," he shot back.

Everyone stopped. We held our breath, waiting to see what

Grandma would say next, but she just smiled at him. "I like this one, Rose. He's got spunk. Not like that other dolt you dated—"

"Ma, please!" Dad interrupted.

"Oh, like Mr. Will doesn't know who his competition is. *Was*," Grandma corrected herself, walking over to him, brushing off his collar and straightening the peony I'd pinned there. "But you are also smart enough to know there is no competition between you and that other boy. Aren't you?" She looked straight up into Will's face.

"Yes, Maggie," he said, smiling.

"Good to hear," she said, and stepped back again to direct the photo shoot. "Confidence is attractive in a man."

Two spots of red appeared on his cheeks and Will turned to me, his eyes growing wide. Then he leaned down and gave me a quick peck. The moment our lips touched I heard a click and a cackle from Grandma. "Now, that's the way to do it. Good boy," she said to Will.

"Grandma! He's not a dog," I protested.

"No, he's not," she responded, and whistled.

"Oh my god," I said, shaking my head, giving her a pleading look. "You are so embarrassing."

"Okay, kids, let's get one group shot and off you go," Dad said, taking over, a fact for which I was grateful. He hobbled to where Grandma and Mrs. Doniger stood to set up the photo, while Kecia, Jim, Will, and I arranged ourselves in front of the peony garden.

"It's about time you stepped up to do your job, James," Grandma Madison said to Dad.

"Ma, leave me alone. You're distracting me from my handsome children and their dates. They don't want to be late for the prom." There were several more clicks as we smiled, then laughed, and then made funny faces and poses while Dad snapped pictures. Finally, after more photos than I ever imagined I'd freely agree to, Dad said, "All right. I think I got some good ones. Time to go. Your limo, or your chariot, or however it is you four are getting to the prom, awaits." Just before we turned to go, he gave Jim and me a hug. "Your mother would have been so proud of you both," he added in a whisper.

The four of us took off across the yard toward the driveway, where Will's truck and Jim's car were parked, my dress, the dress made of stars and wishes and night, trailing along the grass, floating upward with each step. Will's hand held mine, our fingers loosely clasped together, and like I'd done so many times before this last year, I reached for the passenger door to Will's truck. He got to it first, opening it for me, and I climbed inside. He made sure all the layers of my dress were tucked safely by my feet before he shut the door and I watched as he walked around to the driver's side and got in.

"What are you thinking?" he asked.

"I am, right now, taking in this moment. I feel like I need to pinch myself."

"Why?"

"You and I." I stopped to let the full effect of the *us* I'd put together with those two words echo in the space around us. "That would be Rose Madison and Will Doniger. We are going to the prom. Together."

"We definitely are," he said, and gave me a mischievous smile.

"I never would've thought, you know? I never would've guessed. This all has been, I mean . . . I'm just so surprised."

"I'm not," Will said, backing out of the driveway and pulling in front of Jim and Kecia, who were waiting in the road to follow us. "Not at all," he added as we headed on our way.

———

"This goes out to Rose Madison, by special request," I heard the DJ say over the mike. When the first bars of "Dreams" by Van Halen blasted through the speakers I shot Will a look.

"What?" He shrugged his shoulders and raised his hands in a gesture of innocence. Kecia and Krupa burst out laughing and grabbed my hand.

"We can't dance to this," I protested, but they continued to drag me out onto the floor where we'd been dancing all night, through slow songs and fast songs, in groups and couples. We sang at the top of our lungs, occasionally embarrassing our dates with our bad voices—well, except for Krupa.

I couldn't believe the prom was this much fun.

Later on, when Chris Williams was crowned Prom King,

which came as no surprise to anyone, and a girl I thought might be a sophomore or even a freshman was crowned Prom Queen, my friends all turned to me.

"Why," I said, "are you guys looking at me like that?"

Kecia spoke first. "Isn't it obvious?" She nodded toward the wide-open space the crowd had formed for Chris and his queen to have their special dance. "That used to be you. Last year, you were *that* girl."

"Yeah, well, I'm not *that* girl anymore," I said, watching the way she looked up at Chris while they danced. I recognized her, saw an old version of myself in her face, and felt relieved to be in a different place now. I hoped he was happy. "While you guys ogle the royalty over there, Will and I," I said, taking Will's hand, beginning to lead him away from the group, "are going to go find a dark corner."

"We are?" he asked, following after me, both of us glancing back at our friends—Krupa, Tony, Kecia and my brother, and Mary and Tamika, who had already ditched their dates. Will gave everyone a happy sort of shrug. "I guess we are," he said, and soon it was Will pulling me along to a spot against the wall that the lights didn't reach, where we stayed for a long time, during so many songs I stopped counting.

So on that night in May, I found out just the sort of girl I'd become over this year—the one who went to the prom after all and danced the night away with her friends. The girl who hung out with the cheerleaders and dated the star of the hockey team.

The girl whose mother died last year, too early and tragically, a reality that would always bring more sadness than it seemed reasonable to bear. Yet little by little, I was also becoming the girl who was learning to live with this, all of it, letting it weave together with everything else, the good and the bad, as life moved forward, because that's what life did, regardless of whether we were ready for it or not. Before, last spring, when everything began to unravel, it never occurred to me that the girl I'd always been in high school could bend and shift and change without breaking altogether.

But the girl I am now, *this* girl—she survived.

I just needed a little help getting here.

EPILOGUE

June 4
The Kite

40

ALL WILL BE WELL

"You made these for Rose?"

Jim's voice was incredulous, hushed. He watched Will and me tie the last knots, tugging at them to make sure they were tight. Will looked up after we finished. "It was Rose's idea. I just helped with the construction."

Jim nodded. If he felt at all like I did, his throat was too tight to speak.

The day was gorgeous, the breeze was warm but steady, the sun a big round yellow ball in the sky, and the waves of the ocean crashed softly in a gentle, uneven rhythm. An occasional cloud puffed by, like a cotton ball torn in two so that it became wispy at one end. Again I pulled hard on each strand of twine. Will knelt down next to me on the blanket, patient, watching as I scooted back and forth checking and rechecking. He placed a hand on my arm. "They're ready. I promise, Rose."

I stopped and looked over at him, stared into his deep blue eyes. "Okay," I said. Then, "Dad," I called out, my voice carrying on the wind down the beach to where he waited by one of

the lifeguard chairs where Mom set up her blanket and um-
brella when we came to this beach as a family during our summers together. Mom loved the beach. She used to say it was
practically a prerequisite of being a teacher and the big perk of
having summers off. Dad, Jim, and I hadn't come here once last
summer.

But today, for the one-year anniversary, we'd decided to
make the trip.

Dad ambled back toward the blanket, his limp almost gone
now, his eyes squinting in the bright sun. I handed him his sun-
glasses. "Thanks," he said, his voice hoarse, putting them on.

Jim and Dad, Will and I, surveyed the three diamond-shaped
kites that lay flat, side by side on the blanket—three splashes of
color stretched across thin, flexible spines. Will and I had spent
entire afternoons sitting in the back garden, cutting out circles,
squiggly lines, hearts, and stars, and sewing them onto the kites'
sails. Then we gave each one a long, flowing tail, tying ribbons
that would fly out behind them in the wind.

"They're beautiful, Rosey," Jim said, walking from one end
of our setup to the other. "Mom would have loved them."

"I know, right?" I looked up at my brother, shading my eyes
from the brightness of the light.

"So which one is mine?" he asked.

"Let Rose pick first," Dad said. "She made them. She planned
this day."

My eyes shifted from one kite to the next.

"Take your time," Will said, and I reached my hand out, feeling his fingers weave through mine.

But I'd known from the beginning which kite I'd fly today—the one with the bright green sail, on which I'd carefully sewn a silver star, a red heart, a single musical note, a pink flower, and a yellow crayon. Gathering my courage, I reached for my kite, its willowy tail trailing different shades of blue already taken up by the breeze.

"It's your turn," Dad said to Jim, and he immediately went for the bright purple one, leaving the pale blue kite for Dad.

The three of us stood still a moment, the tails of our kites like rainbows reaching toward the ocean. Then we spread out down the beach, moving far enough apart that the three lines of twine wouldn't tangle.

Will handed me the letter I'd given him to keep for this day. I threaded the paper with string and tied it to the spine, this letter to Mom, the one I couldn't bear to write last year at the memorial, the one I was going to send up to her now. When it was attached, I turned to Will. "I'm ready."

"I know," he said, and leaned in to kiss me. Then he stepped away.

I watched as my dad moved down the beach, his kite low at first, then higher and higher as he let out more string. Then Jim, moving faster than Dad, sent his kite jumping quickly toward the sky. And now, my turn. I began to walk forward, stumbling in the soft sand, but as I gained a better footing I felt the kite tug and pull at me in the breeze like a living thing and my steps quickened, and then I let it go.

While it flew up, caught by the wind, I started to run down the beach.

My legs stretched across the sand, my feet leaving prints behind me, carving small hills in the grains. I couldn't help but imagine that the colorful kite was my mother, dancing and twirling and looping high in the sky, letting the wind take her up and down and hopping across the horizon. I called out to her as I leaped down the beach, my words swallowed by the sounds of the ocean.

Dad and Jim stopped by Mom's lifeguard chair, pulling on their spools, letting out the line and then yanking it back to make their kites jump, their eyes on the colorful triangles spinning toward heaven. I watched as my kite popped past the sun, and glanced now and again at my dad and my brother, knowing that Will was here, too, keeping me in his sights, his presence helping me maintain the courage I needed for this day, steadying me.

Then I let my imagination go again. I let myself believe that somehow my mother and I were connected by this string in my hands. That she would know the words I'd written and let go into the sky, that she could hear me call out to her. That she was with me today on this beach where we used to fly kites together. That she was here in the joyous playfulness of this day with my family, a playfulness that we inherited from her, that she gave to us and to so many others during her life.

This is what I imagined as I watched my kite, my beautiful kite, with its heart, its star and crayon, its note and flower glowing from the light of the sun behind it. I felt love and grief and joy and all the emotions in between, letting my weathered broken heart knit itself back together again as I said goodbye to my mother.

Our imaginations are such gifts, she used to say.

So I thanked her for mine.

ROSE MADISON'S PLAYLIST

1. "Can't Go Back Now" by the Weepies
2. "About a Girl" by The Academy Is . . .
3. "My Best Friend" by Weezer
4. "How to Save a Life" by the Fray
5. "Precious Things" by Tori Amos
6. "All at Sea" by Jamie Cullum
7. "Nice Guy" by the Animators
8. "How It Ends" by Mike Errico
9. "Over You" by Echo & the Bunnymen
10. "Fan of Your Eyes" by Tim Blane
11. "Can You Tell" by Ra Ra Riot
12. "Between the Lines" by Sara Bareilles
13. "One of Those Days" by Joshua Radin
14. "Hockey Week" by the Zambonis
15. "My Baby Just Cares for Me" by Nina Simone
16. "Energy" by The Apples in Stereo
17. "Take It Home" by the White Tie Affair
18. "I Stand Corrected" by Vampire Weekend
19. "Bottle It Up" by Sara Bareilles
20. "Private Conversation" by Lyle Lovett
21. "Blue Christmas" by Elvis Presley
22. "Are We Friends or Lovers" by the Zutons
23. "Family Tree" by Julian Velard
24. "All I Want for Christmas Is You" by Mariah Carey

25. "The Heart of Life" by John Mayer

26. "Hard to Explain" by the Strokes

27. "Colorful" by Rocco De Luca & the Burden

28. "Are You Gonna Be My Girl" by Jet

29. "My Heart" by Lizz Wright

30. "Last Nite" by the Strokes

31. "Falling Slowly" by Glen Hansard & Marketa Irglova

32. "Been a Long Day" by Rosi Golan

33. "Not Your Year" by the Weepies

34. "Better" by Toby Lightman

35. "Everybody" by Madonna

36. "Kind and Generous" by Natalie Merchant

37. "Stars" by the Weepies

38. "Midnight Blue" by Lou Gramm

39. "Dreams" by Van Halen

40. "All Will Be Well" by the Gabe Dixon Band

ACKNOWLEDGMENTS

As always, wonderful friends who are also wonderful writers and readers have been indispensable to the existence of this book, most especially Marie Rutkoski, Daphne Grab, Eliot Schrefer, Betsy Bird, Rebecca Stead, and Jill Santopolo. Thank you to Beth Adams and Nicci Hubert for being the eternal cheerleaders for my writing projects; to everyone at FSG and Macmillan, especially Frances Foster, Simon Boughton, and Susan Dobinick; to my amazing agent, Miriam Altshuler; and to my husband, Josh Dodes—I am grateful to you all.

And, Dad, thank you for weathering the difficult and the sad and finding your way to a third act, and, Mom, of course, thank you for having a wild imagination—I wish you could have read this.